THE
CHILDREN
SING

OTHER BOOKS BY MACKINLAY KANTOR

FICTION

BEAUTY BEAST (1968)

STORY TELLER (1967)

SPIRIT LAKE (1961)

IF THE SOUTH HAD WON THE CIVIL
  WAR (1961)

THE WORK OF SAINT FRANCIS
  (1958)

ANDERSONVILLE (1955)
  Pulitzer Prize Novel, 1956

GOD AND MY COUNTRY (1954)

THE DAUGHTER OF BUGLE ANN
  (1953)

WARWHOOP (1952)

DON'T TOUCH ME (1951)

SIGNAL THIRTY-TWO (1950)

ONE WILD OAT (1950)

THE GOOD FAMILY (1949)

WICKED WATER (1949)

MIDNIGHT LACE (1948)

GLORY FOR ME (1945)
  On which the motion picture
  The Best Years of Our Lives
  was based

AUTHOR'S CHOICE (1944)

HAPPY LAND (1943)

GENTLE ANNIE (1942)

CUBA LIBRE (1940)

VALEDICTORY (1939)

HERE LIES HOLLY SPRINGS (1938)

THE NOISE OF THEIR WINGS (1938)

THE ROMANCE OF ROSY RIDGE
  (1937)

AROUSE AND BEWARE (1936)

THE VOICE OF BUGLE ANN (1935)

LONG REMEMBER (1934)

THE JAYBIRD (1932)

EL GOES SOUTH (1930)

DIVERSEY (1928)

JUVENILE

GETTYSBURG (1952)

LEE AND GRANT AT APPOMATTOX (1950)

ANGLEWORMS ON TOAST (1942)

PERSONALIA

I LOVE YOU, IRENE (1972)

HAMILTON COUNTY (1970)
  (With Tim Kantor)

MISSOURI BITTERSWEET (1969)

THE DAY I MET A LION (1968)

MISSION WITH LEMAY (1965)
  (With General Curtis E.
  LeMay)

LOBO (1957)

BUT LOOK, THE MORN (1947)

VERSE

TURKEY IN THE STRAW (1935)

MacKINLAY KANTOR

THE CHILDREN SING

A NOVEL

HAWTHORN BOOKS, INC.

Publishers / NEW YORK

Buddhist quotations in this work are reproduced from "The Teaching of Buddha," copyrighted in 1968 by Bukkyo Dendo Kyokai of Tokyo, Japan, and the author is grateful for the permission extended to him.

To
Tom and Adelaide Garrett

The children sing in far Japan,
The children sing in Spain;
The organ with the organ man
Is singing in the rain.
STEVENSON

THE
CHILDREN
SING

1

In Bangkok there had been some argument about whether or not they wanted to go journeying up *klongs* with the rest of the tourists. *Klongs* was the local name for the canals—some fairly wide, some extremely narrow—which fed tainted water into the Chao Prya River passing through the city.

Donald Lundin and his wife agreed that this might prove to be a filthy episode in their travels. But also they concluded that almost every local adventure constituted a filthy episode—except their witnessing rare graces surrounding the palace and other significant shrines.

Lundin said, "What we see and smell will probably make us sick."

"True enough. But we've been sick before—at least there's nothing permanent about it. We recover with comparative ease. We're still young—"

"Says you."

"Well, compared to the majority of our fellow wanderers, we are."

"But we've still got stomachs, and some degree of taste. What my grandmother used to term our risibilities will be affected."

His wife, called July, laughed reassuringly. "Oh, come on, don't be an old poop."

"Well. Whatever you say."

"My love, if we're to know the Orient, then we've got to know the Orient."

"I don't give a damn about the Orient. You were the one who wanted to come on this trip, not I."

"Don't be an old poop."

"Well."

She was called July by all, although that was not her true name. She was named Ada, but Don never used the word. She had been July to him, and eventually to the rest of their world, since she was in her teens. She had a slightly older sister named June, and Lundin had dated June when he was a boy and first in uniform and first in training. One night he got a pass unexpectedly and borrowed a Pontiac. He drove out to the Banfield house, in the suburbs of a town near which his base was located. He had thought to find June at home, but she had gone on another date. There ensued a flirtatious episode with Ada on the front porch, and she agreed to go out with Don. She would be a pinch hitter although not yet sixteen in age.

They found the prescribed, adjudged, safe dark parking place, and there in the bruised Pontiac he proceeded to investigate Ada's potentials. The potentials turned out to be wild, warm, vigorous. He gasped a little later, "My God, if June's your sister, then certainly you ought to be called July." That was his name for her from then on, and in time became adopted commonly.

Promptly there ensued a brief program dedicated to dodging a somewhat indignant June and the girls' understandably distracted parents. Then Don was ordered away to another training base and shortly thereafter was sent overseas. His infrequent letters came to July, not to June.

As soon as Lundin was returned to the United States and separated from the service, late in 1945, he and July ran off and got married. They disappeared for some days thereafter, and thus the parents were not disposed to break up the union. It was a union of whim, but also of ardor and persistence. They retained their fervent teen-age companionship through stress, and trailer living, and his momentary career as night watchman in a lumberyard (but with a book under his arm). In time they would observe various somewhat elder associates marry and dissolve, marry and dissolve.

After twenty-six and a half years of married life, July was nearly as slim and even more shapely than she had been when they first came together. Her reddish hair was changing into a fluffy gray. Her bright brown eyes still snapped with emotion, and her narrow freckled face was piquant and alert.

Her husband told her frequently that she was the sharpest little piece in town, and he meant what he said. He believed this, and so did many others who looked at her, and so did those who had tried unsuccessfully to seduce her. The power of the Lundins' loyalty was next to phenomenal in the busy circles through which they had grown to move. Financially they prospered further than the majority of their contemporaries. Thus necessarily it came about that a great many of their social companions were of elder years.

Even the woman's parents called her July nowadays. Most people supposed that it was her true given name, that she had no other. An aunt or two still addressed her circumspectly as Ada, and she made faces over this.

She didn't feel at all like an Ada, she felt like a July.

"Don, I should really like to go up the *klongs*, but if you don't want to go, you don't have to. Just forget about it and go off and play with an idol or something."

"They're not idols, they're statues of Buddha. But anyway I'll go *klong*ing if you insist on going."

Lundin had round gray eyes which gave a false impression of hardness and lack of sympathy. Truly they were bullet-firm and held a stare to them. When he was a small boy, he owned access to a book which included accounts of the lives of certain police officers and sheriffs of note, and this volume was illustrated liberally with photographs of the various subjects. His fancy was stricken to recognize that his eyes looked like those of heroes described.

A little later on he experienced contact with other works portraying the lives of notorious bandits, and especially criminals addicted to deeds of violence. Their photographs appeared also—and he was even more fascinated by his own resemblance to them.

"Cop or killer," he told himself in youthful fancy, "I've got those eyes."

Although aware of deception, he tried to play the role with a swagger, until a little common sense was knocked into him. His schoolmates were reluctant to accept him in either capacity. Thus it was necessary for Don to be taught tractability, which he learned after a few encounters, some of them bloody.

Time and wisdom, however, did not cause his eyes to soften apparently or to lose their hard stare. Thus at first meeting he often gave a false impression of brandishing a danger which truly was not in him. In contact, people soon found out that underneath the annealed exterior which seemingly he brandished, he was soft with pity and affection.

These gentilities he exemplified moistly and in filth on this morning among the *klongs*. Those tourists who wished to make the journey traveled in a large red-black-and-blue launch—one of a flotilla clustered adjacent to their hotel.

They passed ragtag business and manufacturing establishments, which lined the wide river on its further bank and contributed their offering of din and fester. Then the launch turned in at a *klong* wide enough to accept two or three vessels of the same size, and later into narrower ones. Here they inched past a descending regatta of native craft poled along with cargoes of everything from melons to coconut husks, or small fish which were cooked or pickled, and purveyed en route.

4

The nearer bank on the right was lined solidly with homes of the Thai-landers (Don thought of them as Siamese—he could not get the term out of his mind). There sprawled family groups on rickety wharves facing this estuary—some half naked, most of the small people wholly naked—bathing, emptying slops, or washing their hair. A bulk of swarming brown children waved prettily and greeted the tourists with charm in a manner which suggested the best of teaching and a pervading kindliness. Still, naughtier elder boys were bound to come plunging over and try to clamber up on the prow, yelling for donations of *bahts* (coins worth a nickel).

Lundin refused to contribute *bahts*, and wished that his fellows would offer none. As a matter of fact, most people on the launch were wise in the ways of travel and knew better than to distribute unessential charity.

One of the gallery inhabitants was much too small to swim a-begging, even if females were permitted to do so, which commonly they weren't. She jigged in a frenzy of appreciation at the vessel's approach. An elder woman—her grandmother, it seemed—had been bathing the child at a round wooden basin, high on disarrayed boards which did duty as a porch in front of the dwelling. The tiny girl, having attained perhaps to a year-and-a-half in age, was joggling up and down delightedly, clapping her hands and chattering at the strangers. Her name was Kitsomboom Malee, or Malee Kitsomboom, and with her grandmother's vigilance relaxed momentarily, she danced in danger, too near the sloping edge of the shelf.

She was a tawny wet plummet going down with hands waggling on high. Her body cut the *klong*'s surface with a tiny incomplete splash.

Older children out in front and along the sides did not see her or hear her, and there was no use in depending upon them anyway. After they achieved a certain size they could swim like water rats, could be water rats, and were. But not this one, not she—she was too small.

Lundin stood up, kicking off his loose moccasins and tossing his wristwatch in the general direction of July's lap. He went head first off the launch, striving in the general direction of the rickety piled wharf-porch. Dimly he heard the first halloo of the grandmother as he struck the water; he imagined in that instant that a series of other howls would come rising behind and above him as he explored black depths with his hands.

Over here?

No, further this way.

Claw out and sweep arms, and stay hunting as long as possible.

He had no time or energy to spare in tasting this sewage, or doing more than sinking and experimenting with it.

Luck sent his elbow astern to brush the child's body. He grabbed her and made his way aloft.

Greasy boys intruded, and he had to keep fending them off with elbows and shoulders as he handed the little figure up into a growth of straining arms and hands. The girl had swallowed quantities of water and was belching, coughing, vomiting, as she tried also to wail. He would remember accurately and with appreciation the straining concern of faces pushed toward him and the dole they uttered, with the grandmother's private wail still creasing high. Malee Kitsomboom was lifted, and elevated to the platform, where water was dumped from her, and she was spatted and shaken. Froth spewed, and she began to give full voice again, as in the case of a puppy encouraged to bay by its elders.

The launch had banged against a couple of small river craft. It was turned to one side, effectually blocking the canal. After ridding himself of the child, Don swam a few strokes and reached the launch, where men clustered to help him aboard.

He saw July smiling and trying to push her way among others. A lot of handkerchiefs and a scarf were offered.

Women cried, "We ought to go right back to the *hotel*."

"Oh, no," Don said, "don't bother, it's not necessary. It's a warm day. Of course," he added, "I probably smell like hell."

"No, you don't."

"Yes, he does," some of the men said. "The whole damn place smells like hell," and laughter sounded.

A foolish widow was braying, "That was just about the bravest thing I ever saw in my *life*," which she knew was stuff and nonsense, and so did some of the others.

Their guide for the day and for all trips about town was a solemn, bespectacled youth named Dang. Dang followed Lundin to the upper deck and prow of the boat, where Don sat down to try to repair the damage. "Please. You wish to return to the hotel?"

"It's not necessary, if the rest of you can stand me. I'll be dry in just a little while."

Back on the dock-house-porch, family and neighbors who had come leaping to the scene were waving or else standing with hands pressed together and heads bowed above the hands. They were calling *sawadee* over and over, although some of the tourists insisted that the term was *sabadee*, and replied in kind. This expression seemed to mean "thank you," and "hello," and "good-bye," and a number of other things, but at least there was appreciation displayed. A number of Americans replied in kind, and Don waved and made an imaginary handshake above his head.

July told him promptly that that was not the thing to do.

"You've got to stand up and put your hands together and say *sabadee*."

"Oh, forget it. The kid's all right. She probably would have been all right anyway. One of those little boys would have gone down and grabbed her. They can all swim."

"Well, why did you go in?"

"I acted on impulse," he said.

"And will probably come down with a creeping, crawling Asiatic crud."

A retired surgeon named Mitzheimer came to sit beside Don in the forward position. He was seventy-six years old and possessed of a second wife—a woman considerably younger than he—who had been a patient of his and whom he had saved from the same obliterating fate which claimed his first bride. Mitz's eyebrows stuck out like horns. Beneath them the eyes were tolerant, the face attractive and dependable.

7

Don asked, "Well, Flight Surgeon, what do I do now?"

"Just wait for the plague to develop. Of course, you've had all the usual shots?"

"We had to get cholera shots for this trip. We do travel a bit, so we both keep up our triple typhoid and tetanus."

"You'll be all right."

"I'm not too worried, Mitz, but I don't think I'll ever feel clean again."

"Your hair'll be the worst to wash. You'll probably have to scrub it twice before you feel all right. But you don't wear it as long as most of the other young punks—"

"Thanks. I haven't been called a young punk all day."

"Wait'll you're my age, and then you'll think that people your age are punks. That little July of yours is a young-young-young punk. Or punk-ess?"

Don had been smoking his pipe before he made the leap, and it had fallen safely to the deck, but his tobacco pouch was in his hip pocket. He now produced the soggy mass and tossed to overboard. Some boys swimming after the launch began to fight and spatter in the water, trying to retrieve the pouch; one finally got it and waved the thing aloft with a yell of triumph.

"For God's sake. What'll he do with that?"

"Eat it," suggested the surgeon.

A wizened lawyer from Akron, a man named Semple, came hurrying to offer his own tobacco to Don.

They went up a series of *klongs* to a sprawling dockside market, and Don trailed ashore with the others. His clothes were drying rapidly, but he felt stench clinging round him. Loyally the rest refused to recognize it. The market was a hullabaloo infested with shyster merchants. Women of the party held small indignant meetings about suggested prices and said that things were cheaper in more seemly modern bazaars close to the hotel, or in finely furbished hallways of the hotel itself.

"You know," Lundin said to Dr. Mitzheimer, "I looked up Siam in the encyclopedia before we started on this trip."

"Siam? Oh, yes—Thailand."

"Siam, according to the old designation. It was a real old encyclopedia. We've got a modern one, naturally enough, but I like to use this ancient one—1916, or somewhere around there —because we had it at home when I was a kid. My sister sent it to me after our parents died and their house was sold."

Mitzheimer prodded him. "So you looked it up."

"Bet I can quote with pretty good accuracy."

"Go ahead."

Lundin closed his eyes in thought. " 'Elephants roam wild, and are also useful. The rhinoceros, tiger, leopard, gaur, water buffalo, flying fox, gibbon, and crocodile are plentiful.' Hey, how's that?"

Mitz wanted to know what a gibbon was.

"Some kind of monkey or ape, isn't it?"

"And what's a gaur?"

"I don't know."

"I don't know either. But let me tell you this: while we were having breakfast this morning I looked out of the window and counted seventeen big smokestacks. Fourteen of them were belching smoke. Black smoke."

"The hell with the gaurs," said Don Lundin.

2

The Lundins' quarters on the fourth floor of the Songkran Hotel were broken by steps and gradations of altitude without any seeming purpose and with annoying effect. The bathroom stood on a level lower than the adjacent bedroom, and you had to watch to avoid barking your shins when you went back and forth.

Don got into the tub with the hose spray. He used up all the hot water and went on with the cold. He said it didn't matter: the temperature was muggy outside—it was midday now, and the sun stood high behind clouds, and all the air bulked stuffy, and the air-conditioning system kept battering below the windows.

"You mustn't catch cold," July warned. "It would be the worst possible thing."

"I won't catch cold. It's just that I don't ever expect to be clean again. I've washed this goddamn head of mine three times and washed my teeth until my mouth's sore."

"Darling, you're now clean as clean can be. It's just that you don't *feel* clean. It'll probably take a while."

"What did you do with my clothes?"

"The room boy took them, but he says they can't be washed until tomorrow. And probably they'll be shrunken, too."

"It doesn't matter."

The Spirit of Buddha is the great compassion and love to save all people by any and all means. It is the nourishing and protective spirit of a mother for her child; it is the spirit that prompts it to be ill with the sickness of people, to suffer with their suffering.

"Your suffering is my suffering and your happiness is my happiness," said Buddha.

Don Lundin burst out finally, "Oh, you know what's the matter with me, and I'm sorry if I offend you, but I can't help burning up about it. I hate Asia and the whole idea of Asiatics. I don't know why the hell they call them Asians today. The newspapers seem to insist on it. Maybe they think it's more polite—I don't know. Little brown people and little yellow people, the swarms and hordes of them—the yellow, and the brown, and their own kind of black. I loathe the whole damn parcel of them. You knew I did before we started on this trip. I said I didn't want to come, but I didn't want you to go alone. I can't stand being without you, anywhere, any time."

"Now, now," she said.

"Don't use that tone of voice when you say 'now, now.' It's as if you were soothing a sick child."

He regretted those words the moment he uttered them; he hadn't thought to say them, they just slipped out. July went over to the window and stood looking at the dry and wet landscape, spread in interest and prettiness near at hand. She seemed to be studying the horizon, with its chimneys, and smoke, and suggestion of tin and rubber and God knew what other commodities. His mention of a sick child had squirted water in her eyes, and goddamn it, why had he ever said such a thing? He hadn't meant to, because in her life there was only one vast double tragedy that could spring to mind when anyone said *sick child*. Because she would think of the two small ones they'd owned who got sick, and sick together, and died of it, and all within four days, and why the hell hadn't Dr. Jonas Salk been born ten years earlier than he was? But he hadn't been, and so the two tiny adopted Lundins had been bent, tortured, smitten on that same vile unsought altar with the millions gone before them, and the few who followed.

He hadn't meant to say it at all, but he was embarked and had to keep on, somehow to justify his original utterance.

He said, "They're treacherous, and vicious, and imitative, and I wouldn't trust any one of them around the corner, not the nicest little Siamese in the world who puts his palms together and bows his head and says 'sawadee.' He's probably trying to think of how he might turn a sacred elephant loose on you. Oh sure, there was a show called Anna and all the rest of it. She was a king or queen or something, and you wanted to go and see it, and I wouldn't go, and I guess you and June went finally; I don't know, you went with somebody.

"When I asked you how you enjoyed it, you said it was swell. So O.K., here we are. Thailand, Siam—call it what you will. Sure, the river has charm out there—you're looking at it now.

But if we look out the other window, we see the streets in front, and just try to count those high-rises. Try to count the machinery that's out there putting up more. What a mess. Those high-rises are some of the worst things we Americans have to offer the world, and O.K.—I'm speaking with guilt right now. Because I've been dependent on them to make a lot of money. I hate high-rises, but indirectly I'm in the business. I started out picking sites for low-rises, and look what happened. We started out low and got into high."

Her voice came to him but weakly. "Now, now."

"Goddamn it," he said. "I didn't want to come on this cock-eyed trip, and here I am, spoiling your good time. All because that worthless little brat fell in the water, and all because— What did I try to do? Make a momentary hero out of myself? I just acted automatically, I tell you. I didn't stop to consider it, I didn't think about all that shit in the water. It's there. By God, I'll smell it on myself for days, I swear to you I will. But I didn't think about it. It was just a case of a child going in and, and— Well, next thing I knew I was down in that cruddy stuff and— Oh, hell."

You could have counted to thirty in the silence that followed, but no one counted.

July asked, "Have you blown your top now?"

"Yes, I guess I've blown."

She turned around and smiled. Her upper cheeks were moist, but he had expected to see them that way. And, oh Christ, why did he have to run off at the mouth when he got, when he got— his mother used to call it "exercised." Yes, that was it. When he got exercised.

"I'm sorry. I just got exercised."

"Ah," she said, "I'm a good person to exorcize that exercise."

"Playing with words." He tried to scoff.

"Yes. But don't I do it nicely?"

"Yes," he said, and hugged her, and she squeezed him tightly, and they were at peace again.

For a moment.

Comparatively.

3

_____

While they were eating dinner at dusk in a downstairs restaurant, their local guide, Dang, came and stood at a short distance from their table. He kept bowing slightly to claim Don's attention. Lundin excused himself and got up and met Dang between the crowded tables.

The guide said, "Please," and led to the nearest doorway. "There are people to see you."

"People to see me?"

"Yes, please. They are on the water."

Lundin was puzzled. "People to see me—on the water?" He laughed. "Are you sure you've got the right guy? I don't think I know anybody out on the water."

"People from this morning."

"And they asked for me?"

"Please to see them? I do not think it will take so long."

Lundin shrugged. "O.K. I'll go back and get my wife."

They told the waiter to hold their coffee, and he fetched July along. Dang escorted them beyond a wide short-cropped lawn to where drinking tables were set along the river's margin. A few launches still lay moored close at hand, but also another craft had poked its way up to the wharf. It was a good-sized dugout, or pirogue, or scow, or Lord knew what they called those things they were always poling around the _klongs_. An earnest-looking young man in a flowered sarong leaned against his oar at the prow, and another youth at the stern. In between were crammed women and children in various styles of traditional and modern dress.

July said, "It's the little girl."

There she was, Malee, whom Lundin had drawn from the ooze that morning. All the Thailanders were smiling, shyly but warmly. Malee was dressed in tiny red pants and a miniature sweatshirt of gray, on the front of which was printed in black letters "Sing Sing State Prison."

Dang said, "They come to thank you."

"How did they know where to find me?"

"Please, they knew our launch comes from this hotel. Everyone knows. They speak of it."

Still grasping his oar, the slim man in the prow bent over and picked up Malee with his left arm. He stood erect and grinning, clutched her to his body, then put the child down gently once more.

"He is her father."

"Yes," said Lundin, "one can see that."

"They have the gift for you."

It was produced—a miniature coop made of split bamboo sticks in which two angry chickens were squashed together. The poultry croaked balefully about their condition.

"Why, look at that," July exclaimed, "that one is white, almost like a white Wyandotte, and the other's sort of mixed. Maybe a Buff Cochin?"

"Apparently an Oriental hen got mixed up with an Occidental rooster."

"Don, you remember that I know chickens. We used to have them out at my grandfather's place. Don't you remember how we went out there to get fresh chickens for a holiday? Well, Don, say something. They're expecting you to say something. They're all smiling."

He found his voice. He tried to do a proper *sabadee*. He put his feet together and his hands together and bowed over his pressed hands and murmured the expression. Then, acting on a better impulse, he stepped down to the barge and extended his hands to the child, still the center of attention. She backed off against her grandmother and hid her face, and the people in the barge laughed at this. Somewhat gingerly Don accepted the hen coop and came back and put it down on the ground. Everyone bowed in salutation again, July and the guide joining in.

Dang chattered rapidly to the Thailanders and then turned to explain. "I tell them that you are pleased with emotion and appreciate much the gift."

"That's fine," said Don. "Bless them all."

At his words the launch was poled out into the river, and the family set out on their return voyage to *klongs* across the way.

July was wiping her eyes. "I can't help crying a little. I'm really overwhelmed. You are too, Don. I can tell it. You're overwhelmed and didn't know what to do or say."

"You're right," said her husband. "I was surely taken by surprise. Now what the hell do I do with these chickens?"

They looked at Dang, and he shook his head rapidly.

"No, no. I am still a student, I do not live at home, I have a room with a family where I live." He seemed to be considering for a moment, then explained, "I do have a girl friend. And she lives with her father and mother."

"Wouldn't they like to have the chickens?"

"Very much," he said in acceptance. "I am so sure, please, that they would like to have them. But you might persuade the hotel chef to prepare them for you?"

July said, "That might be rather difficult. Why don't you take them, Dang?"

"I am grateful."

They looked toward the river and waved their hands, but the people in the dugout were occupied with the task of crossing.

4

Erna Mitzheimer had been a child actress known as Erna Grayce. A child actress, never a child star. She had been married twice before she met up with the surgeon. Of her earlier unions, one husband was a compulsive drunk and the other a compulsive gambler—and a drunk. Through much of her active adult life she had been a proprietress of a small dramatic school in New York City.

She was an excessively tall woman, very thin, who at sixty-two still walked with feline grace. A fluffy blonde wig roosted atop her own hair, which she described as so skimpy that it wasn't worth looking at. "Thank mercy for the popularity of wigs. At least I don't feel like a freak in public. Just in private."

Her mother had been wealthy in her own right, and hustled Erna off to California in early days of the motion pictures. The child was acceptable in bit parts and slender speaking roles, but more often she appeared as an extra. She trotted through well-known pictures such as "Hearts of the World," "Daddy Long Legs," "Pollyanna," "Way Down East," and even "The Kid."

In such capacity she worked (sometimes) in scenes dominated by stars of those days: the Talmadge sisters, the Gish sisters, Mary Pickford, Charlie Chaplin, Jackie Coogan, Rudolph Valentino. She declared that the actor she admired most of all was a child somewhat younger than herself, named Ben Alexander. She confessed to July that the most hateful words of recollection were uttered by her own mother's voice. An imperious demand rang in the background of memory. "Mr. Griffith, I wish to talk to you about my daughter." "Mr. Ince, I wish to talk to you about my daughter." Even, some time later: "Mr. Fleming, I wish to talk to you about my daughter."

"I suppose that what I lacked most of all was any personal ambition. People around me—the admired, important ones— all worked hard as hell. But there was no leisure either for a child hag-ridden by a mother like mine."

Then fate held the steering wheel one foggy California night when a Pierce-Arrow touring car went through a railway warning signal near Santa Monica and Mrs. Grayce could dream and demand no longer. Erna was thrown clear and knocked unconscious but otherwise unharmed. Her weak and amiable father took the young girl back to New York and both were happier from then on.

"You must remember: it was all silent stuff in those old days. I don't know— If I had stuck around or been made to stick around in pictures until sound came in, I might have had a better chance. As it was, all gaunt and leggy, I had become a monster in the silent stuff. But I'd fallen in love with my own voice and liked to *cultivate* it, as voice teachers used to say. It's a horrid word, but still it indicates what I mean."

She had a few small parts on Broadway, but in no play that became a great success. Then, still in her teens, she married wealth and disgrace—and later married wealth and disgrace the second time, and was again divorced.

She founded a voice school, of which she became inordinately proud and wherein she shared enthusiasm with several young actors who went on to eminence.

A few older people in that tourist party remembered motion pictures in which the present Mrs. Mitzheimer had appeared, and were proportionately awed and forever trying to question her about Hollywood, despite her deploring such reminiscences.

In 1960, possessed of a seemingly inoperable cancer, she had gone in desperation to Dr. Mitzheimer at Johns Hopkins. Skill and fortune enabled him to save and extend the life of this patient, whereas his colleagues had been unable to do the same thing in the case of his first wife. Erna and Mitzheimer were married two years later.

They displayed in public, and also in private, that beautiful, somewhat railing relationship of perpetual trust and jest which enriches the lives of those who are equipped to practice it.

In speaking of these people to Don Lundin, July was drawn to quote an anecdote she treasured. It was about a woman who, on hearing the laughter of a stranger, said, "How wonderful to hear a woman laugh like that. How she must have suffered in order to be able to do so!"

Both couples were delighted in the awareness that each had found an opposite team whom they might enjoy under any circumstances. All knew that they would be devoted friends until their dying days. The Mitzheimers had experienced this quick-earned joy on two previous occasions. The Lundins had never known it before, and considered it to be a remarkable quirk.

5

Dang warned the travelers about dangers attendant to sitting out by the waterside after night had fallen. So, also, did the general tour conductor, a Hindu—a man of vast human experience (which many people own, but possessed also of intricate human understanding, which is discovered in lesser quantities).

Both said cautiously that the attack of mosquitoes was unpredictable but in some cases had been known to breed severe results.

"What are they really talking about?" Lundin wanted to know.

Mitz told him, "Some form of filariasis."

"I've heard about that in the American tropics. You're apt to get a recurrent fever, aren't you?"

"Here in the Far East it can have even more severe effects upon the patient. It can go into elephantiasis. You might go stalking around on enormous legs, carrying your balls in a bag over your arm. Lymphangitis and chyluria and chylocele wouldn't be any fun at all."

The women expressed horror, and cried that they were fortunate in that they could not be thus victimized. Both were wearing long skirts and no stockings, but agreed that stockings wouldn't have done any good anyway. A mosquito could bite right through—

"We are definitely not going to sit out here," July announced.

Erna warned, "Remember, Mitz, elephantiasis is grounds for divorce in any court of Thailand. White elephantiasis is much the worst. July, let us retreat to that somewhat ornate and somewhat understaffed restaurant on the top floor. We shall indulge in frappéd liqueurs, and look out and down, and observe our husbands being bitten."

So the women had long since fled and now were safely windowed-in above. Mitz and Lundin still sat by the waterside. They wore slacks and the usual wool socks against tropical heat, and they had their lightweight jackets, and screw the mosquitoes. It was pleasant sitting there, watching the lights and the small craft plowing gracefully in the river.

"These *klongs*," said Mitzheimer. "Do you realize we are probably seeing and participating in the last of them? I saw an old map of the city, and *klongs* were everywhere. Now they're mainly replaced by this high-pressure road system. You've seen the traffic. Unbelievable."

Lundin said that everything was unbelievable. Japan, too.

"Well, we haven't seen too much of Japan. I'm glad we're stopping there for a couple of weeks on the way back. We can really get in a little exploration."

"It's incredible. Remember, Mitz, how we spent that one night there on the way out, in that big hotel not too far from the airport? I was up before dawn. I woke up and couldn't get back to sleep."

"What woke you?"

"You might call it a kind of nervous uncertainty or something like that. I went to our wide windows and drew the curtains back. Then I saw a train, and then I saw another one."

He said that finally he drew up a chair and sat watching trains and the street traffic, which was beginning to dash even at that early hour. Then he went back to the refrigerator and found one of the beers placed there thoughtfully by the Japanese staff; along with a little note and card on which you could designate how much beer you drank, or how much soda or how many soft drinks, so that they could be put on your bill.

They trusted you. Lundin was surprised at that, because he hadn't expected the Japanese to trust anyone, especially Americans. So he got his beer and went back and sat at the window, and watched and watched. He said that he felt dizzy and almost sick at his stomach, because in the expanding dawn the vast skyscrapers and factories were beginning to loom into view across the river. There the trains ran coyly and silently on their elaborate system of tracks.

It got lighter and lighter, and first you'd see a blue train coming, seeming to approach on oil without sound. Just twelve, or fourteen, or sixteen long blue cars sliding into sidings and halting for seconds, discharging masses of people, then going on. Then there'd be a white train of maybe eleven cars coming from the other direction and on another track; on the slope above them on a track heretofore unseen would appear a dark red train, and it too might have sixteen cars, and all of them moving as silently as colored paste being squeezed from tubes.

"I counted. I could see at least five tracks, one above the

other. The ones that halted—they ejected at least ten million passengers. I found it impossible to believe, Mitz."

"Well, why? You knew that the Japanese were extremely capable, and they were builders and had been builders and copycats for a long time."

"Oh, yes. But it wasn't like that, twenty-two years before. Time of the Korean War. Tokyo was still a wasteland."

He remembered a freight train, when he was driving with somebody from the Yokota Air Base, coming in to Tokyo on one of their rare visits. That train went by and then got stalled at the crossing, and they had to sit in the old Japanese-salvaged taxi and wait. A brake on a freight car had been set by mistake, apparently, and the single small grasshopper-shaped brakeman couldn't get it loose.

"He just hung there and pranced up and down, pulling and pulling, trying to move that brake. He looked like an insect trying to apply its weight. We felt sorry for him. We felt we ought to go and help, but we didn't go. Finally he got it loose. That was their railroad system twenty-two years ago. Old freight cars with little men hanging onto big beams to adjust the brakes. How the hell could I believe that I'd ever see these blue and brown and purple and white trains? The New Tokaido Line. You glide along inside the electric-eye doors and you may hit 140 miles an hour. And it isn't just one train. They're oozing with the goddamn things."

Mitzheimer was laughing softly. "Don, you get so disturbed about this stuff."

"I can't help it. In 1945 I helped to burn up Tokyo. I acted in a very small capacity, but I remember every minute of it."

Mitzheimer listened with that patience which he had been taught and which had affected him through long exposure to life and its inevitable projection into terminal mystery. He had witnessed it in the myriad cases which passed silent, or breathing heavily and rigidly, or mumbling beneath or within, or surrounded by the striving of his keen, rubber-clad fingers.

2 1

He had been mindful of the futility of his own dedication, even while he embraced its procedure. He had learned that he must never demand, that there was nothing to be gained by publishing the edictal. He had learned to utter only an innocent request, which might sound flippant to some, but he did not set the request in that fashion.

He would speak only with docility.

"How did it happen? Tell me."

Often there was no method by which he might perform to amend or to heal, and this awareness confirmed an increasingly gentle quality within him.

Now, in old age, frequently he would think like a child in the night—"Oh, I wish that there were somthing I could *do* about it all." His belief in God had been stamped out of him by especially cruel Lutherans when he was young. In the combat zones of war and peace he was unable to pray. But often he wished with factual bitterness that he might pray. The act of praying might provide a bolstering, a reassurance. Take those Buddhists whom Lundin was always glowering about—

But no.

Don said that it was red. Red for a long way ahead. A long *ways* ahead, as he put it.

"Just red against the sky and whatever cloud formations there were. There weren't many. I'd stood right close by when our Aircraft Commander was talking with some other guys. I guess there was a weather officer there, too. They'd said something about not more than two- or three-tenths clouds. That must have been about what we had over Tokyo. Or less. We burned up half of Tokyo that night."

Doctor Mitzheimer, who had his own military recollections of France long before, wanted to know what ordnance they used.

"Mixed loads. We used two types of fire bombs chiefly: napalm and magnesium. And those magnesium bombs came in clusters, and they'd fly off in all directions. They actually made a hotter fire than the napalm. I guess each had its advantages and its disadvantages. But anyway, that was what The Cigar picked to do the job."

"You say The Cigar. Who do you mean?"

"General LeMay. He was in command, and he dreamed up this low-level attack with all the fire and so on. A lot of people were scared that it wouldn't work. I can tell you this: we folks in the B-29's were scared, too. About the idea of coming down to that low altitude."

"How low were you?"

"Most of them went in around eight thousand feet but some were a lot lower. I heard that some of them went in around four or five thousand. I don't think anyone was above eight or ten, except when the hot drafts caught them and bounced them way upstairs."

"You mean the fires in Tokyo were hot enough to do that?"

"We burned up about two hundred and thirty-one thousand buildings."

"*What?*"

"The population went into the canals when the fires started. And into the river, I guess, and Tokyo Bay. But in a lot of places that water didn't do any good. It was so hot that it just boiled. Boiled the people to death."

"You mean the civilian population took refuge there, and lots of people were boiled to death?"

"That is correct."

"But weren't you attacking industries? How on earth all those people— I mean— Civilians?"

"You see, the Japanese industry was dispersed. People were working in their little houses. They had turning lathes and all sorts of machinery there, and everybody would work at the armament industry. Mother and father would work, old people, grandfathers and grandmothers, and all the little kids who were big enough to carry baskets around with nuts and bolts or whatever. They were all part of the war economy."

The doctor thought about it, and then shook his head and said, my God, it sounded something like the atom bomb.

"Oh, it was worse than the atom bomb."

"Now look. I'm talking about the *real atom bomb.*"

"I know, I know. You mean Hiroshima and Nagasaki. Yes, it was worse."

"But those were *atom bomb targets.* Those were the *worst—*"

"No. Tokyo was worse. We killed more people in Tokyo that night or that morning, whatever you want to call it, than were killed in either of the atom bomb attacks. That's not just according to our estimates. It's according to Japanese figures."

The surgeon took the name of Jesus Christ very much in vain, and loudly. Guests seated several tables away turned to look at him and at Lundin.

"Why couldn't they put out the fires?" Mitz demanded.

"Fires were all out of control about twenty minutes after the attack started. The fire department engines and trucks burned up in the streets. You know how it is—like a forest fire. The flames themselves create the drafts, and then they start sucking and roaring and make their own holes in the atmosphere to fan the rest of the flames. More people died horribly in Tokyo that night and morning than died in either of the atom bomb targets."

Mitzheimer said weakly that folks all over the world didn't know that. He wondered why they didn't.

"Because newspapers and magazines and all the great soft hearts on radio and television and so on, through the years, have always concentrated on atom bomb attacks. They've tried to make it appear that we had some sort of strange moral responsibility that we didn't fulfill. They don't try and explore it and ask what would have happened if the Japanese had contrived such bombs, or the Germans, or whether they would have used them. I guess the record of the Germans speaks for itself. I didn't ever fight in Europe. I mean I didn't fight much of anywhere, except to be in the tail of that B-29."

"Don, how old were you?"

"According to Army Air Force records I was nineteen. Actually I was seventeen. I went in when I was barely sixteen, ran away and went in—had to beg permission from my father and all that sort of thing. They said they couldn't take me at sixteen but they'd make it eighteen, so that was the way it was. The recruiting people laughed a little. I mean the guys in the office, but there were a lot of kids coming along like that then. I met a couple who were younger than I was."

The doctor murmured, "Seventeen. Up on top of all that burning and boiling in Tokyo, and there you sat with a tail gun in a B-29."

"I didn't have any tail guns. They had taken out all of our guns to lessen our weight so we could carry more bombs. We were utterly unarmed. Later on they put the guns back in the tails, at least in some of the aircraft. It was a gamble. The Cigar took it, and he won, and we all won."

"Then what were you doing, in the tail?"

"They left us in, without arms, just to observe. And report. That was our function. As a matter of fact, I never would have had an opportunity to use my guns once that night, even if I had had them there. Not one night fighter approached our aircraft."

The doctor kept repeating, "Worse than the atom bomb blasts. Worse than— It's hard to believe."

"You can take my word for it or you can read the official books. It's there in history. The kind of muted history that isn't commonly made public. Or you can ask the Japanese. They will confirm that statement."

"The ones who survived," said Mitzheimer.

Then both were silent for a time.

6

Don Lundin had a bad dream in which he was a Buddhist monk, or studying to be a Buddhist monk, and he went tripping about in a long robe gathered up so that he might walk within its folds. The guidebooks called it saffron or gave it other winsome terminology, while he called it orange.

My robe is orange, he kept repeating aloud, but still in the dream. My legs are bare, except for the cool sandals on my feet. I think they may be made of gibbon skin.

He traveled to all sorts of temples and climbed their high steps, and he went from house to house with a bag to gather up food, which people awarded him. He was told he should not beg. Very well, he would not beg.

Here he was in his orange robe, and he had a pal with him, and the hair on both their heads was mown very short. They halted at one farmhouse, and people were sad. They had nothing to give them. Then they strode past rice paddies and along stony places and came to another house and yes, yes, the woman had fresh fish all cooked, flavored with curious herbs, and these bits she gave to them. They accumulated shreds of coconut as well, and in another farmhouse the women boiled some eggs. They carried the fresh-boiled eggs along until they grew too hungry, and then they sat and had their lunch, or call it dinner or call it breakfast.

When had they eaten last?

What is my name? asked Lundin, the Buddhist monk, of himself and of the Asiatic world.

Is my name Bhumibol? No, no, he is a king, and if I am a monk, I cannot be a king. Ah. My name must be Piebul Songgram. That would be the one.

Later he counseled himself, no, no—it could not be. He was a prime minister and revolutionary, and I am neither. Well, I could be a revolutionary, if I knew exactly what I was revolting against, but I don't know really. Anyway, as a strict Buddhist, I could not think of killing. What about Sarit Thanarat? That would be a good designation for me. No. It couldn't be. In local history he was known as a field marshal.

Still later he had another idea. Let me take my own name and reverse it, according to customary local usage. I shall go Gaelic and be a mild but querulous monk named Lundin Dhomhnuill. Let us look it up in Black's *Surnames of Scotland*, as I did long ago when hunting for my own designation (and it stemmed from the City of London itself). Let us see. There are people named *Lundoniis* in apparent confusion and some named *de Lundin* and *Lundy*. Many people named *Lundy*. And other *Lundies*. And what about that burgess of Glasgow revealed as *Lunder*?

What matters my name truly? Any more than the fact of July's being a July and not an Ada?

Hell with this name business. Let us visit *wats*, if that is the proper plural. Let us go to the Wat Phrakaeo. We did visit that, and we saw the emerald Buddha, thirty-one inches high and so pretty, and way up there on that enormously high altar. But actually he wasn't emerald at all—he was made of jasper, which is a green chalcedony, whatever chalcedony may be. I had to take off my shoes to go in, and there was a nice little old man who put them away neatly in little bins—everybody's shoes each on its little shelf or in its bin, and he didn't ask for money but he had a dish on a table nearby, and it was full of all sorts of money from different countries. We put in a dollar bill. July and I had taken off our shoes, and she put on plastic slippers she was carrying in her bag, but I had to go around in my stockinged feet. I should have brought along some plastic slippers.

But that was before I knew that I was a Buddhist monk and would have these sandals.

I remember that three-tiered roof from the outside, and the gold, the gold. I didn't care much for the murals inside, but I did enjoy the fact that tourists weren't allowed to take pictures inside the chapel. No click, click, click. It isn't that I wish to deny people the pleasure of possessing and going back and reviewing their momentary Oriental past, if that is what they truly intend to do. It's just that it gets to be such an infernal bore to see them going around with all those cameras hanging around their necks and over their shoulders and forever click, click, click.

Will they sit and dream dreams over those pictures?

I doubt it.

Hasten to another *wat*. It is called the Wat Arun. Sounds rather Irish. And it has five of those towers. Five! Imagine.

Khmer-style pagodas.

Would you like to be decorated with chunks of broken dishes? No more should I.

Very well. Let us not be Khmer-style pagodas. Let us not be—

What did I say we were?

Buddhist monks?

Present your bag now, or your bowl. Maybe the housewife will give you some cooked white elephant meat. Then off you must go.

Not begging. No.

Never begging, but just clogging up to the door to see.

If she's got food, she will give you some.

You may eat it if you are hungry.

Hungry, monk?

Hungry?

He awoke. It had taken a piteously long time to descend into that quagmire of imaginings, and to become evasive, and to rise again. To participate in mysteries of the East, and then disclaim any desire to know more about them.

An air-conditioning unit beneath the window was making a motorcycle noise, and Lundin went groggily over and tried to adjust it so the sound would not be so severe.

July woke up and asked him what he was doing.

"Just trying to fix the air conditioning." There was no way to describe his delusive dream, and by the next day he had almost forgotten it anyway.

However, he had endured and would endure a great many strange dreams throughout his life. Once he even dreamed that he was an ox in a Certain Stable.

7

In earlier years Lundin had been plagued by that commonly prevailing ambition—he had thought that he might write books. Indeed he had written one, working between demands of family and family responsibility (an entirely separate and dully economic demand) and moping at night or in infrequent daytimes when he was so sleepy that his head sagged above the paper.

It was an atrocious book, and he had come to realize it. He submitted it to six publishers and two agencies and received stolid rejection in every case. July did not encourage him in this striving. She remained aloof and was concerned only about his physical health. She understood keenly and immediately that he was bitten with the desire to be a writer, but not with any overruling ambition to write.

Don considered earlier that his youth and the scorching he'd undergone in war and bereavement were a charm sufficient to attract readers. He had a flair and liking for words. He enjoyed using them cannily in conversation, when he was in the mood, but he could not tell any story unless he was concerned emotionally with it because of experience. He could recite anecdotes but could not invent them. He might relate in fashion to require attention what happened to the flight engineer when he got into a brawl at the Top Three Club, but unless the master-sergeant actually came from Ventress, Louisiana, Don did not want to say that he came from Ventress, Louisana.

Under other circumstances Lundin might have found minor success as a journalist, but he was not fit to practice the eternal process of invention. Only occasionally at night in sleep had he contrived weird adventures surrounding himself, but these musings vanished with the light of day, and he felt no inclination to recreate them on paper. Nor would he have been a competent recorder of his own fancied experience. A hardened truthful fact he could recite orally; in ungoverned moments he exploded with emotion, but again, orally. He felt deeply even when he was bound in misshapen prejudice, but the feeling was one thing and the ability to array it in type quite another.

"Suppose I clung to that ambition to be a writer. Suppose I were till possessed by it," he said to July. "I wonder what our situation would be."

Calmly she told him, "We would have starved to death. Or maybe we would have been divorced. I doubt that I could live in happiness with any man, be he ever so noble, more noble than you, if possible— Live with him for twenty-six years, if all the while he were consumed by unfulfilled ambition."

"Well, I've got a lot of unfulfilled ambition. Who hasn't?"

"Name yours, please."

"Well— For one thing, I'd like— I wish that I— Oh hell. What I'd like to have is serenity. You know— Greater calm. Mitzheimer has that serenity. He's been through everything. He *knows*. He recognizes changes, he can appreciate evil, but above all is that towering serenity. I wish I had it."

"Darling, wait till you, too, are seventy-six. You may acquire it. I rather imagine that it takes time. We're too young yet. We can recognize time, but haven't yielded to it."

"I don't intend to yield to anything I don't want to yield to."

"See? Like I said, you're still young."

Lundin had maintained his status in the organized reserves until he was twenty-two and the Korean War exploded. Promptly he was summoned to active duty, and through a variety of flukes that occur even in the most constricted military organizations, he found himself flying with a Strategic Air Command crew as early as August. Low-priority wings were first loaned by SAC to the Far East Air Force, and the 92nd Bomb Wing was one of those. Every other man in the crew was a regular SAC type, but by this time Don had achieved lieutenancy and also acquired a log of radar time. He attacked with the 92nd as long as they attacked, which was only until late in that same year. Then he came back to Spokane with them.

There was serious illness in his family. Through exertion of compassionate leave and the American Red Cross he was separated and returned to civilian life and sick beds, death beds —but always with the engrossed companionship of July.

He owned a friend in another crew whose aircraft exploded and burned over western Korea. This man, a widower, left tiny twins, a boy and a girl. It was apparent now, both through physical experience and the judgment of specialists and laboratories, that July would never be able to bear children. The Lundins took the twins and were joyed in fervent companionship until 1953, when polio swept in. This was barely short of the time when news of the Salk vaccine gladdened the world. To July and Don it brought stubborn bitterness.

A few silly acquaintances urged them to Try Again, but the Lundins shook their heads and always changed the subject as soon as possible. Wiser friends (and some of the elder and more experienced who observed them) witnessed what gentling effect a combination of tragedies may have upon people whose souls are equipped to bear it. But they were glad to leave the North, where emotional blows had fallen with dire frequency.

A bombardier from MacDill, with whom Don had formerly flown, and his father were proprietors of a gasoline station in Tampa. The Lundins went down there when Don was offered a job. Then the father suffered a paralytic stroke, and all within five active months Don found himself managing the station.

He kept his ears open and heard what his customers had to say. Many of them delved in insurance, real estate, the building business. Whenever opportunity afforded—not too frequently—he and July combed the lower west coast of Florida. They scrutinized the commercial situation in villages strung there and through countryside which still boasted its pines and live oaks, and mangroves along the shores. They leased their first property near a hamlet called Conch Point, then bought it, and shortly were off to the financial races.

The site attracted the attention of developers who were anxious to build a haven for retired members of a men's lodge, but they had not acted promptly enough. They offered Don a substantial profit if he would sell. He said No Sale, and the would-be builders declared that they would comb the area rather than yield to highway robbery. Don was perfectly willing to be a highway robber. Eventually the company could find no other site which satisfied them as well and came back to Lundin again. He gouged to the end, and profited in fashion unholy to the developers but holy to himself.

He proceeded in the stern belief that there was only so much sea water to be had and only so many shore sites available throughout the semisettled area south of Tampa and north of the surviving wilderness below Naples. He did not enter into the building business himself, except through stocks awarded as a portion of sale—when he had made stubborn study of the situation—in a few organizations. He recognized also that expensive beach land could not be marketed frugally, and thus necessarily the up-building of those areas would continue for miles into the interior.

He selected properties east of Venice, far east of Sarasota, and watched them become more and more desirable. Several times it seemed to him and to July that they would pauperize themselves in paying horrendous taxes on newly acquired land. Changes in valuation and zoning occurred in normal fashion but sometimes at abnormal speed. In several cases the Lundins had to sell out at a loss, standing so severely in the need for ready cash. But rapine of the landscape raged on and on. Within twelve years from their start the Lundins were wealthy.

Their lawyers and two bankers with whom they dealt used the term "independently wealthy."

Don said, "There isn't any such thing."

"But— See, if you were to terminate all competition and investment activity at this moment—"

"What's the dollar worth nowadays? By some terms of reckoning it's worth thirty-odd cents right now. What if it went down to a dime?"

"Then, on the basis of actual cost, all commodities would be down accordingly. If your dollars became dimes, you'd still have the dimes."

"But July and I could never be independent of the actual structure of the economy. Nor could anyone else. So what's all this guff about *independently*?"

"Well—"

"Well!"

8

In this party, identified in current travel annals as Graduate Tours Incorporated, were several wisps, but all were wives or widows, except Miss Sarah Buckles. She was so shy that she squeaked when she talked, and in human charity the assured and outspoken companions adopted her as they might have waxed generous to any wet and starved furry creature which scuttled up to their back doors, mewing for shelter and milk.

"What was your school, Miss Buckles?"

"Vassar."

So long ago.

"We couldn't afford it. But my father was still alive then, and he wanted me to go. And I won a scholarship."

"Wasn't that wonderful!"

Chirping away, and concerned forever with her mighty past, which truly was as threadbare as any past could be, and yet of ruling importance because she had no present worth mentioning, and her future was contained in that tight little box which elder people own.

"I was gone from the United States only once before. In 1939. To Central America. I hadn't expected to go again. To—to anywhere. But my nephew died suddenly of a heart attack. He was a bachelor, and there weren't any other—heirs or heiresses. I guess I'm an heiress. I never thought I would be one."

"It's wonderful that you can be one!"

Her memory ran detailed and taut, and she tasted it readily, and comforted herself with memory by night when she lay alone. By night she had always lain alone.

Erna Mitzheimer called her "the Divine Sarah."

People said "Baggage? Baggage?" to Sarah Buckles before she climbed out of her taxicab. Men reached and waited, men importuned her, and she was frightened because she didn't know whether the men could be trusted or not. She knew Red Caps —they could be trusted—but none of these men wore a red cap. They had striped denim jackets and little black-billed caps, they had some kind of badges on, badges with numbers. These looked official enough, so finally she let one man bring her things.

He was strong, with a swarthy face and great round shoulders, and he made no burden out of the three bags that she had struggled to bring down the stairway at home in Oakwood, New Jersey. There was her own oblong brown bag, and a black suitcase of shiny imitation leather, which her mother had bought some years before and had seldom used. These, with a striped linen case belonging to her landlady's niece, held the clothing and traveler's necessities which Sarah Buckles was taking on her journey. In addition she carried a raincoat, a plaid auto robe, a box camera, and a paper shopping bag, which held a few articles she had forgotten until the last minute.

With her arms full of these things, Sarah followed the baggage man to a long counter inside the building. This was the pier, but it didn't look like the Jersey Central ferry pier. She tried to remember how the pier of the Cunard Line had looked when she and Evvy went to see Dora McCune off on the *Berengaria*. Perhaps it had looked like this (although she could not remember), with baggage men standing about and other people producing tickets at the counter where now she, Sarah Buckles, was asked to produce hers.

But she remembered the postcards Dora had sent from England and Scotland. *Spent last night at a delightful Inn, rooms named after Shakespearean characters. Miss W. and I* slept in *"Romeo and Juliet." Wish you could see Wales & peaceful countryside. Affectionately D.* And she remembered another card from Edinburgh. *Saw Holyrood Castle and scenes made famous by Mary Q. of S. Now we are to take bus trip through Trossachs. You would adore it all. Affectionately D.* For a long time Sarah had kept these cards on her dresser, after showing them to people at Mrs. Sanford's rooming house. She had stuck them into her mirror by their corners, and thus for months she was able to look at Ann Hathaway's Cottage and Pipers of Gordon Highlanders, Edinburgh Castle—even after Dora McCune was back in Oakwood, telling her civics students about it.

Now that she herself was on the point of embarking for a foreign port (for no less than *three* foreign ports) it was impossible for Sarah to experience any feeling of elation. Surprise at her willfulness, extravagance, and physical temerity had eaten resistance from her being. Thus unnourished, her surprise had vanished utterly. She was not amazed that her most noticeable sensation was a sense of shame. Sarah Buckles had no business in paying money to the International Fruit Importing Company and embarking on one of the vessels of their Great Golden Fleet. She kept seeing the flowers on the polished lid of her mother's burial casket, as it sank away from her twenty-two days before, when she looked for a last time at the meek gray house where her mother would find longer comfort than she had found at Mrs. Sanford's. She thought of her bankbook, the unfamiliar inky figures danced and shriveled in her mind. $3,961.82. No, that wasn't right, that was before she had sent a check to Mr. Marsh in Fanwood for that ancient bill of her father's, which Mr. Marsh had been kind enough not to mention before. $3,911.82? She would look again at her bankbook when she got on the ship.

It seemed that she was trangressing, that she was assuming portentous obligation, that she was pretending to be somebody else and should be arrested for it. She was pretending to be Dora McCune, who had been once to the Mediterranean and once to the British Isles and now even talked of South America.

Or she was posing as one of those women who strode, eternally twenty-one and eternally smiling, through pink and gold and black prospectuses of the Golden Fleet cruises—who basked, shapely and gracious and sought after, in pink-engraved pools and who played deck tennis in daring shorts—women who traveled with enormous piles of bright-labeled luggage, women who knew how to swim and dance and drink, how to operate Leica cameras, and—above all—how to win the interest, admiration, and desire of the bland, tanned, grinning men who surrounded them.

Some person looked at her ticket, another person's voice said, "All right. Straight ahead." She was lifted in an elevator, and then she walked and walked, and the man was there, he had her bags. The shopping bag started to slip from under her elbow, and she gripped it more tightly. The man went ahead and set her suitcases down—they had passed through a wide door—and here was another desk with two men and a girl behind it. She saw uniforms—some of these people were ship's officers, maybe —and out on the Hudson River behind them and behind the thick pier walls and behind the Golden Fleet ship that waited for her, Sarah Buckles heard a whistle blast, deep-throated, resonant, straining to get away.

They wanted to know her name.

"Miss Sarah Buckles." She was afraid that she might whisper it, that they might not understand, so she spoke her name clearly and vehemently.

They wanted her ticket. "Let's see. Thirty-five."

"No," she said, startled. "I'm—"

"Cabin thirty-five. That's right."

"She didn't sign this, Duke."

He looked at a paper. "Yes, that's right. This wasn't all filled out. No, give me the other. Now, Miss Buckles, your address is 411 Elm Street, Oakwood, New Jersey?"

"Yes."

"Occupation?"

"I'm a librarian."

"Where were you born, Miss Buckles?"

"Fanwood, New Jersey."

"And the date, please."

She gave the date.

"All right. Sign here."

She signed, and they smiled and waved her on. The baggage man was already walking ahead, carrying her bags as if they were not heavy, walking as if this were nothing new or important, walking as if he had carried many bags to many boats. (She called them alternately boats and ships.)

"But—" That wasn't her voice. It wasn't Dora McCune's voice either, or the voice of one of those smiling women in the pink-and-gold-and-black folders. "Don't I take my ticket on the boat?"

"It'll be there, Miss. The purser'll have it."

She had a vision of a purser, a stern man with a large steel safe filled completely with purses. And stewards—she had never had anything much to do with stewards. And waiters—in restaurants there were waiters, and in hotels there were clerks and bellboys (some people called them bellhops, but that sounded uncouth, Sarah thought) and chambermaids. They had a steward at the Bonny Crest Golf & Country Club near Oakwood. Sarah had been there three times.

In this narrow corridor, lined on the floor with rubber matting, her feet sounded clandestine and secretive. She looked down at the toes of her shiny brown slippers. Her coat also was brown, with a red fox collar. It was a good coat, warm and well lined, though it made Sarah seem wider at the waist and hips than she really was. She wondered how soon people could take off their winter things when a boat headed south. Maybe when the ship was opposite Carolina? The Mabries in Oakwood went to Carolina every winter, to Southern Pines. It must be warm down there, but perhaps it might be cooler at the same degree of latitude on the ocean.

Sarah's knees shivered momentarily, though no one could have seen them shiver under her coat and under the pale green woolen dress. She was going on the ocean, and certainly she had no right to go. The tunnel of the corridor became shorter and shorter, there were figures moving at the end of it. And there, behind wide panes of glass built to shut out the cold and through open spaces where soon she would walk came a burst of glistening brass and polished rails and stanchions, white painted pipes, striped canvas, varnished hardwood, the amazing flat and snowy doughnuts of life preservers (they were real— they actually had and used them—they were like the ones in movies, like life preservers on the stage at the Oakwood Municipal Auditorium when the glee clubs gave "H.M.S. *Pinafore*"). Surrounding all, glaring and gleaming with a sunshine that lived in its pigment and did not need to pierce from the gray ceiling of early December, was the banana-colored paint of the International Fruit Importing Company—the skin and dressing of its steamship *Utilla*—the uniform of the Golden Fleet.

Sarah Buckles slipped as she turned left under the arch of bright canvas; she must have looked foolish, slipping that way, but it was uncertain underfoot, with those funny cleats on the gangplank. Nevertheless she must have looked ungainly—people would think she was a plain idiot. The man, the sailor-kind-of-man in a blue uniform, caught her arm quickly and saved her from falling; he seemed to dissolve her flesh and squeeze it into the armbone, and of course he didn't mean to hurt her.

"Oh, thank you," she gasped, and then she went up the gangplank, walking fearfully and unnaturally, and another sailor-kind-of-man helped her at the top. She walked into lights and warmth, into the sound of moving feet. Somewhere beyond this room an orchestra was playing "The Beer Barrel Polka," and Sarah Buckles had seen pictures of orchestras in the ads, but just the same she hadn't realized that there would truly be an orchestra on such a small boat. Maybe they would get off before the boat sailed.

Here were lights and glass and a wide desk with a uniformed man behind it, and there was a little slice of glass sign illuminated above.

"Purser. *Contador*." "That's Spanish," Sarah whispered in

her mind. "I suppose Spanish people do use these boats. South American people, not just Americans. Well, of course I guess they're Americans, too. And Central Americans" *Contador.* The baggage man had stopped there and so she stopped, too, and peered in at the purser who waited behind the desk. He wasn't very stern-looking—he didn't look as if he had a hoard of purses that he wouldn't let their owners have back again. He wore spectacles. He looked something like one of the boys in Jarvis's drug store in Oakwood.

There was a carbon copy list spread before him.

He smiled and said, "Good morning."

"I'm Miss Sarah Buckles."

"Let's seeeeee." He kept whistling softly, while he examined the list. "Buckles, Miss Sarah. Cabin thirty-five. Thirty-five, Marty." A blue-uniformed arm slid out from behind the partition and gave him a big key with a wafer dangling from it, for all the world like a hotel key. "I believe there's some mail already down in your cabin, Miss Buckles."

She said, "Mail. For *me?*" A lump stood in her throat. It seemed that somebody—the bank, or the library board, or Mrs. Sanford even—somebody might have sent a letter or a summons or a legal document to restrain her from sailing on the *Utilla.* It hadn't been real, wasn't real now. Maybe nothing was real— Oakwood, or the library, or those two rooms at Mrs. Sanford's for the past nine years since the Building & Loan took their house away from them, or the scream of brakes in Elm Street on the early evening of November 7, or her mother's black felt hat all mashed in on the side, or the special automobile insurance policy which Mr. Braunsdorf persuaded her mother that she ought to take out, back in 1935.

"Maybe a telegram, Miss Buckles. I remember sending something down there. No, behind you. Corridor on the left. That's it."

The baggage man was far ahead, turning and looking back. He saw her coming, jerked his head to summon her, and then she went after him through shadows, under electric lights. There were numerals on the doors: "19," "21," "23."

Sarah thought, "Odd numbers on this side of the ship. I suppose they have to have a system for these things, just like when we catalog books at the library." Opposite "23" was another of those illuminated glass signs, and this one said, "Women. *Señoras.*" Sarah looked up at it and then down quickly, for fear someone might see her. Now there was a new terror in her mind. She didn't have a private bath; she couldn't afford that. She would have to use the public toilet rooms.

A women's toilet room wouldn't be so bad, but—*Señoras.* She didn't know any *señoras.* It seemed that the ship company people ought to have separate toilet rooms—some for women, some for *señoras.* Sarah prided herself that she could stay abreast of the times, and she had read voluminously about venereal diseases—in fact, she read every book or pamphlet about venereal disease which she could get hold of. She recalled that such diseases were plentiful in ship ports, where sailors and other low characters gathered together for the purpose of— of dissipation.

She was afraid to enter a ladies' room marked with this strange Spanish name, it sounded something like *señorita,* which of course meant "Miss" instead of "Mrs." But she remembered books by Ernest Hemingway, or James M. Cain, or somebody, and there was always a lot of talk about barring Hemingway from the Oakwood library, and they wouldn't consider one of those Cain books for a single moment, and some of the *Señoritas* in such books—

Danger piled on danger as she went forward. She followed her baggage man across another little vestibule or lounge and into the corridor (a very dark corridor this was, with a closed door at the end of it) and here was her Cabin 35, and opposite loomed a bright-lighted sign. "Men. *Caballeros.*"

Well, she wouldn't be going in *there,* but it was almost directly across the hall, and it was bad enough to have Men there. *Caballeros.* Some kind of an awful song about them. She had heard Mike Sanford, Mrs. Sanford's nephew, and some of his friends from Rutgers—they were sitting in a car down in front of the Broad Street diner one night when she passed, and she was almost certain that they had been drinking—they were singing a song. She remembered it . . . how could she forget it, anyway?

> *Oh, I was a gay caballero*
> *Embarking from Rio Janiero,*
> *Bearing with me*
> *My ly-trum-bo-lee,*
> *And also my ly-trum-bo-lar-os.*

It was simply terrible for those boys to sit around in a car, singing a song like that. She had been worried about Mike Sanford; she thought that he was in bad company and probably something awful would happen to him. But he seemed to settle down after he graduated. He was working in New York at a branch of the Bank of Manhattan, and he was said to be engaged to Lois Enright—she was really an awfully sweet little girl—and Sarah herself had seen Mike being very nice to his mother, who was lame, and helping her carefully out of her car in front of the A&P store.

> *Oh, I was a gay caballero . . .*

She dared not look at the sign again. She had given her key to the baggage man, and he was fumbling with the door. The door swung open, heavy, smooth, solid. Everything seemed heavy and smooth and solid aboard this ship: partitions and doorknobs and hinges were fabricated of thicker material than was used in houses ashore. The man put her bags down, and Sarah spread the things that she was carrying upon the bed built beneath the two windows. Light came on, brilliant and warm and strong— The baggage man had found the switch.

"Well," she said. "Thanks an awful lot."

He stood looking at her, smiling a little; he seemed to be waiting for something. Well, she bet she knew what he was waiting for. Dora McCune had explained to her in detail: there was no tipping on a boat, until you had crossed the ocean and had arrived at wherever you were going, or until you had come home if you were on a cruise. You shouldn't tip the man in the dining room or the chambermaid, or whatever they called her, or anybody. But maybe this baggage man was different.

"You're not on the *Utilla?*" she asked abruptly. He still looked at her. "I mean, you don't work here? You're not a sailor or a porter on this ship, I mean?"

He shook his head and pointed. "I go off."

Sarah realized then that he was some kind of foreigner, for he could barely talk English. Probably she had been cheated, probably she should have waited for one of the sailors to carry her bags aboard. She calculated rapidly: three bags. That should be ten cents apiece: thirty cents total. She hunted in her purse. The taxicab had taken most of her small change. She found two quarters and dropped them into the wide yellow hand which he lifted toward her.

"I hope you have some change," she started to say, but he had touched his hat and had gone out, closing the door carefully behind him. "Well!" she gasped, and it seemed that her money wouldn't last long at this rate.

Sarah had removed one glove, to search for change. Now she dropped her bag on the bed and slowly peeled off the other little brown glove. She thought of what the purser had told her and looked about quickly. Yes, there it was—on the desk. Or was this a dresser? It must be her dressing table, though it looked something like a desk. Oh, here were all sorts of things! A yellow Western Union envelope, and a letter, and a basket with paper all around it. The basket was big—it was almost a foot high. Sarah wriggled out of her coat and snatched up the telegram. The message appeared before her eyes; the little strips of printing were pasted on a special blank—all sorts of crazy designs and—

HOPE YOU HAVE A FINE TRIP
LOVE EMMA SANFORD

Why, she hadn't expected Mrs. Sanford to actually send a telegram. She bet that was the reason Mrs. Sanford looked so sort of mysterious during breakfast this morning. Hot tears began to sting Sarah's eyes, but resolutely she blinked the tears away and picked up the letter.

There was a knock at her door. She went and opened it. A burly man in a white coat stood there with a vase of carnations.

"Yes, ma'am," he said, smiling. "I've brought your flowers. Thought I'd better get them in a vase *pronto*."

"Flowers? I didn't have— Are you—?" And he came in, so purposefully that she stood aside and let him place the vase on the dressing table. He said over his shoulder, "I'm your steward, ma'am. The name's over there on that card by the door: Bruce. Now, if you want anything at all you just ring one ring, and that'll fetch me *pronto*. Two rings if you want the stewardess for anything. I neglected to bring your drinking water." He whisked over to take a shining flask from its bracket on the wall, and then he went out, still winking and smiling and saluting Sarah Buckles with his pink forefinger.

Flowers. She tore open an envelope and learned about them. "Dear Sade," Dora McCune had written,

I'm praying you have a *divine* time, every moment, and come back the week before Xmas as brown as a berry! I'm sending carnations—I trust they reach the boat in time. Not very *swanky*, no? But carnations last and last and *last*.

The tears were on Sarah's cheeks now. She supposed that Dora McCune was really the best friend she had in Oakwood, or in all the world. She was really very fond of Dora, though once in a while Dora frightened her a little when she kissed her hello or good-bye on some special occasion. She felt a little sick, when Dora kissed her like that. She wondered if— There was that book. She read it long ago, but the board had decided that it must not be admitted to the library. It was about a girl who— Oh, what was she thinking of, thinking such things about a dear sweet girl like Dora?

Her hands tore at the purple paper wrappings of the parcel, and a shimmering mass of cellophane, ribbons, and glistening fruit came to view. She gasped when she saw it. It was wonderful that trivial things like oranges, apples, and pears could look so positively elegant when they were arranged so prettily. And raisins and dates, and almonds. Here was a little box. She pulled it out. Preserved ginger. Well, she just hated preserved ginger, but it was simply wonderful of—

Who—who could have done it? She thought of men at the bank—they had been awfully nice to her. Or maybe Dr. Shelton. Here was a small white envelope. Her trembling fingers began to open it. There sounded a rap at the door, and before she could speak the door was open and the steward had reappeared with her water flask.

He set the jug carefully in its bracket above the washbasin. "Nothing else, Miss?" He had called her "Ma'am" before but now he called her "Miss," and there was something odd about that. "Just ring if you want anything," he said soothingly, and then he had closed the door again.

She unfolded a slip of stationery. "Bon Voyage," it read, "from The Gang!" Their names were written below: Miss K., Edna, Evvy, Lucille, Ralph. Why, even Ralph had joined in and helped to send this basket; he was the old janitor at the library —they had got everybody in on it. Miss Klabbe, the head, was awfully stern and stuffy—she wasn't a bit modern or anything— but it had been nice of her to think of this. Edna and Lucille were just girls who worked there part time, and Evvy used to be in the library all the time before she got married.

Sarah stepped slowly backward until she felt the bed behind her, and she sat down. She was insensitive to the newness and wonder of physical objects nearby, she saw them, she knew they were there, and yet she could neither examine nor marvel at them. Mirrors, little silver cranks below the windows, shining railing above the washbowl, neat gold and brown spread on the bed, floor rug with "I.F.I.C." woven together in elaborate spirals . . . the electric fan, the terrifying framed placard that showed you how to put on your life-jacket: none of these was for the moment a part of Sarah Buckles' life. She was struggling against her better judgment, to return to Oakwood and once more sink into its meager certainties.

This was her trip—everyone had urged her to take it—she had the money, she owed no one in the world and had almost four thousand dollars in cash besides, and yet a wild chorus of voices screamed to tell her that she was doing wrong. She thought of her mother's blank face, all powdered amid lilac-colored satin puckers and white flowers. This was mother's money, it was blood money, mother was gone, Mr. Braunsdorf had sold her that automobile accident policy, she had paid five dollars a year for it, it had seemed foolish. And now mother was gone, and here was Sarah Buckles doing what she had never dared dream of doing, and she was crying. She had the little note from "The Gang" clasped in her hand, she lay down across her things on the bed, and she kept crying. The box camera was underneath, she was afraid she might crush it, but still she couldn't move; she just went on crying.

9

On their second morning in Singapore the bulk of the tourists set off by bus for a round of the waterfront, which was to include a visit to the Chinese market. Mitzheimer and Lundin accompanied the party, Lundin going with amazing docility—it seemed that no temples were involved. July remained behind at the tall hotel where they were ensconced on one of the hills swelling out of the high-rise jumble.

"Tower cranes, building new buildings. I counted eleven from our window."

"They used to call them South American cranes."

"I know."

Erna could not go on the trip, Erna could not go on any trip, and July told the men that she would stay behind to keep Erna company.

Erna wore a long robe of flowered crepe, and her wig was a trifle on one side. She stalked her room, brandishing a white flask in hand. In native form she went into Shakespearian quotation. " 'And some, when the bagpipe squeals i' the nose, cannot contain their urine for affection.' Well, urine's not my problem. There's something else I can't contain. Shoemakers' children never have shoes, and doctors' wives get the trots."

"Wasn't there anything Mitz could give you?"

"Some loathsome little pills, which he declared were drastic and just the thing. They gave me a vile attack of Weirdies in the night. I thought I was Little Orphant Annie pursued by Gobble-uns. Thank you, no. No more of that crap. Excuse me: I used the wrong word. Where in heaven did I put my spoon? Ah, here it is. I filched a large spoon from my breakfast tray, although I have no idea in this world why I ate any breakfast, since it won't, shall we say, stay put."

July said that both Mr. and Mrs. Anstrum had bad cases of diarrhea before they left Thailand. "And I heard that some of the others were suffering from it, too. I don't know just who they were."

Erna waved her flask aloft. "Kaopectate! That's the stuff. It was good for me when we went to Treetops in Africa to see the elephants drink water, and what do you suppose would happen to an elephant if it, too, acquired a tendency toward diarrhea? The thought is too appalling. But let us forget elephants. We're graduated from Thailand."

She quoted from the label with appropriate flourish. " 'Do not use for more than two days.' Good God, does that mean I'm going to have this for more than *two days*?" She quoted again. " 'Or in the presence of high fever.' Mitz took my temperature, and it was actually subnormal. 'Or in infants or children under three years of age.' I'm somewhat above that bracket. 'Unless directed by a physician.' And my own private physician gave me the pills and they only made me see Things Standin' In A Row. This Upjohn Company is really something. And where do they come from? Kalamazoo, Michigan, of all places. Up Upjohn! My dear July, you should have gone along with the others on the bus trip."

July said weakly, "Actually I think I will go out for a while."

"Wait a minute," said her friend, "until I retreat to the bathroom."

When Erna came back she was waving the Kaopectate flask once more. "Up here at the top in raised letters it says 'Shake Well.' Does that mean shake the patient well? Don't do it, July, don't touch me. If I were shaken now the results would be indescribable."

"If I could do you any good by staying—"

"Certainly you cannot. 'Flee as a bird to yon mountain!' Also I have acquired a glorious book, entitled *The Second Rebellion*. It's about the draft riots in New York in 1863. If these frizzly punks who think they can change the world to suit themselves by staging riots nowadays— Ha. They should read this one. The punks in 1863 really knew how to stage a riot, so I shall concern myself with them and let you run along. Where are you bound?"

"I thought I'd go and see the orchids in the Botanical Garden."

"Bring me an orchid. I need one to salve my something."

July's heart was pounding. She thought that she felt a little like an international spy, although she was not confident that she knew how international spies were supposed to feel. She could only guess at it. She stopped briefly in her own room, and while there went into the bathroom, raised the lid of the toilet seat, and looked into the bowl. She was driven by no such inclination as ruled her friend so ruinously this time. She just wanted to look and see. No, of course, the residue was all gone down, there was nothing left to see. Gone and washed away, long since gone.

She had memorized the note and then burned it. In pieces. In an ashtray. And washed the fragments down, then foolishly rinsed and dried the ashtray itself.

A young woman in a golden pants suit had come to her. "Mrs. Lundin, please?"

"Yes?"

"You are Mrs. Lundin?"

"Yes I am."

"I am from public secretary office downstairs. I have here a note which I was instructed to give you. To only you. Not to your husband. No. Please?"

The golden young woman had hurried away, turning once for a brief smile and then hastening on, concluding that she was an intimate instrument in romance, and dying to serve as such.

Dear July:
    Saw your names on the list of passengers arriving and should like very much to talk with you. Should like also to see Don but Negative, not this trip. Will linger among other orchids in the orchid colony at the Botanical Garden, tomorrow forenoon at eleven. Do hope you can make it.
                                                                            As ever, Cliff.

She told the doorman where she wanted to go, and he summoned a taxi driver and instructed him. The driver knew some English. He wanted to talk about the glories of Singapore and point out all the new buildings that were going up. On every side you could hear the clank and jamming of construction. Traffic was choked at the red lights, and often in between. Nevertheless July had allotted more time for the journey than was needed and reached the gardens at twenty minutes to eleven.

She was told where to go to find the orchids and went up the hill, amid mighty trees. Trees were the haven of some chattering buzzing herd of inhabitants that she could hear, even while they remained hidden and unseen. A few people went past, talking in English, and some said that creatures overhead were squirrels, some said monkeys, no one seemed to know which.

A greater throng of tourists was on the point of leaving the region where exotic colors exploded in suspended merriment—potted color, hanging potted frenzy. They gloated and chuckled at the munificence. Women were crying, "My eyes are glazed, I can't believe there could be so many varieties, I wish our Goldfarb dealer at home could see this, he'd faint dead away." July waited at one side until aisles had thinned under the housing and then ventured her own exploration. Pink, umber, mossy, tints of other-named flowers, like lavender and violet—the opulence was stifling. And workmen went about their delicate task of tending as if they also walked in dream.

She tried to paraphrase words of Alfred Noyes, learned in high school years: "Come down to Singapore— In orchid time. . . ."

A gardener had removed some pots from a trestle where they'd rested temporarily. In critical friendly fashion he looked at the woman and was affected by her manner of rapture. He wiped the area clean and dry, and motioned. She could sit down. So she rested and gave way to this delicate torrent around and above her.

When it came to orchids July, like many people, recognized the difference between a *Cymbidium* and a *Cypripedium* and that was about all. These in their wealth she wished she might embrace and wallow in. Often as a child she had experienced that luxurious inclination when confronted with a mass of beauty, and now she recalled vividly a yielding to such sin.

At the farm where her grandparents lived there grew a brake of lilac bushes—her grandmother called them English lilacs, as opposed to a darker variety, termed Persian—and the scent of the blossoms in their season held the positive flavor of a medicine. It rendered her intoxicated and unable to move or reason.

Early one May morning when July, then a mere Ada, was

visiting her elders, she pursued a pet kitten, which was supposed to be addicted to fits; earnestly she wanted to see the cat having a fit, because this malady had been mentioned in terrifying terms which attracted a child all the more. The cat's course of flight led among lilac bushes, but suddenly the small chaser halted, overcome. Bowing masses of pale blossoms were so heavy in their bloom that the scent was almost visible. The girl shivered physically as she put her face among them and felt their genteel moisture; she drew the scent through her nostrils and then through her open mouth; she wanted to eat them, drink them, be lost permanently amid their fragrance and their gift. Drunkenly she extended trembling arms— Thin, frail arms by common reckoning but now seeming mighty as an athlete's. Her hands strained upward, inward, quivering, crushing. O God and all World and all Heaven and all Nature; it was hymn and overwhelming ballad, she felt like an angel and demon united, as she pressed and strained amid the mass.

"*Ada!*" screamed the grandmother, who had come unseen behind her. "What are you doing to the *lilacs*?"

"I— I—" She tried to turn and appeal, but had no knowledge of how to present such a plea. She said in needing to explain, "I was chasing Kit-Kat to see if she'd have a fit, and I kind of ran into the bushes."

"But to tear them down, you naughty girl! To break them, maul them like you just done! Why, you got those poor little petals all *over* you! Look at that—you actually busted some branches right off! You got poor little lilacs all over your face! Them lovely flowers never done nothing to you, did they? They never hurt you, never was mean to you! Why, I never saw anything like this in all my born days! I'm going to give you a good shaking right now!" And Grandma grabbed her by the shoulders and shook and shook.

Squirting tears, the child fell away. "You don't understand," was her shriek. "You don't understand. They're so beautiful! Oh-ho-ho," in the eternal broken bellowing of the spoiled or angry or sinned-against young, and she ran stamping to the house, and burrowed among dust rolls under the bed in their carelessly kept guest room, and sobbed for long.

Later she heard Grandma telling Grandpa in the kitchen about her wicked prank and the punishment which followed, but he only said mildly, "Oh, Callie, I don't think you should ha' done that," and when she and June were taken along to the village that afternoon, he bought them chocolate nut sundaes as a treat. Mostly he was apt to yield to miserly inclinations, but in some way the infant's alleged crime and conviction had touched his heart. Still, there existed a wrong that could not be forgotten. Years later July would tend the grandmother faithfully through an exhausting and smelly last illness and hear herself be blessed for it.

This notion from the past exerted itself as she waited for Lawrence Cliffert. It reappeared quickly in recollection, and then was put away. She was amazed to learn that the man had happened to be in Singapore, of all places, at the precise moment of their arrival. Still, when one considered the dictates of his profession, it probably wasn't so odd after all.

How did she look? Her dress was white, with the skirt permanently pleated, and she should have worn walking shoes, but couldn't resist these blue ones, because she loved the blue strapped bag which accompanied them, and she had that matching blue chiffon scarf to tie over her hair if the wind played tricks. Her flossy, wiry hair was carroty and gray together. Even at what she rowdily called her advanced age, she saw the gardeners examine her with approval as they strove among the orchids. What might one call an orchid gardener? An orchidacean, perhaps? The men admired her trim figure, she saw them looking at her legs. Thank mercy, her legs were not yet shriveled or mottled with exposed veins, like the legs of many other touring ladies, poor things. The feet were narrow, highly arched, the ankles slim and tapering, her calves swelled into abrupt roundness. Don Lundin said that they looked like the legs of a high-priced Parisian whore, and she hoped they did, department called 'Senior Staff Changes.' I knew that you were a general officer now."

"Major-General Selectee," he said with pride. "Guess it hasn't been published yet."

"But I thought you were with the Strategic Air Command."

"Haven't been, for a good while."

"I didn't know that Singapore would permit American military personnel to come in here," she said honestly.

Cliff was silent. July whispered, "Sorry. I just stepped on your cloak."

"And kicked my dagger."

"Cliff, we actually flew across Vietnam on our way to Bangkok. I was a scaredy cat. Kept looking out of the window in fear and trembling."

"And you saw a great big round red Japanese sun painted on the wing, which was the reason you were there. The Japs have a special corridor through which their commercial aircraft are permitted to pass at certain altitudes."

"I kept looking for flak or fighters or something, and all the rest were laughing at me."

He told her, "Maybe some fine day somebody will goof and knock down one of those airplanes. Hasn't happened yet. At least to our knowledge."

"Cliff—"

"I just like to sit here looking at you. Yep?"

"How's Inez?"

"Meaner than a can of cutworms, probably. I don't know. I haven't seen her in several years. The girls are both married, though Shirley and her husband are still corn-husking at the University of Nebraska. Inez and I were divorced years ago."

July caught her breath, turned her face away, and shook her head blindly.

"We were divorced— Let's see. 1963. Maybe they ought to include divorces among the news notes in the *Air Force Magazine/Space Digest*, but they don't."

When still she didn't speak, Cliff said, "Well, you *are* sur-

"Because you wouldn't have come to meet me in a private one. Would you?"

"I— Guess I don't know."

"Well, you wouldn't."

"No. I mean—"

"Would or wouldn't?"

"I would have been too frightened and upset to have come."

"If in private—"

"Yes."

"That's what I thought. So, in suggesting our rendezvous here, if a group of your own touring party members had happened to arrive at the same time, I could have strolled right past you, and no one would have suspected."

"Cliff, it's so kind of cloak-and-daggerish."

"Seriously I thought of this garden because I had to go to a private address near here, for a conference. One character talked a little longer than was expected. Hence, I was late, and apologize accordingly."

"But to think that you knew we were on this trip—"

"July, the lists of arriving Americans—also some others—are tightly screened and passed around. I doubt that there are any other Don Lundins in the world."

"It still sounds like old-fashioned Bolsheviks with great big round bombs. With fuses sputtering."

Cliff made grizzled sputtering noises, and they both felt more affable, and found a slightly secluded place where they could sit down. Strollers came past constantly—you could hear their talking, it came to you in little yelps and spurts of various languages—though the strollers could not hear you when your conversation was muted, and this conversation was quiet if not lulling.

"I've kept track of you a little bit, Cliff."

"Delighted to hear it—"

"Just militarily speaking. Don belongs to the Air Force Association, of course, and gets that *Air Force/Space Digest* magazine, so when I see one around, I look at it. They have that the elder of Don Lundin. Also he was larger and more powerful physically. He had no sons, he had daughters, but if he had had sons of high school or college age, you'd imagine him heaving a football with them, and passing farther and more accurately than the youths themselves. He had disliked the name Lawrence from the moment he first became aware that he owned it—just why, he could not have told—and was Cliff to all and sundry. When July and Don knew him, he had been married to a slender brunette named Inez, who was appropriately given to sultry and gypsyish poses. She wore more-than-a-little-expensive earrings and bracelets and jangles and bangles, and you could hear her coming clanking into a room before you saw her. She was sly and adroit up to any point where her emotions were not involved, but once they became involved she acted the role of hell-cat—on wheels—said the members of the officers' wives clubs along the line.

Now Cliffert walked nearer in his crisp Oriental-tailored suit, and his battered rebuilt nose looked almost handsome, wads or no wads, and his brightly burnished blue eyes were close to disappearance as he smiled and spoke her name.

"Why, Cliff!" Almost as if amazed to see him.

"Sorry I was late. As a good secretary always says about her boss, I was in conference."

The orchid man whispered, *"Adios, Señora,"* and scuttled away. July called her thanks after him.

"He told me some wonderful things about orchids. I wish I could have understood more of what he was saying. Did you know that vanilla is an orchid, too?"

"Yes," Cliffert said. "Do I get to kiss you?"

She tilted up her face, and they kissed. "Wow," he said, and they both laughed shakily.

"Up the hill and then down that other slope. We can find a place to sit beside the pond, pool, water, river, whatever it is. We can't talk here; here comes another gang of tourists."

"Why did you ask me to meet you in such a public place?"

but considered also that her husband's acquaintance with high-priced Parisian whores was strictly limited.

One of the nearer orchid tenders looked like a Filipino. She could not estimate the nativity of another, yet was certain that they conversed in some form of Spanish. During one recent summer the Lundins had taken a house for ten weeks on the coast of Andalucia, near the village of Los Boliches; Don would not study Spanish, but July engaged herself in a series of lessons with a local bicycle repairman who had picked up English during previous sea-going days. Her Spanish was regional and fragmentary and studded with high school Latin, but now she essayed a comment. "*Las floras estan muy bonita—*" and a bit more, which brought the Filipino scrambling as if he had discovered a long lost friend. He uttered a crammed botanical discourse, replete with Latin and mostly beyond July's understanding; she did not have to reply, except to nod wisely and venture an occasional faltering question. She had never guessed that there could be as many as fifteen thousand species of orchids, but the man said that there were. She had used vanilla throughout her cooking days, which began early, and had never dreamed that *Vanilla planifolia* was an orchid, but now she was informed about this, and she cried, "*Me allegro mucho, porque me gusta mucho la vanilla,*" and the gardener swore that he loved vanilla also, especially in ice cream.

During this cozy episode Lawrence Cliffert arrived, ten minutes later than intended, and he stood for a time a short distance away, watching July with admiration undiminished by the years that had passed since last he saw her: she was unique, it was a marvel that she could appear so girlish and uninhibited.

Cliffert wore a brown-striped seersucker suit and might have been awarded compliments on his own youthful appearance (but only when watched from a little distance away). He held a black belt in judo and struggled sternly to maintain his claim to such distinction. In some lights he looked blond, in some lights silver-haired—the silver had the better of it at last, but still he boasted a thick crop of hair, even though he was some years prised. You thought she still had me. By the balls," he added with deliberate brutality.

"I didn't think she'd let you go—easily."

"She didn't. July, that letter she wrote—"

"Don't let's talk about it," she said quickly. "Don't let's."

"But I mean— Don himself—"

"He doesn't know a thing about it. He never did. I never told him."

"My God!" said Cliff.

He was married again, this time to a Meg. "She's a darling. I remember how my mother used to say: 'Fair, fat and forty-ish.' Two boys and a girl, now all away at school. Home is in Hawaii, that's where we met. It was when General Hunter Harris was commanding in the Pacific, and I met Meg at a dinner party at the Harrises'. She claims that Mrs. Harris invited me on purpose. I don't know, wives are always doing such things. After all, it was the general's father or mother who first introduced the original Eisenhowers, and Meg says we shouldn't be far behind. We have a lot of joking on the subject."

"Joking's nice."

"Yes, nice. I practically never had any with Inez."

July wanted to say that that was obvious, but held her tongue.

"Why do poor officers feel inclined to marry rich women? I've been married to two of them—"

July said that perhaps many poor officers were of the greedy type.

"But I would have married you if I'd come along in time, before Lundin, instead of years after. And you weren't rich. I mean, if you would have been willing to have me."

"Thank you, Cliff. I don't know whether I'd have been eager to marry you or not."

"Sure you would."

"Cliff," she said, "you're a CMP. No, a goddamn CCMP. Charismatic chauvinistic military pig."

"No, I'm not."

"Yes, you are. What was Meg's first husband: a banker or something like that? A Wall Street broker?"

"He had a stroke and conked off when only fifty-one. He was of Italian parentage, from the Piedmont, and owned wineries up around Santa Rosa. Also he liked to grow orchids as a hobby, and he taught Meg a lot about it, and Meg has taught me some bits and dabs. She's got her own collection on Oahu where we live. One time I had some accumulated R&R coming, and I had been wounded again, not badly, but I had a blood problem for a while—"

"Vietnam?"

Cliffert looked at his watch, as if seeking the answer. "It was when they first got those Sam sites operating. If they had listened to LeMay there wouldn't have been any Sam sites operating, or any protracted war. But politicians never listen to people who know the most about the business. I don't believe that McNamara ever listened to anything or anybody except his own conscience, and I can't even guess what that little instrument revs at.

"One time in SAC I got fresh and asked General LeMay if he remembered McNamara in his B-29 days in the Pacific. He took his cigar out of his mouth, and looked at it, and put it back in. 'Some major at a desk,' he says. Listen, woman, excuse me. I keep shooting off my mouth like this, and I'll be busting into Jack Anderson's column."

What he did not explain to July was that, in addition to another cluster for his Purple Heart ribbon, he had acquired the Air Force Cross as a result of the Vietnam incident.

"So I skipped school. Meg met me at Clark, where she waited with friends until I was ready to come, and then we came down here and saw these orchids. Or their uncles and aunts."

He was looking at his watch again.

July said, "Cliff, you've got to go."

"Luncheon date. It can't be wiped off the board either. July, sweetheart, sometimes I think I'd like to talk to Don. Try to explain—"

She cried in shrillness, but struggling to mute her voice, "Don't think of it, Cliff! Don't you dare, don't you dare! He doesn't know a thing! I've never—"

She stood up, and he stood up. He squinted his eyes shut and shook his head, as if trying to discourage intolerable insects that no one, except himself, might see or feel. "Sweetheart, I wish you were going to Hong Kong."

She thought, Line in a play, trivial play, I must tell Erna, no, I can't. "But we are going to Hong Kong."

Rigid as a post, big blond-gray gray-blond-topped post. "When?"

July opened her bag and took out a printed card. "Here's the itinerary. They gave us all these little lists to carry. We fly from here to Bali. We're there until the fifth. Then we fly to Hong Kong."

"Where'll you be?"

"Hotel Queen."

"Golly damn. I'll move to Kowloon."

"Where's that?"

"Just across the harbor. Across the water. Takes a few crowded minutes by ferry."

July began a preachment. "Cliff, I don't think it would be wise. I mean, that we should see each other again—"

"Shut up," he said, "and stand still. If you don't stand still I'm going to lift you up in my arms. I'm going to kiss you good-bye."

He kissed her, gave her no chance to cry protest, to say that there were people coming past, Dutch or Germans coming past —no, not Dutch, you're supposed to call them Hollanders— and he was kissing her long and fiercely. He did lift her up in his arms—held her swinging free, and then her body swung against his—and when he let her down at last the intimate breath of him was still in her.

"See you in Hong Kong. Kowloon," and then he had left, and was marching away down the path, and she was all woman at this minute, watching a man going away from her, as always women are compelled to watch men going away, going away.

For a little while.

Hong Kong?

Kowloon?

10

Waiting since the very beginning of Time—Time as far as humans are concerned, Time as far as life itself was concerned, waiting for the first moment of separation and differentiation of the sexes: when there would be two cells instead of one.

The female cell cried within herself, Oh, please to unite with me.

Although never might she say it, never should she approach the male demanding. She should feign to be pursued, she should desire him and lie in wait, but pretending elaborately that she did not wish to be sought out or copulated with.

Lingering.

Tarrying in light of a flare he'd made for her, seeing its vague, frightened gush upon the cavern wall, dreading what lay in shadows outside the realm of reflection, lamenting to herself.

Will he return?

To me?

Has some dread monster gobbled him?

I don't care if it is his own fault. I need him to come back, need him to assuage my dry, lonely desperation.

My tissues and my notion cry for his presence.

When will he come?

And abiding not only in those dim, violent, terrified moments before the beginnings of history, but also earlier, before the beginnings of womanhood.

Waiting for womanhood itself.

Saying, I am no longer a child.

They all treat me as if I were a child!

Don't they know? I am beyond childhood, holding myself in readiness for the first evidence of woman's mortal attributes and her mortal curse.

Saying, God, God, why don't they understand? Why do they insist upon and persist in treating me this way?

Witnessing herself in a mirror (if by now she has progressed to the use of mirrors), shivering as she detects pubescence, keening softly like a professional mourner and even then not understanding why she wails.

Please, Nature, dictate to me. But dictate with authentication. Let me know what I have attained. Let me know that I must speak and move and feel with woman's authority.

And anguishing again when the miracle of transformation is complete. Bleeding— is this indeed it, is this what I sought and relished in imagination; is this the state I desired? This, only this? Mercy sakes, it's *murder*. The cramps— I did not know it would be like *this*!

Then relishing the entire course, aware of her own figure, her own perfume, her own compulsive softness.

I was created and matured for men. Especially for A Man.

Where is he?

Why doesn't he come?

Is this he? No, this is not he.

Is *this* he?

Impossible.

Is this—?

Well, perhaps. Maybe. I don't know, I can't be sure. I'm still uncertain, still waiting.

He says—

Yes, he says—

I don't know whether to believe him. Should I?

Is it true?

And then agreeing that it is true. Beginning and culmination, all at once.

I have never been so happy, no one else has ever been so happy, no one in the future can ever be so happy! I own this, hold it, embrace it. It is bliss, bliss, bliss!

My voice is vibrant, my hair shines, my eyes shine.

*Dar*ling!

Later (perhaps not very much later, perhaps a long time later, but sure to offend)—

Something's happened. Something is disordered, something wrong. I can't quite believe it is true, yet it seems to be happening.

Why, I didn't think it would be like this. What am I waiting for?

Not—that—man!

Certainly not.

He's betrayed me. I loathe him.

He has shown himself to be heedless, perhaps advisedly cruel. Yes, I'm positive he's cruel.

He did this with deliberation. He—

He didn't appear. He didn't come.

He stayed away in mobbish purpose. In full knowledge of the fact that I was alone, trusting, simple. A fool, waiting for him.

He's abusive. I never would have admitted it before. Yet the truth seemed expanding and forcing itself upon me, even while I dwelt with him.

God expunge this solemn memory. *Even when I lay with him, and he was within me.*

Beast!

A woman stays at home, the man is nowhere about. He is

gone abruptly, and ignoring—perhaps even forgetting—the woman. He is gone off, resounding in violence.

Perhaps there is a child. The child is ill.

Oh God, won't he come home? Won't he come? Possessed by lunacy I need him.

The child is in abomination, child blinks his febrile eyes. Child says, Pa. I want Pa.

Why doesn't he want Ma? No. He doesn't want Ma, or thinks he doesn't, and Ma has been there tending him all along, hovering, doing everything, everything. But it's Pa he wants, Pa he moans for.

Then Pa comes, and the child dies with Pa holding him. Pa says later to his friends, says in blundering agony, He died in my arms. Charley died in my arms.

It happens again. One more traditional torture (life is all torture, life piles torture on torture, because a woman has to wait, and wait alone).

You hear him say, Charlotte died. Lotty died in my arms.

You have the ugly suspicion that it is all pretense on his part; that he doesn't feel, doesn't know, can never know or feel as you knew and felt; and thus his grief is assumed. You are wicked enough to let him know that you feel it is assumed.

He looks at you—

As if he were saying, You think I didn't feel? You think I didn't know?

Nightmare, nightmare! It didn't happen that way.

But suppose it had?

It must have happened that way to some other women.

Many other women.

Poor souls.

They didn't have Don, dear good Don, faithful and attentive, so loyal, so very loyal, anyone without a Don Lundin is a poor soul, yet none of the other women in our party has him, and I'm confident that few of them consider themselves to be poor souls, and if they do they're so cringing and woebegone that it's a sentence to even have to sit with them.

11

July carried the requested flower to Erna Mitzheimer, who was still Second Rebellioning avidly through the streets of New York, amid howling and flame.

"The mobs have just broken into Brooks Brothers," she reported, "and they're all dressing up in fancy shirts and underwear. What a riot is this riot! You lovable creature—you did bring me an orchid! Gimme, gimme, gimme!"

It was russet and purple, heavy of head, bowing under its glory. "It is," the donor reported authoritatively, "a *Phajus*, or an epiphyte, or a *Vanda*."

"How do you know so very much about this cuddlesome thing?"

"I don't, really. Those are just names I picked up. Of course, it was impossible to fetch one from the garden itself, but there was a little Chinese man out by the street where I got a taxi. He had a cart and he was selling orchids like crazy. Maybe he grew them at home or something. A lot of them were pretty much the worse for wear, but this looked more hardy. I asked how much, and he said, 'Two dollar, lady.'

"I thought that was a little steep for being right in the orchid country, but when I got out the first dollar bill he snatched it and turned away to wait on other customers. They were all around; I think they were Germans or Hollanders. Anyway what he meant was two Singapore dollars instead of ours. That meant the orchid cost a whole sixty-seven cents. So I pretended that the other thirty-three cents could be a tip."

Erna crowed that July was an extravagant hussy but that if she predeceased her, Erna would place a placating orchid on July's bier.

"I am certain at the moment that you will predecease me, even as tender young as you are. This morning I thought it would be well to flush my entire body away and be done with it. My dear, can you tell me the name of the traditional little Dutch boy who stopped that threatening fissure in the dike with his busy digit?"

"Of course, I can't. I know it wasn't Hans Brinker."

"His name was Upjohn, not down the john. Your speaking of Hollanders brought it to mind. And after he grew up, Upjohn had a son and heir named Koapectate. Believe it or not, I— haven't—*once* more!"

"You mean—since I left?"

"Not once. I've endured a few quivers, but fought them off with gallantry. Do you suppose there are any wholesale drug importers in Singapore? I should like to buy a case or cases of Kaopectate and present a bottle to every fellow member of our touring party. Overseer Mitzheimer can tell Sambo and Quimbo to take his precious little pills out and feed them to the hogs. I stood in fell need— I mean to say, I *sat* in fell need of a cork or a little Dutch boy or something, and I found it in that white flask yonder.

"Mentioning the Netherlands, let me relate something delectable. You know—or perhaps I've never mentioned it—that Mrs. Eleanor Roosevelt was a pupil of mine, years ago. She was working on her voice for purposes of public utterance, and I must put her down as a very staunch toiler indeed. She was kind enough to invite me up to Hyde Park for luncheon one day; Princess Juliana of the Netherlands, later to become Queen Juliana, had come a-visiting in wartime refugee fashion, and naturally I was excited at the prospect of meeting her.

"I parked my car dutifully where a gardener, or maybe he was a Secret Service man pretending to be a gardener, instructed me to park it. On my way in I encountered a fresh-faced, beaming, plump, peasant-type nursemaid wheeling one baby girl in a carriage and shepherding another tot alongside. Such delightful children, and I knelt down to see them closer. These would be the small daughters of Juliana, without doubt. What fun to see them thus, just ordinary plump-faced sturdy Dutch children.

" 'The little dears,' I said, or some similar banality. And then added proudly, 'I'm on my way to have lunch with their mother.' '*Ja*,' says the also-beaming buxom nursemaid type, 'I am *dere moeder*.' "

12

At the beginning of the trip, after the tour conductor had greeted each incoming contingent from Graduate Tours Incorporated at a Tokyo airport and while he was escorting them to their hotel, he would identify himself. He had contrived a speech intended to guard, guide, counsel, and reassure them generally.

He would say, "I am your tour conductor, and I will be with you through the tribulations and glories of Tokyo, Thailand, Singapore, Bali, Hong Kong, and back to Japan again, where we will visit various places. My name is Wye Rabarti Wong. I like to think of myself as Rab, and I hope you will call me by my pet name. There was written long ago in Great Britain, by Mr. John Brown, a book about a dog called *Rab and His Friends*. So I am Rab, and I hope that we are now friends immediately and will remain friends through existence."

He continued, "As for my name itself, Wye comes because my father dwelt in a Kentish town of that name when he was studying at Canterbury. He rode a bicycle back and forth, and he loved the little town of Wye so well that he gave it to me for a first name. My middle name, Rabarti, is a family name. As for the Wong, when I was very small my mother said that I was well named because I seldom, being a Wong, did wight. Now thank you for the small laugh; it could have been louder but no harm done. I will brief you on procedures at the hotel tonight, and for our reassembly tomorrow."

He did not know how many times he had been told that he ought to write a book about his experiences. But he had learned a truth. The majority of people whose lives are crammed with human experience cannot sit down to write about it. They must be out on the trail, freshly hunting for new experiences or, more enduringly, having the same experiences over and over again. In any event there was too much that he could not tell, and there were some things which he did not even like to relive in memory when they recurred to him, as they were bound to do. He put them away hastily, pretending they were snakes fallen from his private basket. (But still he could not bring himself to kill them.)

Rab thought but did not say, "Yes. Among other things, I have become a snake-charmer too. My cobras were named Peter and Cassie and Murray, and they came along on the trip together—a honeymoon trip for Peter and Cassie. It seemed peculiar to others in the party that they should have a friend honeymooning along with them. Some of the more suspicious souls among the women raised their eyebrows as high as any suspicious women could raise them, and then squinted those same eyes and guessed in fevered whispers that the little bride Cassie was sleeping with both men. This was not quite the case."

Rab was called by airport officials on one lonely night in a certain tropic town and informed that Cassie was trying in hysteria to board an out-bound airplane without benefit of ticket, cash, or passport. Rab made his long trip to the airport by taxi and found a wailing, shivering, tatter-haired girl in the women's washroom, guarded by a female official.

"You'd have to hit me over the head and knock me cold to take me back to that hotel again. I want to get aboard an airplane here and now, and I don't care about my things—they're just things. You can give them away if you want to. My father will send you a check, but *please get me aboard the airplane.*"

When finally Rab had wrenched the story from her, he agreed. He went back to the hotel and had the clerk dig up Cassie's passport, which was temporarily on file, and provide her with necessary capital, and Rab wrote out a voucher for the ticket. Murray had accompanied the honeymooners because he was in love with Peter and wouldn't be parted from him by Peter's marriage.

"I had never dreamed of it! Never dreamed! Didn't know that such a thing could exist! I just thought they were good friends and Murray would come along on the honeymoon for a lark," she said. "So I couldn't find Peter anywhere and then I went to Murray's room and the door wasn't locked. There was Peter in bed with Murray. They were— They were—"

She began screaming again and had to be given an injection by a native doctor who was summoned for the purpose before she could be put aboard the airplane, as indeed she was put aboard. True enough, her father paid for everything, and it was suggested politely that Peter and Murray leave the party then and there or face local charges. They departed the next day for a different destination, after considerable pouting and quibbling on the subject.

Rab told his other customers, "Cassie became ill in the night and had to leave." That was all he would say on the subject. When Rab said that he didn't wish to be questioned, it took an awful fool to try to question him and there weren't too many awful fools on that particular excursion.

He had grown to regard as minor problems those incidents when a flight was canceled or when a bag was lost or stolen (that happened sometimes). People became ill often, and people fainted away, and men got in fistfights on some occasions, especially when liquor had been too free in flowing. When they missed a day here, they'd have to make up a day there. Customers complained and complained and complained. They were dumped down at one richly upholstered inn to find that the resident manager had been fired by his company only forty hours previously, and that principal individuals of the staff had left along with him, and that some of them had stolen files or records, and there was no room at this inn, Your Honor. Chaos ruled, and his little brother Bedlam. Thirty-eight tourists had to be farmed out to other hotels in this last minute, and how were they to be wined and dined and transported and coddled and shown the pretty sights they'd come all those thousands of miles to see? Quite a phenomenon, this travel business.

How about Mrs. Fegge? She was something to remember. At each port she would buy and buy and buy and also would buy new bags in which to put her acquisitions. She was told that these purchases could be shipped home—it would only take a month or two, even if they went by ship—but she said that she must be allowed to fetch her treasures with her, and began hallooing and trembling as if she were coming down with a plague when told that she could not lug them along. Other ladies gathered to pet and reassure her. Never a dull moment at the Wandering Orphanage.

In steadily recurring fashion it seemed to Wye Rabarti Wong that, when he roamed huge hotels as it was essential to roam them, he moved in the guise of a Reverend Mother. He had observed such souls in hospitals most of his life and had known mean and surly specimens, as well as those who were willingly Torn by the Wheel (they practiced saintliness which many of the saints themselves might have respected if not envied). He himself held no mean or surly cell in his composition, but he could be tough when the demand for toughness was forced upon him.

He held a secret still boyish ambition to serve capably in

the State Department of some nation, almost any powerful nation. He desired to see gangsters exterminated (and situations curried to prevent their future reproduction); he prayed that food could be made available to all populations, so that they might eat adequately, and unused sources should be tapped to provide food.

He felt drawn to Don Lundin personally, but thought Don's commonly expressed attitudes infantile and senseless. Nations and races were bound to intermingle and had been doing so for a long time, and would continue to do so. Rab himself was a roving proof of the fact.

He was proud of whatever courage and humility he might practice but tried earnestly not to show his pride.

He walked his hotel floors as nuns walk hospital floors. Sometimes it seemed that he must run out of fresh advice and understanding, and where might he acquire more?

Mrs. Groyne was positive that she had been cheated, back in Bangkok, at a shop which she insisted was recommended enthusiastically to all oncoming patrons by Graduate Tours Incorporated itself or themselves. It turned out after examination that Graduate Tours Incorporated had recommended no shops whatsoever in Bangkok or anywhere else and that Mrs. Groyne had gleaned any information she possessed from a printed folder she picked up in the lobby. Still, she reiterated the threat that she would talk to "my lawyer" (the attorney retained by her husband's soft drink bottling company) as soon as she got back to Nashville.

Mr. Root had developed an ulcerated snag in his lower jaw and wondered why the management declined to call a dentist for him in the middle of the night.

Mr. Koot complained that his wife had been given apricot brandy instead of apple brandy in the night club bar, and she was allergic to apricot brandy; she had been groaning and throwing up and suffering nightmares, and Mr. Koot wished to have the bartender fired that very night.

Mrs. Loot had bought an emerald that had the proper flaw in

it, but she had just been examining the stone with her own little microscope—"he didn't even guess that I had such a glass"—and could discover no revealing flaw, and Mrs. Loot was positive that a factory-produced emerald had been substituted for the authentic gem, and Mrs. Loot wished to have the police called immediately; they were to ascertain the residence of the cheating jeweler and take him into custody.

Mr. Scoot, traveling alone, wondered if there were any— Well, did they have any— He meant that, possibly, there in the hotel, they might have a girl or two who— Money was no object, Scoot declared. No, no, no, he wasn't going out to any of those bars or joints or places along Bugis Street. He might look dumb, but he wasn't any chicken. He knew his way around. He wanted a good clean girl right there in the hotel, they were there, he'd seen them in the lobby, nobody needed to take him for a sucker.

Mrs. Boast had had her traveling bags rifled and robbed when she was in Antwerp—no, maybe it was Amsterdam—eleven years before, and since that time she had made it a rule to lock all of her bags—and she really meant that: *all of them*—whenever she left her room. And now she had come back to her room, and all her bags sat there still locked, and where were her keys? They weren't in her purse, and she had been carrying that gold lamé purse, the new one she bought in Tokyo at the beginning of the trip, and the keys weren't in her purse, and she remembered distinctly putting the keys to her big bags in her little gold lamé bag before she went out to dinner, but now they weren't there, look, she'd opened the little bag and dumped out everything, *everything*, and the keys to the other bags were gone, they weren't dangling from a kind of little plastic mother-of-pearl key thing, and look, *they're not there*, and she'd been parted from that little bag only for a few minutes, perhaps she was careless, she should have carried it with her when she danced, she'd danced only that one time when Mr. Gloast asked her to dance with him, and she left the gold lamé thing lying beside her *couvert*, and she remembered later that she'd noticed how the waiter had seemed to scrutinize it and her, and now she was positive that the waiter had slyly opened the little purse while she was dancing, for probably there were a few minutes when every single one of the guests was away from the table, and there would have been ample opportunity for the waiter to take her keys, and then he might have a private deal with one of those chambermaids (or was it a chamberboy? They do have boys taking care of the rooms sometimes)—and then, if the waiter passed the keys along to *her* or *him*, why they might have already opened the big bags and taken what they wanted and then locked them up again before she came back to her room; Ben Boast, her husband, was still down at that night club place, and she'd tried to get him on the phone, but *they wouldn't even answer the telephone down there*, and wasn't there something suspicious about that, and anyway she knew well enough that she hadn't given her keys to Ben because she always kept keys her own self (Ben was very careless about trifles, because in Albany other people always looked after him so carefully—she did, and his secretary did, and at home their houseman did), so she knew Ben didn't have her bag keys, she'd carried them herself, but now they'd obviously been stolen and—

"Did you have your room key with you, Mrs. Boast?"

In triumph. "Certainly not, Mr. Wong. That great big heavy thing! Certainly not! I left it at the reception desk and picked it up there."

"Ah, yes, I saw you going through the lobby. Let's see. You were wearing a flowered jacket—"

"That's it, right there on the foot of my bed."

"Would it be possible, Mrs. Boast, that you have a pocket in your jacket? Allow me to pick it up—"

Jingle, jingle.

The Jews, always the Jews, a parade and pageant of them, the eternal wandering Jews, they wandered nowadays under Mr. Wong's tutelage. He thought that his favorite was then and would forever be a watch dealer named Solomon Cohen. And he supposed that there were thousands and thousands of Solomon Cohens in this world, perhaps a hundred thousand Cohens, or more, or less, and so many of them named Solomon or Levi or maybe Sam. Sometimes it seemed to Rab that at least one Cohen came in each of his herds; but no one of them ever claimed his heart and his attention like this one small man.

Sol Cohen had come from Vienna, and he was a watchmaker, and his father had been a watchmaker, and his grandfather had been a watchmaker.

"When I was a boy, I had no choice. Early I was apprenticed. To do what? You guessed it. Watchmaking! Always, always the watches."

He repaired watches, handled watches, sold watches. While still very young he was sent to Switzerland to study intricacies of the trade there. Shortly after Sol returned to Vienna his father died. He inherited his father's house, he lived in the old house, and there eventually he made himself an oracle.

"To make this oracle I go into the library at night and close the door. Mind you, this is immediately before the *Anschluss*, when Nazi soldiers are coming in. I stand in the middle of the library and close my eyes, and turn round and round slowly until I do not know what direction I am turning. When I am stopped turning round and round, I walk slowly—my arm is outstretched, so; one finger is pointed, so; and when that one finger comes in contact to a book on the shelf, then only do I open my eyes and take down the book. I do not look to see what is the book, but now I go and sit down in a chair. Then once more I close my eyes and sit turning pages slowly of the book until I think, 'Now I stop turning pages.' So, still not seeing, I put my finger on a page of the open book and move my finger on the page until I think 'Now I stop.'

"For the first time again I open my eyes, and look at my finger where it is stopped, for this will be my oracle. The book I hold is an old encyclopedia belonging long ago to my grandfather, and under my finger is the story of a man's life. It is a man I never heard of before, a name I never heard. He was a philosopher of the sixteenth century, and under my finger it says that he was hanged because of his beliefs. Hmmm, what an oracle! I go upstairs, and my wife wakes up as I am crawling into bed.

"I tell my wife, 'Anna, you got to get up early in the morning, for we are going to the United States, and you got to get ready.' We dare take nothing, nothing, and also it is so difficult about the money. Already they are searching people who depart and making it so difficult to go. Everything we leave, everything! Except one teacup I have in my bag.

"They say to me, 'What you got here, wrapped up in your nightshirt?' I tell them, 'One empty teacup. It belonged to my mother and—see—here is a white Fujiyama on the green cup. Let me please take my Fujiyama teacup.' They say, 'O.K., no harm done. You take your teacup.' So I take along my Fujiyama teacup, and I am laughing, laughing sadly that this is all I am allowed to bring to the United States."

Where was the cup now?

"Safe at home in Brooklyn."

Then, thank God, it hadn't been broken.

"Hell, no. It is, like they told me when I left, O.K. And now on this trip, for the first time I will get to see Fujiyama as on the cup. Hmmm, what a sight that will be!"

The Cohens were very old now. One son had charge of the watch shop on West Forty-seventh Street in Manhattan, and all was well there; the other son had charge of the importing end of the business, and managed national distribution of a fine, solid, hardy two-hundred-dollar Swiss watch, and all was well with him.

Mrs. Cohen walked almost blindly, and her ancient eyes swam behind lenses thick as window plate, but her talkative little husband led her everywhere, dutifully, but also proudly. So they went to see Fujiyama at last, and it was a perfect day for the bus trip up from Hakone, and they got out at the viewing stand, and walked away from the bus, and climbed to the wide platform, and there, oh there, swam Mount Fuji-no-Yama in all his opulence. He seemed higher than any mountain in the world—Alp or Canadian or Himalayan—and truly he wasn't higher or nearly as high as some others but he seemed to be; he wore his sacred circlet of clouds, his scrolled peak was thrusting up out of the cloud collar, pink and rusty and bluish rippled peak against paler blue of the gracious sky, and snow or glaciers dripping down from his hair.

Hmmm. Like on the teacup. But the color was different.

So Solomon Cohen saw Fujiyama and savored every minute of the viewing, and then they all went back to the bus and made more trips around that day, and Solomon Cohen helped his wife up and down steps, and he looked very tired at dinner that night, but still was chirping amiably to companions, and then he guided his wife to the elevator and they went up to their room and went to bed. Wye Rabarti Wong always considered that Mr. Cohen must have been thinking of Mount Fuji-san with wonder and worship, just like on the teacup, but a different color. And then it was early morning, and Anna Cohen had managed to grope her way to the telephone and call Mr. Wong in his own room, and she was crying, and saying, "Mr. Wong. I can't wake Sol. He won't wake up. I can't *wake* him."

The lonely, the lovely, the un-lovely, the blank, the frenzied; gabblers, babblers, cheats; the blatant, the cringing; the ones who sought to impress Rab by the munificence of their tips; the ones who never tipped at all, and cried within Rab's hearing that they had already paid more than the journey was worth, and why didn't Graduate Tours Incorporated pay the conductor an adequate salary and not leave it up to the customers; the timid, the ill, the scrawny and trembling, looking at their last landscapes; the boasters, the truculent; the leering old apes whose enlarged prostates sent them on the prowl; the beldams who tried to buy Rab's affection by waving cash in front of him (oh yes, that happened several times); the frightened, the affable, the belligerent; the scoffers who constantly compared foreign scenes to the glories of Akron, Wayzata, Lambertville—and to the discredit of the former; the acquisitive, the doubtful, the impetuous; the striving bargainers; the earnest, the sedate, those dreaming calmly; those put into sobbing by beauty; Rab and his friends, Rab and his enemies, Rab and his never-changing and ever-changing tribe.

13

Don Lundin was not the only man in the party who decried an infernal round of Balinese masques and mimes scheduled for tourist attraction. The belief was held by several others that there was too much of such posturing set forth to regale them, just as there had been too many girl-girl displays and girl-boy antics in Thailand.

Ray Papinsky, a wholesale grocer from Long Island, was especially rabid on the subject; Ray Papinsky was bald, thick-necked, thick-spectacled; he had a grim little wife named Lil to whom the tour was one vast shopping expedition and who kept the bus waiting at most of the stops because she had scuttled into some store or market and could not be found, and the tour director or local guides would need to comb the neighborhood for her. Ray Papinsky said that the Thailand antics of slim young males, who postured and performed native combat by knifing and leaping and kicking at each other, constituted one vast falsification in the world of sports.

"If they're taught to fight like that, then God have pity on them if they ever get in a brawl with some Westerner of their size and weight, see? When I was a kid I went to Princeton for a couple of years before my Dad died, and we ran out of dough and I had to go to work in Gristede's. It was one Saturday night after a big game, maybe with Columbia, and we all went into Joe King's Rathskeller— you know, down on Third Avenue, what they used to call the German-American— and we had one character who was a big bruiser, a real big guy, Butch something-or-other.

"Butch had had a lot of drinks and was feeling no pain. Most of our gang sat at tables in front of the bar, but there got to be a vacant space at the bar right next to a real pretty little blonde babe, and old Butch he went for that like a homing pigeon or something. He said, 'Hey, that's strictly for me,' and he went over and sat on the vacant bar stool, and tried to make out with this little babe sitting next to him.

"There's a small, slim, grayish guy sitting just beyond, and the girl is with him, see? This slim little guy is about the size of those characters we saw jumping around with knives and hitting with their feet—you know, jumping up in the air and kicking each other and so on. The girl doesn't want to talk to our big old Butch, and she keeps trying to turn away from him and talk instead to the little oldish guy she's with. Because he's her date, see?

"So pretty soon the little guy says to Butch, real politely he says it, something about, 'Listen, friend, the lady doesn't want to talk to you, so lay off, please.' Says 'please' like our Oriental friends around here are always saying 'please.' Old Butch he says something about I've got a right to talk to anyone I want to talk to and this is a free country and so forth. Little guy says, 'Look, the lady is my date, so just leave her alone.'

"And Butch rises off his bar stool, all two hundred and whatever pounds of him, and he comes around to the little guy and says something about, 'Do you want to make something out of it?' Little guy gets up, see? You can't even see his fist move because it's so fast: just punch-punch-punch, like that, maybe

7 7

three or four times, while Butch is still going down. He goes down all right—he's out cold, completely knocked out, dead to the world. Joe King, the proprietor, comes over and says, 'All right, you Princeton guys. Get him out of here,' and we take hold of Butch and drag him back to the men's room and lay him out on the floor, and he's still dead to the world, see?

"Joe King gets some water and flings it in Butch's face. Joe King has seen plenty of guys knocked out because he used to be a boxer, and he was a bouncer in that same Rathskeller before he became manager and finally bought the joint. So he keeps splashing water on Butch, and pretty soon Butch sits up and shakes his head and blinks his eyes and looks all around and realizes that he's on the floor there in the men's room.

"Big old football Butch says, 'What happened to me?' Joe King says, 'Benny Leonard.' Lightweight champion of the world for seven years. And I'm telling you this: Benny Leonard could have taken that whole gang of Oriental kids with their kicking and swords and screwball stuff. Believe me, yes. Benny Leonard could have."

Don Lundin wrote a play about Balinese plays, or rather wrote a descriptive summary. He felt that they'd suffered too many Balinese plays stuffed down their throats, or into their minds, and was resolved to protest, and to have fun while he protested. The weird misspelled folders explaining or attempting to explain plot and symbolism were more than he could bear. Don had no awareness that he was being sly and nasty; he thought that he was being rowdy but utterly harmless insofar as the natives were concerned. He read and reread one of the original folders to begin with.

BARONG AND KRISS DANCE
The Barongplay represents the eternal fight between good and evil.
BARONG, the mythological animal represents the good spirit, while RANGDA, another mythological animal represents the evil one.

Barong is represented by a lion - like figure carried by two men Rangda. the evil witch, is represented by a female figure with flowing white hair, a long tongue and ricious fangs.

During the fight there is one moment when the victory of the Barong seems to be doubtful. Then his followers draw their krisses (daggers) and attack the Rangda, but the magic of the Rangda is too powerful.

Their attempts are returned back to themselves. This episode in which they are put in a trance and stab themselvess with their own krisses is called "ngurek".

ACT. I:

Two girl-dancers appear, respresenting the servants of the Rangda, and they look for the servants of Dewi Kunti who are on their way to meet their Patih (Prime Minister).

ACT. II:

The servants of Dewi Kunti appear. One of the servants of Rangda changes herself into a spirit and enters both servants of Dewi Kunti to infuriate them.

The Patih and both servants return to Dewi Kunti.

ACT. III:

Dewi Kunti and her son Sedewa make their entrance. She has promised the Rangda to sacrifice Sedewa. A spirit appear and enters her. She becomes angry and orders the Patih to take Sedewa into the forest. The Patih is also entered by the spirit and his pity for Sedewa turns into an intence dislike Then Sedewa is taken into the forest and tied to a tree.

July said, "Don, what on earth are you doing? You're scribbling and scribbling ever since I came back to the room. And you hardly spoke to me."

"I'm writing a play."

"Nonsense."

"No nonsense about it. They drag us around to see all this symbolic stuff, don't they? We get hauled from one monster to another every waking moment. Some sleeping moments, too. At that last mummery-bummery old Davey O'Hearn was sitting right in front of me, and he went to sleep after about six or seven minutes and slept through the entire production, resisting all gentle efforts of the Mrs. to wake him up. If I'm compelled to witness these overdressed pageants then I've got a right to write about them. Especially when there's a lady character named Dewi Kunti."

"Don! *Really!*"

"Well, there is. She was there in the damn play, and her name was printed on the program. Big as life. Dewi Kunti."

"*Don!* Isn't there enough wretched obscenity in the world these days without your going around creating more?"

"I didn't create her, they created her. The Balinese did it, not poor old Don. And they're anti-Semitic, too. In a couple of other places in a couple of other plays they've got a character spelled Hanoman, H-a-n-o-m-a-n, or Hanuman, H-a-n-u-m-a-n, which is a direct attempt to cast discredit on our glorious fellow-touring-party-member, Mr. Sidney Hennmen of Ohio, and his good wife, Becky. Sid and Becky are not out of *Tom Sawyer,* they're out of Cleveland. Without Sid and Becky to ask the guides statistical questions about urban housing in these parts, I don't know where we'd be. And they make him commander of an army of monkeys, no less. A clear attempt to link Jews and apes. What do they think we are—a gang of Russians, a gang of Arabs? And what about that king of the demons named Rawana? A clear attempt to discredit Rowena, the beautiful heroine created by Sir Walter Scott—"

"I think you're perfectly horrid," said July, who was on the verge of laughing herself into fits. "I'm going shopping. Good-bye."

"What are you shopping for?"

"Wood carvings, maybe. They have loads of them here in the hotel shops. Our neighbor Dolores Vendig at home commissioned me especially to send one to her."

"Get one of Dewi Kunti."

Don worked on his play for the better part of two days. Mitzheimer, on hearing of what was projected, said that it sounded to him like Don was working for the worst part of two days. Don declined to witness any more mummeries, or what he called glummeries, but went along on trips. While the others were exploring or witnessing he sat alone in the bus, scribbling. He was cool and serene when the rest returned, earnestly fanning away insects or begging children, who were even more annoying than the insects. The party was led for lunch to a hillside hotel in a village named Ubud.

"I didn't make up the name of this village," Don insisted. "July will say that I did, but it was named that all along."

The Mitzes and Lundins and a few others had sense enough to eat only crackers, cheese, bananas, and the *djeroek* (huge, solid, dryish red-pulped fruit which grew in the region); but some of the party announced that they were starving, and they fished and fleshed and fowled on whatever the management put before them.

Bathroom facilities at their own spick-and-span hotel were overworked from then on; pills were gobbled, Erna became a high priestess of Kaopectate but the supply fell exhausted promptly; the three medical men in the group (two of them retired) were preyed upon for advice and assistance. Thus the assemblage was nearly halved when it came to a nighttime presentation—by reading only—of Lundin's play.

Word of his venture was bound to circulate, and women became pestiferous. He had planned initially to share this project only with Mitz and Semple and a few other men. They told their wives what was up, then clamor arose.

"You ought to let us in on it, Don."

"No, Evelyn. You'd be shocked."

"No, I wouldn't."

"If you think Evvie would be shocked, Mr. Lundin, how about *me*? I'm a tough old turkey-hen, I am. I've reared one husband and three great big mean sons and—"

"Don, you ought to let us girls *try* it, at least. If any girl thinks it's too strong stuff for her, she can leave sedately, and no hard feelings—"

"You should at least let us be *exposed*."

Don said limply, "I don't think it's as bad as all that."

"Well, then. In a world where people are permitted to witness public fornication in the movies—"

"Darling, did you say *permitted*? *Compelled* would be better. Tell you, we'll ask July. Has July read it, Don?"

"No, I wouldn't let her. I hid the manuscript, and she couldn't find it. I was afraid she'd blab and carry on."

"Don, I didn't try to find your lousy little manuscript. I did nothing of the kind!"

"Did."

"Didn't!"

Finally in general consultation it was agreed that women might be present if they chose to be and could be excused for exit at any time if they desired. The reading took place in a small private dining room on the top floor, but removed some distance from the supper club where an orchestra, with girl singers in hot-pants outfits, crashed and snarled until dawn, to the social enrichment of visiting Turkish and Australian delegations. As a matter of fact, two women did leave before Don had read for long, but whether because of diarrhea or disapproval no one was certain.

BALI BELLY
A Tale
(Or a Piece Thereof)

Dewi Kunti, the queen of Upchuk, desires that her daughter Rebecca shall be escorted to Mecca in order to be wooed by Hennman, who pretends to the throne of Cleveland. The queen calls upon her son Shitta to do the escorting, but Shitta declares that he would rather be turned into a frog. Lacksmuni, a wandering impoverished magician, is called upon to perform this feat, but Lacksmuni desires that Rebecca should be his own bride instead, because she is wealthy. He changes Shitta into a toad instead of a frog.

Shitta, still believing that he has been turned into a frog, hops into the water. He cannot swim, and is on the point of drowning, when he is rescued by a pair of dwarfs, Wunballi and Twoballi. For reward, Dewi Kunti allows the dwarfs to perform their famous religious dance known as Belly High. Lacksmuni feels that he has been cheated and is enraged. He changes himself into a dragon and eats up Wunballi and Twoballi.

Everything is now ballixed up. Shitta, who has recently eaten lunch at the hotel in Ubud, comes down with severe cramps. Shitta cries urgently for a magic powder, which is the only known cure for what ails him and will also cause the dragon to disgorge the two dwarfs. Queen Dewi Kunti, annoyed by her son's demonstrated weakness, says that she will escort Rebecca to Mecca her own self.

In a rage she bursts into tears and cries so savagely that a pool of water is formed on the ground. Lacksmuni, still in the shape of a dragon, slips and falls in the pool of tears, and in his struggles he gets a coughing fit and coughs up Wunballi and Twoballi. They are a little the worse for wear, but basically unharmed. The angry dragon flounders out of the pool of tears and tries to reswallow the protesting dwarfs.

Just in the nick of time they are rescued through the arrival of a Cleveland Indian, who has been dispatched to the scene by Hennmen, who has been wondering why Rebecca was so damn long in coming to be wooed. The Cleveland Indian hits Lacksmuni the dragon with a magic baseball bat. All the other characters converge from the dugouts, and a general fight ensues. It is broken up by the appearance of Hennmen himself, who couldn't stand all this delay in the courtship.

In separating the battlers Hennmen is also struck on the head by the magic bat and promptly turns into a magic bat of the winged variety. He flies away, squawking for help. (Question at this point: Do bats actually squawk?) Anyway bats are alleged to have built-in radar systems, and that is what is employed. Through using this instantaneous system of communication, he summons Dr. Waldo Kayce from Scottsdale, Arizona, the eminent gynecologist.

Kayce protests at being called to the scene, saying that he is a retired gynecologist and no longer available to the public. Retired or not, declares the assemblage, Kayce is the only person capable of operating on Dewi Kunti and turning her into a Dryee instead of a Dewi. Kayce goes into a chant—

Don considered that Mr. Sidney Hennmen would be amused at finding himself a character in this extravaganza, but Hennmen was not to be beguiled. He contrived a frosty grin, tacked it on his countenance, and sat immobile throughout the reading. His wife, Becky, watched and listened in expressionless silence. Once Lundin looked up from his script to observe her whispering to a husband whose lips barely twitched in reply. Obviously she was saying "Let's leave," and he was saying, "Guess we can't." And Don supposed that Dr. Kayce, himself addicted to storytelling when men got together without any women present, might yield to at least a chuckle in finding himself operating on Dewi Kunti. Kayce only looked embarrassed and bored; his own wife was not present, she was one of the absent sufferers.

Before he reached the end of his reading Lundin wanted to yell, "The hell with it," and tear sheets of paper into well-deserved fragments. But basic stubbornness persisted, and he read on to the bitter end, which indeed was more than bitter for him and the rest. There came a weak scattering of applause, probably initiated by Mitz, and the group dispersed rapidly.

"Aren't you coming to bed?" asked July.

"Not yet. I'm going to have a drink."

"You can have one in the room. And I won't utter any curtain lectures," she added as others came close.

He said, "I'll be down in the room very soon."

Several of his friends gathered and cried, "Well, well," and "That was a riot." Lundin knew better than anyone else that it was no riot. All the women by this time had departed. A fellow or two suggested another drink, but Don said he had to go to the men's room. When finally he approached the big bar, with its view of serene countryside spattered with village lights and the docile Indian Ocean making mystery beyond, he was alone.

He wanted to yell quits. He held a momentary demented desire to trot from room to room, knocking on doors and summoning people in their robes and pyjamas, making apology, seeking to extenuate himself. I'm sorry, I didn't mean it truly, it was just a childish resentful stunt, you all wanted to hear me read it, you sought to have it read to you, I succumbed through my miserable creepy vanity. I'm no playwright, no humorist in print or scrawling, and why I took great pains to scratch out such a trivial smear, I have no true idea. It was just an expression of dyed-in-the-wool resentment against Asiatics. All right, Asians if you will. I was juvenile, am juvenile, and will you please forgive me for boring you and attempting to be cute at the local inhabitants' expense.

He knew that he could not and would not go traipsing with such apology, yet the wish was there.

He drank one drink, hesitated, ordered a second, promising that it would be his nightcap. A giant, bearded, long-black-plastic-haired Australian stumbled against the bar stool next to him, lurched to seat himself on the stool, ordered whisky, and eyed Don Lundin intolerantly.

"I say, mate. Are you an American?"

Don admitted to being an American.

(So my own intolerable intolerance comes to haunt me in kangaroo guise.)

"I say, mate. I don't like Americans."

Don sipped at his drink and made no reply.

"I say. Did you hear me?"

Don finished drinking.

"Don't—like—Americans."

Don motioned for his check, signed it when it came. The tip was included automatically—you didn't need to tip in the Silver Seas International; they had orders to refuse all cash tips, and most of the help carried out such instruction to the letter.

"I—think—Yanks—are—*shit*."

Don got up, preparing to leave.

"Matey," said the bearded one. "Want to—what do you blokes say—make something out of it?"

Don said, "Yes. Stand up." He was no Benny Leonard but he was still cherishing the anecdote related by Papinsky.

The bearded one struggled to arise, finally achieved the feat, loomed hulking. Don knocked him flat, and he seemed to jar bar and bottles and Bali when he went down. Don stood looking at him and suddenly wanted to weep. "That wasn't a very bright thing to do," he said, both to himself and to the world at large and close at hand. "A drunken Aussie is a pushover." Then he held up his hand to stem the rush of waiters who appeared. "Sorry. I won't be back," and he walked out of the room.

14

I am reluctant, Lundin declared to himself. But if prejudice permitted I'd honor them for imagination and serious purpose and for having the wit to be walking seashells.

Seashells? How come?

The people of Bali are not dedicated seagoers as are the inhabitants of some other islands not far away. They fish a bit, but prefer the inland rivers, prefer the small fish and eels they take in such landlocked waters; and where they swim as well, usually in late afternoon, the males splash in physical contention below the little bridge, the females with less raillery above the bridge. They all will stand and hoot and wave their arms when we go by; the males yell louder, the females look serene and give a milder wave.

Still now in ceremonial significance I would call them shells. Because they are extravagantly coated with their patina, they march in solemnity and dedication, carrying weight upon their heads which I could not bear, you could not bear, they yield in majesty to the tonnage and accept and treasure it. The burden is their self-contrived offering to their Buddha, and they lug it to the temple in serenity, marching high and proud in long lines, and a hundred pace from this direction and two hundred from that, and their menfolks tread along respectfully.

I am a pink conch.

What carry you?

Biscuits made of ground melon seed.

I am a tan angel-wing, I am edible, a clam of shiny mien.

What bring you for offering to the Buddha and his minions?

A pudding baked firm but still with juice. It has bananas in it, and flavoring of cane.

My sister and I tread in violet. Heavy and delicious are the burdens on our heads. Crusty with their flavored innards, the pickled tiny eels we bear.

Outlander, outlander, stranger come to see! Witness the pride in which we sway!

Our cousins tread in violet, we all bought violet cloth, we sewed and stitched, we cut a fringe, we put the blossoms in our hard-wound hair and in the baskets when we garnished them.

Call us the violet club, the violet cortege if you would speak so fanciful.

Rice-cookies sweet, and rice-cookies salted, and rice-cookies made more tasty with nuts, we bring on this great march because it is a march in a salute to the Buddha.

See how praiseworthy we pace. We walk in fresh sarongs of emerald. We come from Ubud.

We from Pedjeng. Hibiscus in our hair.

We from Bedulu.

Coconut cakes with colored seeds atop.

This is the first day of the month. The moon rises in full gold tonight. Full moon, full moon.

But listen to the gamelan a-playing!

We wear magenta, and we walk from Bona, and we have crab cakes with spices on them, in them, and the choicest fruit and frangipani blossoms.

If one wishes to follow the Buddha's teaching one must not be egoistic or self-willed, but should cherish feelings of goodwill to all alike; one should respect those who are worthy of respect; one should serve those who are worthy of service and treat everyone with uniform kindness.

I am a dark snail, compact and whorled.

The blossoms that we wear, the perfume that they issue, the perfume of ourselves.

Well, he sat there in the bus, pretending to the rest that he was bothered by outside heat, and wanted to bask in the air conditioning, which hummed. Other men had chuckled and cried, "Look at old Don, he ain't going to no more God damn temples."

"He might meet Dewi Kunti," added one of the bolder ones. Don grinned and waved them away.

He did not feel like grinning. *You're being an actor. Didn't you get enough of acting fifteen hours ago? When reading aloud your doggerel?*

Around him other buses pulled up, some of them lopsided, all with bundles under tarpaulins upon the roofs. Station wagons crowded in; there were assembled trucks, old cars, a few new cars, foreign cars, cars which might have been put together by a colony of wood-carvers; and every vehicle had been populated with patronage to surfeit—and oh, the galaxies of offerings they bore.

Hoist them on high, and march away.

And in due time come parading back, offerings and all.

This evening we will dine on pickled melon seeds.

In symbolism they were offered to the Buddha but in honesty we eat them up ourselves.

Banana fluff, Don thought.

Rice surprise, rice canapés, rice gingerbread.

And floating-island pudding stuffed with eels. Boo.

So this was all a picnic of their church. He'd been to church picnics in his own fair time. He'd gone to picnics of the Baptist Young People's Union, "BYPU" they called it, and ornery little boys ranted forth the letters when they were having fun or thought they were having fun and said bee wy pee-*yooooo*! But they'd had picnics (but no flowery adornments in the girls' hair or if they'd had flowers he couldn't remember the flowers—but surely no hibiscus), and it was all the traditional rural American festival, replete with dishes fetched from home, and each family bringing what they called "a dish to pass," and sandwiches and ham and the wealthier families bringing along big jars of olives, deviled eggs, and potato salad in good stone crocks or wooden bowls, and don't forget the cold baked beans.

I wish, he thought in weary idleness, that I could taste them now.

Presently a spindly shape emerged alone from all the crowding. He looked again, centered his gaze upon her, saw that this was Erna. Were all the others coming back so soon? But no July. No others. Only Erna. She saw him watching her and waved, then pressed on through the thronging to the bus. The door stood open, though the air conditioning still sang. She entered, and Don was standing as she came. She motioned him back into the seat and then pressed down beside him.

Erna said, "I want to talk and do all or most of the talking, and I want you to just sit here and listen and take it while I dish it out."

"Go ahead."

Erna said: "It isn't the matter of your molesting anybody else with your attitude. You may or may not annoy them. But what I despise is the kind of mental and artistic suicide which you're carrying out. You don't like brown and yellow people, and have proclaimed it frequently, and made us all aware of the fetish which you lug around. July can stand it or at least bear with it, that's obvious, so I'm not attempting any worthy works in defense of July. It is yourself with whom I'm chiefly concerned.

"You're deliberately cutting yourself away from something which might prove to be a revel and a benefit. I yield you my permission to hold your own opinion about Thailand and Singapore. I don't think I like the high-rises any better than you do, or all the scrambling for the fast buck, or fast Singapore dollar, or fast rupee. I guess it's rupiahs here, and since they're worth something like a quarter of a cent apiece the scramble becomes less necessitous.

"Allow me to refer first to that cute little enterprise you conducted last night, when you read aloud to us your fiddle-faddle relating to native dances and traditions. But those weren't fotch-on; they were for real. They were and are part of the landscape. I don't know where our bus driver is now— Oh, yes, there he is, over there in that crowd, talking to some friend who's driving another bus. But he or his kid brother might be the spook or the king's henchman or the monkey's matron-of-honor in the very next masque which you go to see, if indeed you will permit yourself to be dragged to another.

"These people have an inborn pervasive and persuasive talent for pantomime and mimicry. It is absolutely astounding. I wasn't keenly aware of it before. That feature hadn't been emphasized sufficiently in anything I'd read about Bali. The intense Mr. Wayne Semple has toted along a somewhat elderly book about Bali, which everybody is scrambling to examine. It was photographed and compiled and written by one Philip Hiss, but something like a third of a century since, and anyway I'm far down the list. But as for dramatic presentation, whole families work at it here, entire villages full of people. That's not done anywhere else in existence—never has been done before, unless perhaps you except a novel by J. B. Priestley, or a family gang of strolling players displayed through the talent of a Shakespeare. Old Sik Sak San may be a rice grower, or a coconut grower, or some kind of grower in the daytime, but when he comes on at seven or eight o'clock in the evening as an ancient court prophet overwhelmed by apes, then by God he is an ancient court prophet overwhelmed by apes, and no mistake about it.

"As for the girls, without fail they're all lithe and winsome. They're little flowers, they're made of brown silk—they may appear ludicrous to your intense cold gray cop-or-criminal eyes, or to my fair orbs, because nowadays they're putting on bras in order to cover up their divinely ornate mammary glands. It used not to be done, but this is just another step in the conversion of a dainty and primitive people into hideous international perfidy. I wish I could have seen Bali years ago before the gals started putting on the bras, and it's my own God damn fault that I didn't come and see it and them. But still we are getting to see it all after a fashion, and that's no intentional pun.

"Instead of withdrawing and giving way to ludicrous discourse on the subject, you ought to get those prejudiced films off your staring eyes and be seeing the place honestly, as it's meant to be seen. I'm concerned about you and probably you won't love me anymore so the hell with that. But I'm concerned about you because it's your own light that you're standing in, and without any excuse or reason. You never bombed these people, you never punished them with napalm or phosphorous in remembrance of Pearl Harbor. They didn't do anything to you, but they did plenty to each other. You realize that only six or seven years ago they killed fifty thousand Communists on this very island? They wiped out entire villages, burned them to the ground. It was their own way of keeping house—a savage and vicious and intolerant and insolent piece of housekeeping. But they did it, by God and by Jesus, and you ought to be out there applauding them and kissing their feet. Because if the struggle against Communism is a world battle, with the good guys against the bad guys, then these were and are some of the good guys. This green mountainous island, lapped by the azure seas and lit by the golden sun and the silver moon—it ran red and make no mistake about it.

"You like dogs, don't you? I know you do, because you've got two at home, and you're always showing their pictures. Have you ever seen so many dogs on one little island? No you haven't, and I'll bet no one else ever has. They're all trusting and confident and good-natured, and they go wagging here and wagging there, and 98 percent of them are either white, black, or black-and-white. Once in a blue moon you see a hound, and I've seen one German Shepherd, but he was a lone sentry kept strictly to himself on a leash or a chain or something. The Balinese dogs are in every yard and on every step, up every lane, down every path, and wherever there is a shrine or a temple or a memorial of some kind along the highway, there are twenty-one dogs to the square foot. Have you seen one that was run over? One dead dog, along any of the roads that we've traveled?

No more have I, and I'll bet we don't see one up to the last minute. I'll be brokenhearted if we do. They bear a charmed life, and so do all the islanders who have survived.

"I don't say the fifty thousand Communists bore charmed lives—obviously they didn't. But I'd rather see the island the way it is at this moment than to see it with fifty thousand Communists dragging themselves and everybody else around. I've seen modern Russians en masse, and of all the dull heavy gloomy globs— They seem to be fabricated from a mixture of putty and oxalic acid and—to employ a masculine rough-and-ready term—cow shit.

"Why won't you observe and estimate these island people the way they truly are, instead of curling your lip at them? Nobody starves, nobody goes hungry. The fruit and vegetables and fish and eels are practically for free. I never had much curiosity about the Garden of Eden, but if it were anything like this, then I'd like to move there post haste. Even if Eve insists nowadays on putting on a Penney-store bra to cover up the fonts that nature gave her. This is all delectable and delicious and for pity's sake let loose and enjoy it.

"If you were asked to epitomize the strength of America, you'd have to take recourse in the common testimony that we are a band of brothers from distant countries come, or different countries, or something like that. Well, it ought to warm your heart as an American to recognize that the Balinese people are the same sort of mixture. They've got all sorts of tribes in them —they've got Malay in them, they've got Indian in them, they've got Chinese. Yet they have ignored the graphic influences of these elder cultures and made their own, just the way we Americans did.

"If a society of artists and actors is good for the world, then Bali ought to be the best in the business. Everybody can act or sing or dance or do remarkable things with pens or knives, and when I say knives I'm not referring to the fifty thousand dead Communists. If the Balinese make something for you to wear around your neck, then they make something utterly glorious for you to wear around your neck. If they're going to get screwed up by an influx from other current civilizations—and I'm afraid they are—it is we from the outside world who are going to screw them up.

"Take a glance at our gorgeous Silver Seas International Hotel on the beach. I looked over the staff of dignitaries: the general manager is a Swiss, the resident manager was born in Bali itself, the front office manager is French, the chief engineer a German, the assistant manager a Japanese, and the assistant food and beverage manager came from India. There is a combination of East and West that looks a little dangerous, since they're already working on a big addition to the hotel, down the beach just over west, over there beyond the little artistic pool and elevated food bar. This is an amalgamation of Eastern and Western talent that I for one find quite frightening to behold.

"Balinese children before they change at puberty are considered to be holy. I agree with you, probably, that they're emphatically not. They don't seem very holy when they come swarming around the bus at every stop the bus makes, yelling for money. Or tendering a twist of rice straw for sale and saying 'Dollar, dollar.' I think that's a lot of crap, and the brats probably know it's a lot of crap, but some silly people have been stupid enough to give in to them before and will do so increasingly. By strange fate, *after* puberty they're supposed to be earnest, hard-working individuals, and I guess they are, because all the adults seem to be earnest and hard-working. Not too long have too many resident managers come from Zurich! Probably you will never come back to Bali again, and neither will I. 'Life is real! Life is earnest! And the grave is not its goal.' Which is something I was compelled to learn to recite before I had halted my own individual holiness in puberty. So for Dewi Kunti's sake, Don Lundin, quit corpse-sitting and get out and mingle with the mystic multitude."

After several moments of silence Lundin ventured in caution, "What I say to July frequently. And what she says to me. 'Have you blown your top?' "

"I've blown."

He leaned forward and took her hands and worried them as if he were a puppy and kissed them. "Erna, I love you. I will love you to the death."

15

Sarah Buckles existed in constant terror of space. Commonly she felt out of touch with peoples of the earth, creatures of the sea, and that journeying portion of the world's congregation who braved it. At this season there was prevailing overcast that blanked out the planet beneath her, and she endured pain and stuffed-up hearing in altering altitudes.

She had flown very few times previously and never at such a height; the 747's put her in panic at their humming size and arrangement and the DC-8's were nearly as formidable. Where was the nearest continent, the nearest isle? She could look out at cotton wool, and that was all. Where was humanity, where were sharks, where were the flying fish? She burrowed deeper and deeper into the one previous traveling assurance she had ever owned (and still it had been mystery and fright, and even physical aching was associated with it). But in comparison the recollection bore a fragrance of youth, although that experience had befallen a third of a century before. She could understand and relish the food she had eaten in a December so long ago. Then the nation's attention was fastened on what was happening in Finland, as Soviet troops advanced and Finns fought a bloody retreat. France had not yet collapsed, the Battle of Britain was yet to be.

Sarah could not tolerate the food that was proffered to her nowadays aboard these burdensome jet airliners: biscuits that looked delicious but oo they were made of dead fish; congealed masses of green stuff vended in long narrow tin-cans, ooo, they seemed to be *worms*, and rice was packed alongside duly, and there were chopsticks in fringed paper envelopes, ooo, oooo.

She had been compelled to totter a promiscuous path through the Chinese market in Singapore, sliding on fish carcasses, her very sandals slimed with residue from disemboweled ducks—her vision blurred, her weak little breath coming short. She thought that no sad soul who'd ever gone skating on such stench in the Singapore Chinese market would ever consider the bare thought of chop suey again. She wished to faint, it would have been such relief; she had never fainted in public in all her pinched life (and only once in private), but she dared not faint because she would have fallen into the pools of decaying broth that lapped round her.

And then next morning, sustained only by tea and toast and marmalade (it tasted kind of, oooo, Chinesey too) there'd waited the mighty aircraft, with its engines ready to suck and fume and haul her and the rest to awful strata where there lived no friendly sea or lands to lean upon, nothing but racing clouds beneath, or solid clouds to block the windows. *Menace,* boomed this present agony, *I am menace here enfolding you.* Yes, she was now an heiress, a rattling little skeleton of an heiress; she'd wanted so to come, she'd squealed within herself at the prospect, she'd thought it would be fun, it wasn't any fun.

Only a murdering withdrawal ruled her.

How soon can I go home?

Yet where was—

Where was *home?*

She'd had people in her life before, that other distant time she went a-voyaging. She had no people now. The starkness of

95

the realization took her breath away. She wanted to weep, she couldn't weep, she just sat staring.

"Dear Mrs. Sanford," wrote Sarah Buckles in 1939,

> I could scarcely wait to thank you for your thoughtfulness & kindness in sending me a Bon Voyage telegram. You have been so kind I hardly know what to say. Please tell Madeline I will take extra special care of her big suitcase, and try to see that it is brought back safe with "Nary a Scar" on its pretty sides. It was so kind of her and of you to lend it.
>
> It is late—oh, so late—but I am still so excited that I cannot sleep, so am propped up here in my berth—imagine me in a berth!—writing letters to you & other friends. Goodness, I nearly forgot to tell you something. Mr. Paley phoned from the up-holstering place and said he would deliver the settee whenever you wish. If I mail this by "Air Mail" you will no doubt have it very soon thereafter, but doubtless you have grown worried e'er this and phoned him yourself. I am very sorry I neglected to tell you, but in all my rush of departure I very nearly "lost my wits."
>
> Please give my regards to Mr. Sanford. I hope his asthma is somewhat improved.
>
> Maybe I can write a bit more before we reach our first port. If so I will add a "P.S." If not, I send many, many thanks.
>
> With love,
> Sarah

She thought of Mrs. Sanford waddling out on the porch for the mail. She thought of her drawing envelopes and papers out of the box and hastening back into the house, with the steam of her breath blowing in clouds. Mrs. Sanford would hang up her old plush coat on a gilt hook beside the golden-oak mirror frame, and then, turning her attention to the mail, she would exclaim, "Well, well, well—here's a letter from Sade. Papa," she would call to her sickly husband in the living room, "here's a letter from Sade."

"From Sade?"

"Yes. It's from—let me see—Papa, it's from Havana."

And it would have a foreign stamp (imagine Sarah Buckles licking a foreign stamp; no, no she would not lick it—she would moisten her finger first and then moisten the stamp carefully) and it would have that traveled, smudged, cryptic look of a letter come from far away.

Sarah's shoulders quivered under her pink dressing gown. She began to write again.

Miss Edna Ord
Stanley Drive
Oakwood, N.J.

Dear Edna,

What a wonderful surprise when I untied the wrappings and found the delightful "surprise." It fairly took my breath away. I do not know how to express my thanks to you and the others, but rest assured the luscious fruits & candies are being eagerly eaten and appreciated.

This is a perfectly lovely boat. The food is lovely too, although I must whisper a secret—I felt a bit "squeamish" at dinner tonight and did not eat much. However I shall soon recover. What do sailors call it? When they get their "sea-legs"—is that it? Ha, ha.

Will send you some snaps or postal cards soon. My regards to your family.

Sincerely,
Sarah

Next she thought of Lucille Wayne. Lucille was only a senior in the Oakwood high school, but she was a very intelligent girl. She had some ideas that startled Sarah Buckles and which would have caused the head librarian to eject Lucille from the library bodily had she known that Lucille cherished such ideas. All about—well, freedom in life and what Lucille called a changing moral code. Lucille seemed to speak through theory rather than from actual experience.

Sarah did not believe that Lucille was really loose with boys of her high school group. Sometimes she wondered what Lucille's life would be like if the girl were not so scraggly of figure and if she did not have such prominent front teeth. Lucille was not pretty, but the loyal Sarah Buckles thought that she was intrinsically so sweet that even her treacherous beliefs could not betray her.

Miss Lucille Wayne
Garth Apartments
Oakwood, N.J.

Dear Lucille,

What a thrill lay in wait for me in my little cabin! You
were so sly—all of you—that I had no idea. Now I shall simply
gorge myself with delicacies & nuts while en route to tropic ports.
Beaucoup thanks, *Mademoiselle* Wayne! Will you still be the
"star" of your French class when I return? I sincerely hope so.

There are signs on this ship, in both Spanish and English—

She considered that for a while and then scratched the line
out. That looked messy, so at last Sarah copied the note upon a
fresh sheet of paper, and added:

I observed a girl on this ship very near your own age and shall
hope to become acquainted. Beware of snapshots in the mail—
I have my Brownie with me! Please give my regards to your
aunt & uncle.

Sincerely, your friend,

Sarah

She was writing on a folder of imitation leather—a traveling
correspondence case, it was called, and she had bought it at
Kresge's the week before. There were pockets for envelopes,
stamps, and accessories. The notepaper was in a large slab—it
was fun to write a page and then tear it off, tearing along the
perforations. You might write letters forever and ever on such
a correspondence pad, without growing weary or annoyed—
without experiencing any sensation but that of placid pleasure
and generosity.

For it seemed to Sarah Buckles that she was giving something
of herself and her palpitating experience when she gave letters
to those who were her friends and who had been kind to her.
She was sharing, as her mother had always told her that she
should share. She did not regard her mother, in shocked
memory, as a tyrant who had persuaded Sarah that she should
not marry Lowell Eberle, the only man who ever asked her to

marry him. Nor as a fat, gasping, whining wretch whose attacks of indigestion were staged on the rainiest nights, with Jarvis's drug store nearly a mile away and the medicine bottle empty. Nor as a dough-faced martyr who shook a tear off her spectacles and picked up her crocheting with weary hands. "No, no, Sadie. I wouldn't want you to stay home. Mamma doesn't want to be selfish, Sadie. Now, you just go along to the movies with Dora. That's all right—Mamma'll just sit here alone and do a little fancy-work. No, it's all right. Now, Sadie, don't take off your coat, or Mamma'll feel bad. I've been here in this room all day, but I don't mind. I'll just listen to Mr. Anthony on the radio. Oh, I don't mind being alone."

Those recollections did not provoke her. If they suggested themselves even slightly, Sarah Buckles was sturdy enough to batter them back into hiding. She choose, fervently and with full heart, to regard her mother as an elder saint—one who was butchered on the public highway at the behest of an inscrutable Providence who selected the wisest, the sweetest, and noblest of mortals to populate Heaven.

Her mother had told her to share, to sacrifice, to always think of others.

She thought of them devotedly.

Mrs. R. J. Raumeister
640 East Broad Street
Oakwood, N.J.

Dear Evvy,
It was a truly wonderful treat! I actually don't know how to thank you dear girls for the luscious basket of "goodies." Such tangerines and grapes, to say nothing of raisins! It fairly took my breath away.

This is a charming steamship, with the best of service & food. I have had a few "qualms" but we are not going very fast—on account of fog, so they say. The foghorn is blowing constantly: toot-toot. Hear it?

She drew a tiny picture of a horn, blowing, saying *Toot*.

99

Remember me to your husband and to little Shirley. You will hear from me anon. And thank you for your share in the "treat."

Sincerely,
Sarah

She must write to Ralph. She did not know his address; she knew that he lived across the Jersey Central tracks and that he lived with a son who was unemployed. She began to worry about Ralph, as she tried to think what his address might be. She hoped that Miss Klabbe had not accepted too large a contribution from Ralph, because certainly the old man could not afford to contribute a great deal of money.

A quarter. She hoped that Ralph had not put in more than a quarter.

She would bring him a present when she returned. Something from Cuba or—cigars. Men smoked cigars; at least her father used to, and old Mr. Sanford used to also before his asthma got so bad.

Sarah thought of cigars in a little paper sack. She would buy cigars in Cuba; she had read that the best cigars came from there. They would have to be packed carefully, so that they would not be crushed.

She could address Ralph at the library.

Mr. Ralph O'Neill
Clark Memorial Library
Oakwood, N.J.

Dear Ralph,

How charmed I was by the lovely present and by the kind thoughts of the givers! Seldom have I received a gift which I have enjoyed so much and am enjoying still. Many, many, thanks indeed.

Were you ever a traveler on a steamship? I never was before. Such endless corridors & stairways and such shining brass! It must keep a small army of men busy sweeping and polishing.

I recall that you were in the Span.-Amer. War although not sent out of the United States. I shall send you a postcard from Havana, and while there—

1 0 0

She thought for a long time about this. She had envisioned the soldiers who went to free Cuba as being bronzed young men: rough riders, athletes, soldiers-of-fortune. She thought of Richard Harding Davis. And Ralph (when he was much younger, before he began to be bothered by arthritis, before his breath got so bad) had very nearly been sent to free Cuba.

I shall think of the heroes of other days, and of the brave men who volunteered to save Cuba from the "Nazis" of Spain. My kindest regards to your relatives & you. Sincerely, Sarah Buckles.

The infallible foghorn kept on blowing. Sarah held her wristwatch close to her eyes, until it was brightly illuminated by the reading light that shone across her shoulder. She followed the second hand around its tiny dial and discovered that the foghorn was blowing five or six seconds out of every minute. She had thought that it was more than that.

Sarah crept out of bed and made a great chore of going to the washroom. She put on her slippers, wound herself in ample folds of her dressing gown, and made sure that the sash was tied. Before the mirror she hovered for a moment, trying desperately to make something less horrible of her hair—she had it bundled into a net. She slipped into the corridor, locking her door carefully and planting the key in the pocket of her gown.

Señoras.

She was still appalled by that sign, though the washroom and bathroom had both been shining and scrubbed and though she had not met any *señoras* in either place.

It was late—it was late to be up, to be prowling an unfamiliar hallway, listening to wild squeak and grumble of wood and steel, to enormous swish of ocean and night and emptiness.

Shivering, Sarah Buckles crawled into bed again and then got out once more to make sure that she had locked her cabin door. It was midnight, but she could not sleep.

Miss Klabbe's letter required more care than the others. Miss

Klabbe had ruled Sarah mercilessly for many years. Sarah was afraid of her, and in her heart knew that if she hated anyone in this world she hated Miss Klabbe. She thought of those hard, glistening eyes with their whites turned oyster-yellow; she thought of the slit mouth and the huge bosom adorned with lace and chains. She heard Miss Klabbe saying, "I regret that I can't agree with you, Miss Buckles! Nevertheless I'll do as you request— I'll take it up with the board. I hope that you'll bear in mind that this is the Clark Memorial Public Library— not a rental library in a corner store!" Sometimes she thought that if Miss Klabbe had not stood so tall and weighed 187 pounds, she would not have been so afraid of her, board or no board.

She wrote:

Dear Miss Klabbe,
  Truly, I was nearly swept off my feet! I did not expect such a charming remembrance from you and the others, and I only hope I can reciprocate in kind when you take your vacation.

Miss Klabbe always went to the Berkshires for her vacation. Sarah had never been to the Berkshires, but she was a little afraid of them, too. Miss Klabbe called them "the Buck-shizz." There was a poem of Joyce Kilmer's. "He was the luckiest fisherman in the Berkshire Hills, I think."

Time after time Sarah tried to associate Kilmer's gentle dream with the thought of Miss Klabbe. She had never been able to manage it. She decided that Miss Klabbe's part of the Berkshire Hills was a very particular part, and one into which Kilmer had never dared to stray, even though he had dared to join the army and be killed in France.

I find the *Utilla* is a charming boat. There is not a superfluity of outward-bound tourists at this season, but all seem to be of a very high type. Not many books in evidence, I regret to say. I saw one man reading Vincent Sheean, and one woman with a copy of "The Nazarene."

Before I forget, Mrs. Parowsky wants to renew "All This And Heaven Too." She phoned Friday. I meant to mark it on her card, but may have neglected to do so. I am sorry.

Once more, my heartiest thanks for your kindness. Fruit and candies and almonds—a "rare treat" indeed!

Most sincerely,
Sarah Buckles

Now her duties were accomplished. Joy would rule, the next day or evening, when she wrote her first letter to Dora McCune. The writing of these other letters was an arduous chore, though Sarah made that admission scamper from her mind the instant it revealed itself. She was blessed, she insisted, with a troop of friends. How many people there must have been, on other ships, other voyages, whose cabins were destitute of telegrams, flowers, or gifts. How many lonely women might have been gladdened by one slight expression of regard or affection! And she—she thought of her friends tenderly, dwelling over their names and remembered faces and remembered figures as a devout Catholic telling her beads. Sarah thought of the sun dial in Dora's parents' garden, out in the Wychwood Addition. Graven on the face of the dial were the words "I Count Only The Sunny Hours." It was as if she wore that dial planted within her now. She could record, she would record only the beauty which lived in her life, and that other beauty so recently departed from it.

She tried to whisper the words. "My mother. Oh, my dear mother. She was so wonderful." She could make no sound. Her lips moved, that was all. But she cherished the delusion and invited it to lie warmly in bed with her. Sarah Buckles believed that some great love was rooted in each woman's life. She could find no one else who was the person she loved, unless it might have been her mother.

Dora was her best friend. But a friend was different, a friend could not represent the kind of love of which she dreamed. Dora was alert, talkative, confident—brazen, sometimes—in her willingness to face life and stare it out of countenance. Dora was only five feet tall and as wide and strong as a truck horse.

She was ugly; her skin made Sarah think of buttered toast (to her infinite regret).

Sarah could imagine Dora McCune grown old in years to come, she could hear her voice ringing across years not yet formed or dissolved, and still that voice was stalwart, even as it quacked from an empty future. Dora would be a "character"— "Old Miss McCune," people would call her, who lived in the Georgian colonial house in which her parents had finally rusted away. She would be busy with everything from Girl Scouts to the Fine Arts Department of the Oakwood Women's Club, and back again to the Little Theatre, St. Paul's Episcopal Church, and the Fortnightly Travel Club.

She would deliver her annual program in the form of a lecture: "Days and Nights Amang the Scottish Highlands and Heather," illustrated with postal cards, snapshots, and guide-books that she had brought back with her from Scotland. She would quote alike from an old volume of Clifton Johnson and from a study of Glasgow housing conditions prepared by a Leftist Member of Parliament.

Sarah thought with pride of how Dora—*her* Dora—was one of the three members of the Fortnightly Travel Club who had the courage to serve sherry or cocktails when entertaining the club. True, the cocktails were very mild—they did not taste at all like the cocktail Sarah had sipped that afternoon—and none of the ladies ever drank more than two, and neither did Dora herself.

And Sarah remembered, again with pride, how Dora stepped into the breach when the school board wanted to discharge that little Miss Hingle, who taught in the first grade, because she was seen smoking cigarettes at a party.

"I smoke," Dora had roared. "No one has suggested discharging me! Is it because my father was six times mayor of this town, and because he's a director of the Oakwood Savings Bank and a former member of the Board of Education? Is that the reason? Who says a woman can't be a good teacher merely because she smokes?"

Oakwood was stirred by Dora's heroism (or loud talk and

vulgar boasting, as her action was interpreted by some) and Sarah Buckles was thrilled more than the rest. On the occasions when she substituted for Edna Ord in the children's department of the library, Sarah never stamped a "date due" on the slip inside one of the three stained fat volumes of *Little Women* without seeing Jo March rise in her mind as Dora McCune in straw bonnet and poplin.

Oh, this was love of a kind, but it was not the Great Love that had ruled her until November 7, until young Edward Kasovitch went speeding toward Fanwood in his father's Dodge truck and Mrs. Buckles stepped off the Elm Street curbstone. In time Sarah might be able to consider her dismal romance with Lowell Eberle as a sacrifice ordained by a Power higher than her mother, a Power with whom her mother was now on intimate and nearly equal terms. Sarah loved the old hymn, "God Moves in a Mysterious Way," and it held pertinence now. She felt that the sacrifice demanded of her was almost too bitter and enormous to be borne in silence, but that, surviving the hurt, she would become a better woman.

For whom (she wondered with the strained intent of a weary person who tries to relax amid unfamiliar surroundings) would she be a better woman? For Dora? In a way, yes. A better woman to write, amid fever and exultation, those thousands of words to be crammed into envelopes with foreign stamps on them. A better woman to endure the joy of telling Dora everything.

(Again she thought of Dora's good-bye kiss. And love Dora as she might, Sarah shivered in fright at the remembrance.)

A better woman for Miss Klabbe and the folks at the library? For Lowell Eberle? He was in the insurance business in Newark—not doing so well, Sarah had heard—and he had a wife and three children. Sarah used to receive seasonal cards: small formal cards, with "We wish you a Very Merry Christmas and a Happy New Year. Trudy and Lowell Eberle." But she hadn't received one in recent years. She hadn't set eyes on Lowell Eberle, even to passing him on a street in Oakwood, for at least four years.

She lay in darkness—the light snapped out, and the *Utilla*

pounding and swelling its way down the coast—and she strove to discover for whom she might be a better woman.

Her arm hurt.

Sara got up on one elbow and pinched the light switch. (It was such fun to have a proper reading lamp set in the wall behind one's head. In her room at Mrs. Sanford's she had only an old bridge lamp with Scotty dogs on the shade. Her bed had no headboard, and there was no way to fasten a bed lamp.) Her arm ached, and to her amazement Sarah saw a discolored area just above the elbow. How strange that she had not noticed that bruise while she was bathing. But everything was strange to her in that public bathroom, and she was worrying about *señoras*, and—

The man at the gangplank, the sailor who grasped her arm when she tripped and stumbled! His fingers had done that to her. She remembered now. A man, a man she never saw before, had done something painful to the delicate tissue of her body. He did not mean to hurt her. She slipped. He seized her arm, he said something—

Again she turned out the light and slid beneath covers.

A man. Lived there a man for whom she could be a better woman—for whom, even, she could be the ordinary woman she had always considered herself to be? What might he do with her? Crunch flesh, color it with the force of his maleness?

Sarah's hand slid across her chest. She turned upon her back until she could press her fingers against the small ache, the sore place. This was the first man who had ever bruised her body. She could not remember if— No. Not Lowell. He never had. And he had kissed her only twice. In school boys never tried to kiss her. Lowell was the only one.

Perhaps she had never been in love with him, even in a small way. If she had been, she might not have yielded so graciously to the flood of mother love which rushed across her youth.

Perhaps, when passing in a doorway or on the sidewalk or on a stair, a man jostled her, had jarred her shin. That must have happened one time or another. Still, she could not remember.

This was the first. Perhaps it would be the only time.

Perhaps it was sinful of her to think these thoughts. Yes, oh yes, it was wrong. A form of mental self-abuse. Something out of a case history, something out of one of those books that didn't circulate through the Clark Memorial Public Library.

Firmly, decisively, Sarah took her hand away from the black-and-blue arm and stretched both arms at her sides. She lay, breathing regularly, trying to relax, drawing in deep breaths slowly, seeking to go to sleep. But her body was rolled from side to side by action of the sea. A crack of corridor light appeared beneath her cabin door. It stayed there; it had been there all the time but she hadn't noticed it until now. This could not be a storm. No hurricane blast, only the ordinary disturbance of ship and water coming together, the ordinary vibration of great machines that shoved the vessel forward.

This was what it meant to sleep aboard a ship. It was very hard to do.

Her mind went out and explored a midnight wilderness of salt water and black vapor and found no comfort there. She was far from land; she was locked in a cabin on B-deck. If the ship went down or upset, she would be drowned quickly. Before she came to bed Sarah had peered shyly over the rail of the promenade deck, and she had seen long white streamers that came against the hull and rose aloft and spread and flew into spray and turned loose from the hull once more.

There were creatures down below, far below, and sometimes they had been photographed by William Beebe—Sarah Buckles had seen their pictures. There were fish and crabs, electric eels, devilfish, clams, lobsters, rays—crawling things, hulks of cold white meat, tangles of scales and feelers, horny crusts of shell. The notion of them made her lie even stiffer on her bed; the thought of them made her dig her heels into the firmness of smooth, warm linen.

Her thoughts swam aloft and coursed farther and farther. The other ships upon the sea (a great dark danger it was), the other seas interlocking, the straits and bays and blue spoon-shaped places on the maps, the relics of elder ships that lay soggy among coral foundations, the gulls which flew screaming. These were all a fear and a mystery.

This ship, the *Utilla*, with many strangers sleeping (perhaps only three feet away, perhaps through this wall at the head of her bed there was a passenger asleep in the next cabin. Was the passenger a woman or a man?) and many strangers walking halls and decks above, and sailors of varied colors and duties—some asleep and some "on watch." And cargoes—bales and tons and hundreds of tons of it—crated or heaped in cargo chambers, and the immense engines laboring against restraint of water outside the keel. The shore, the kind American shore that she loved in that moment more zealously than ever before, studded with names she had read or even some places she had seen—Seabright, Atlantic City, Tom's River, Rehobeth, Cape May, Cape Race, Kitty Hawk, Cape This, Cape That. And all the power of surf lashing on sand, and made more angry by remote vessels that pressed against more distant waters; and all the other people on those gleaming or rusty boats; and the mass of humanity which swarmed the lands touched by this same ocean, and all the wars they fought, and all the flesh they bruised.

16

Mail at the Hotel Queen in Hong Kong included for the Lundins two radiograms for Don and three letters for July.

"Anything breathtaking?"

He said: "Oh, it's about that piece away out east on the Bee Ridge Road. Pelzer has an offer for it. Here's the wire or whatever you call it. It's some company from Jacksonville I never heard of. You know. That so-called landfill is practically next door. It's going to be a public dump, and that's all there is to it. You remember—we both felt a little hesitant when we bought the property."

"You were more hesitant than I—"

"Look at all the pretty ships," said Don at the window.

Through habit and labor and seemingly endless consideration they had evolved manner and system. Don refused to ponder a proposed transaction without consulting July (and often bowed to her decisions, which were not infallible but usually worthy of review). The righteous July would have become offended if he'd neglected to consult her, even when she was secretly aware that the details of a suggested enterprise or withdrawal were puzzles beyond definition. She felt accurate but uncharitable in recognizing that most domestic unions were dependent on mere habit or, at the best, romantic pursuit and acquiescence. She was confident that she and Don constituted an entity ready to resist any challenge from the outside. Accordingly she held her head on high.

They both watched pretty ships awhile.

"Look. That must be a Chinese junk."

"I don't think it's big enough. They call them rangoons or something like that."

"Couldn't be rangoon. That's a place."

"Or balloons or something."

"July, that's Kowloon over there. Mass of buildings. Near where we landed."

Kowloon, Kowloon, Kowloon,
You make such a wonderful tune—

"What are we going to do about the Bee Ridge property, Don?"

"Take the offer, get it off our hands. We won't make much, but we'll make a little. We shouldn't have gone fooling around with stuff near any dumps."

"And we'll feel relieved."

"Yes. I'll cable him tonight. I mean radiogram him. Oh, the other cable was from Rod Bixley. Wants to know if we'd be interested buying that piece on Manasota Key. You remember —the old Rayburg property. This is the third time he's tried to sell it to us. But I feel almost positive that the zoning changes won't go through."

July said, "Tell Rod to take a quick scoot."

"Hey, that'll be good. Just send him a two-word message. 'Scoot, Rod.' Or 'Rod, scoot.' I'm glad we agree."

"What would happen if we didn't?"

"Dunno."

"We'd be like Mr. and Mrs. Franconia in our group. We'd be fighting every minute. And loving it, I suppose, the way they do. They're not just sodden and dull. Like, say, the Javenders."

"By God, that George Javender is a pompous old fart."

"*Don!* Really! And poor little Mrs. Javender looks so weak and unresisting. I bet he gives her an awful time, and she just doesn't even have the power to resent it, poor little thing."

Don said, "I'm forgetting. What's in your mail?"

July read aloud a faithful report from Rosette. Before leaving home she had marked two dates on the kitchen calendar for Rosette to send domestic news, and had left envelopes prepared and addressed, with stamps affixed. Rosette's father had run away with another woman when the girl was tiny, and her disgruntled mother had not bothered to send her to school. Some years later Rosette learned to read and write, taught by her own daughter.

She was a loyal woman, gentle but still capable of firmness, and generous by natural inclination and through faith. Her husband, Lucian, had been an alcoholic in younger years, had disembowled a man in a brawl, and was converted in a veritable downpouring of Light while serving time in the penitentiary. Nowadays he devoted himself capably to yard, garage, house, and grounds at the Lundins'. But sacred Sundays were a realm apart. Then he acted as a lay preacher before any one of several small congregations scattered throughout two counties.

Jeffrey has been running away a good deal I gess he was interested in a lady friend but Lydia has been xcellent about staying home as is usual with her she is a good dog. Mr Morgan came about those plummin valves they are still acking up but he thinks it not nessary to buy new pump yet and only nessary to put in a new valve or two. We got a small leak in tool house roof durin rains but Lucian has already fix it up with new stuff on top and no more leak altho we had two and three tenth inches rain Friday night accordin to the gage. My sister Ellin in Arcadia has got ulsers they fear and she is on a strick diet. Lucian is worryd about what he calls nemmy-todes on the rose bushes and is trying a new spray. Other wise all is well and peece full here at home and we pray the same for you both on your trip as always. Lucian says you send him a heethen and he will garntee to convert him or her.

July said: "Then there's just a brief note from June. Ed has to attend a convention in Copenhagen, and she's going to fly over there with him. I guess— Yes, they must have already gone."

"Anything else?"

"A note from a modiste over there in— In Kowloon. Soliciting patronage. I suppose," she added boldly, "that each of the women in our group got one."

"Probably."

Lawrence Cliffert had ascended into the extravagance of having a letterhead engraved in pale ink. It was printed on heavy silky paper stock and read *The Orchid Bazaar Room 462 Hotel Skye Kowloon*

Dear Mrs. Lundin,

We crave the privilege of showing you our new line of orchid-tinted gowns and fabrics. We have consulted your schedule, and note that Monday the 8th is marked as a Day of Leisure for members of your party. In Hong Kong and Kowloon a Day of Leisure means Day of Shopping. Accordingly your own individual appointment—it is essential that such be arranged on an individual basis—has been set for 1100 hrs. on that date, or any convenient time thereafter. Also we trust that you will feel free to join us at lunch.

Sincerely,
The Orchid Bazaar
Mme. Wow, Proprietress.

"But if I want to look at things in Kowloon I don't have to go until Monday. I've forgotten what's on the program for today."

Don said: "Got my own schedule right here in my pocket." He read aloud: " '10 a.m. Tour of Hong Kong Island including Victoria waterfront and Repulse Bay. Cable car ride climbing 1300 feet to The Peak for magnificent views.' Guess we'd better hurry up and go down to the lobby before the bus gets here. I saw Rab there a while ago. He was cautioning everybody to be on time as the trip is a long one. That damn George K. Javender was questioning him about it, the old fart."

"*Don*! That disgusting word!"

"Well, he *is* an old fart."

July nodded amiably in agreement. "And that poor little wife of his looks so sad and kind of beaten down by it all. And weak and uncomplaining."

17

From Mrs. George K. Javender, in intimate consideration of life and death, especially her own; and in consideration also of violent desire for the demise of her husband; to all peoples herein concerned, GREETING.

I could push him off. He's standing real close to the edge, and if only some of these others around here were to walk away and go around that little corner down there near where the cable car is waiting, and new cable cars coming with new people to sightsee on this high place and— That's Kowloon over there, and look at all the tall buildings— And they said that ship lying out in the harbor was the *Queen Elizabeth*. The old one. Just lying there on her side. They said seven fires broke out simultaneously aboard the vessel, and somebody else said there were eight fires and they were all set by Communists or at least set by somebody who wanted the ship to lie on her side in the harbor or bay or whatever they call it.

If I pushed George hard enough, he would go right over the edge. It's a long drop down. Nobody would survive it. George could not survive it, and he'd be gone for good, and how many times have I wanted him to be gone for good? I couldn't possibly count them myself, or couldn't tell Saint Peter or whoever is going to greet me when I Change. Because when I Change, I'll be a different person and I hope a happier person. But nobody could be happy with George. No one.

I remember something my grandmother said to my mother very long ago when I was just a girl—a slim thing, really skinny. But George said he liked the skinny ones, and I will never forget the night after we were married, in all its horror, and all the other horrible nights that have gone on and ensued, and I suppose if I don't push George off the edge right here and now, there will be more such horrible nights to be endured. Well, not so many now, since we are older.

He hasn't tried to do It to me in a long long while, because he has those girls down at the office, and they probably would be afraid to refuse him if he solicited them. But if that were the only reason I wanted to push him off the edge, it wouldn't be reason enough, because women who do things like that should be motivated by something stronger than mere female jealousy, and I am motivated by something stronger. Those people all walked away, all four of them, and there's just that one other man standing alone—I guess he's Chinese or Malay or a Jap—and then that little gang of women who are holding their children back from the edge so they won't fall. George would fall a terminal distance, and I wouldn't want to be there when he hit on those rocks or barricades or whatever is down below near that house so far away so far down.

But I remember what my grandmother and mother said to each other about Mr. Holterick, and Mother said to Grandmother, "Well, I see Mr. Holterick is moving out of the neighborhood and moving away, and it's a mighty good riddance," or something like that. And Grandma said to her, "Why Tilly, how can you say such a thing!" And Mother answered, "How could I not say such a thing? He's just brutal. He's perfectly wicked, and I'm glad to see him go and be rid of him." And Grandma said, "Oh Tilly, you don't say things like that!" And Mother said to Grandma, "You know perfectly well that I'm speaking the bitter truth, and any of the other neighbors or anyone who knows that man would say so, too. Good grief, Mother, he drove his sons right out of the house just through sheer meanness, and he drove his daughter out of his life because he was so jealous of her that he was always trying to chase away her boyfriends, and she finally had to run away from home. And he wore his wife to the bone, poor little thing, she was always cringing around and looking terrible.

"And what about his partner? What about Mr. Martin? He looked worse and worse, and finally he told his wife and the doctor. He thought Holterick was cheating him, and sure enough, Holterick was. Holterick took all the profits of the firm and gambled them away on the stock market or mercantile exchange or whatever he was speculating in. And good grief, Mother, how he hates dogs and cats. He puts out poison for them. We all know he did, because the afternoon that the Cravens' poodle was poisoned, the Jewitts' dog right next door died in the same way, and they both had been playing together, running around the neighborhood the way dogs do, and I saw them playing in the Holterick yard just before they got to vomiting, so that's where they picked it up.

"So what is he? Vile! And you have the nerve to try to apologize for him. Well, I don't think it's very nice. You ought to call a spade a spade or a wicked, cruel man a wicked, cruel man and be done with it."

And then Grandma said, "Oh, I don't know why I'm defending him. But he always seemed to me like such a nice *big* man."

That was Grandma for you. Because Grandpa was a very little man and he wasn't very nice either. I think of that now when I look at George standing here with his back to me. And I keep thinking just one little push—one little pat—and he'd be gone. How many times have I thought of doing away with him by other means? Oh yes, I have. Again and again and again, and I've got to admit it to myself. But when I do admit it to myself, it gives me an attack of cold chills and I tremble inside. Even if my hands are quiet and cold and even if I don't move, still deep inside I'm trembling with a kind of panic. My panic is the very idea of a world in which there exists no George Javender, and what a fine world that would be.

So, like Mr. Holterick—what has he done? He's driven everybody away from him and from me. Everybody. Our children hate him with the hate of hell, and won't even come home to us. Even after he built our big new house in Lake Forest. No amount of fine new cars or anything like that could make any possible difference in the world. It couldn't bring the children back. It couldn't bring anybody back to him. If he were to ruin his business, it couldn't bring back his business after he ruined it.

But he hasn't ruined it. He isn't any stock market gambler like Holterick. He's a tightwad. He's always been a tightwad, and how on earth he yielded to my plea to go on this trip I'll never know. I guess maybe it was weariness. George has just grown plain weary of being the way he is. I've never accused him of dog poisoning or cat chasing or whatever mild little nastiness like that you want to suggest. I've never accused him of anything that he wasn't, because already he's so many bad things all at once.

Why I've never had the nerve to leave him, I'll never know. I guess I'm a quivering coward at heart, and that's all there is to it. If I hadn't been a quivering coward a heart, I wouldn't have married him in the first place. Talk about having somebody rammed down your throat. Substantial, substantial, substantial! That was the word my dear stupid father was always using about George. Substantial! Agh. If I weren't such a quivering little coward at heart, right now I would be pushing him off that edge.

Let me take another step closer. Another. I'm coming up behind him. Still he stands staring into the distance, looking this way and that, with that silly, flat, vacant grin of his. I think he's counting the buildings, and wishing he could buy them and make money out of them, the way he does all of his resale business and everything falsely labeled that he sells and markets and advertises. Because he sells books nobody wants to read. He buys them up in odd lots from disappointed publishers and sells them cheap, and he sells imitation records for playing on the victrola or hi-fi or whatever you want to call it.

The records are stolen from some source or other. He loves to steal because it gives him a delicious feeling. The records are all fakes. They may sound like beautiful music, and they are beautiful music, but they're stolen. Stolen by hired thieves George's company sends around. They have little secret recorders, they sit up close to the platform, close to the musician's performance, and record what he's performing, and then this is bootlegged away. How George leers when he talks about the time he was a bootlegger during his days at Northwestern, and how he'd make up cheap gin and wasn't at all particular about what kind of alcohol he used, and sell it around, and how much money he made while the other boys were going out on parties and spending money. Not George. He wasn't going to waste his substance that way. That is another expression he's always used—talking about wasting his substance. Well, if I were to push him now—and I want to push him now—his substance would go spattering when he hit.

I can never forget that time the window washer fell, and it was only half a block down the street from where I was walking, and like all the other pedestrians I ran to see what the excitement was, because someone said a child was sick and maybe we thought we could be of help. The police hadn't arrived yet, and there was that window washer all over the sidewalk, and the way he was spattered, and the way his head was opened up and everything had just shot out of his head. That's the way George would look if I pushed him now. Oh, if those people would only go away with their yapping little children—these Chinese people or whoever they are, looking at the view—if they'd take the children and go away.

All this is happening so fast, and my inclination is so high, and if I'd had a chance to push him without anyone seeing me, he'd be dead already, with his head all opened up the way that window washer's head was opened, and I'll never forget it. George would be bankrupt. He's been a dealer in bankruptcies, as he likes to boast and brag through all his adult, savage, narrow-minded, sneaking, sneering life. Now those people are turning away, they're actually turning— Oh, mercy, if I had the strength to discipline myself. I don't need much physical strength. It would only take one mere push, and he'd be gone.

Now I am thinking of the cablegrams I could send—or is it radiograms? Send to all three of the children. *Your father died suddenly today.* Or should I say that he was killed in a fall. *Your father died in accidental fall today. Bringing body home.* Or would they let me bring it home? I don't know, and I don't care. Maybe they could bury him out there in the harbor where the *Queen Elizabeth* lies helplessly and hopelessly upon her side. Apparently they haven't yet decided how to get her out of there or how to cut her up into little pieces.

For all I care, they could take George and cut him up into little pieces, and I'd just stand there and laugh. Oh no, I wouldn't because I'd have to pretend to be the weeping widow. Maybe I could put on weeds—and why do they call them widow's weeds? Or maybe he could be cremated right here in Hong Kong, and the ashes could go home in a box, and for once in his bugaboo little life, or bugaboo little death, George would not be thinking about anything. He would be those ashes. Those ashes would be George, just as the only memories anyone

1 1 7

holds of him are ashes, dry and tasteless, and come to think about it I've never seen any human ashes. I wonder what they look like.

Mercy, here come some more people. A whole new delegation and I know I'll never get to do it, not the way I want to.

I'm dying to do it, but I'll never do it, because there won't be another opportunity like this anywhere along the line. If we were going to Egypt, there might be a chance on top of a pyramid maybe. But we're not going to Egypt, and it would be impossible to push him out of a hotel window because he's so big and I'm so little—just a cringing, miserable, little old woman. I know how I look. I don't have to tell myself how I look because I know already, and here come some more people. Merciful saints in Heaven, more people, and so I'll never have another opportunity like this. I know it. Never before I Change.

That brings a new terror because after I Change will I be possessed and confused and treated badly by George after he too is Changed, if I Change before he Changes? He's made his fortune by dealing in bankruptcies, but never cared for five minutes or even five seconds about his own love and his own life being bankrupt, while he dealt in bankrupt stocks, everything from flower books to cook books to doctor books and back again to Western books, and then on to fiction and dictionaries and always the remainders—always going to remainder this or remainder that—until he himself looked like a big gaunt remainder, with his stony stare and stony grin that meant nothing at all and means nothing at all at this moment.

He's probably grinning at Kowloon and grinning at the *Queen Elizabeth*, flat on her side, and grinning down at the tall hotels so far below. But now more tribes have migrated here, and others are going and coming. My breath feels short and hot within me, and I try to lift my hands— Why, I could faint! I could pretend to faint and fall against him. I think I'll do that. I could put my hand to my brow and stagger a little, and the people would see me stagger, and they'd know that I was feeling sickly or passing out—I could just stagger over against George and then he'd be gone. I wouldn't dare stagger too much because then I'd go with him, and I don't want to do that.

I don't want to Change, I just want a little scrap of existence left to me in which George does not figure, and which George does not dominate, but an opportunity like this will never come again. Never, never. And there come some more people; I'll never get another chance like this. But now the chance is gone, and we'll take that tramcar back down the steep slopes, and people will talk about its getting loose, and laugh, and say what would happen to us if it started slipping and sliding.

Then we'll get down to the bottom, and climb in our bus, and then we'll ride down through more hills, and the guides will talk about the movie companies having been here on location, and which movie stars there were and who was here and Jennifer This lived in that house, Sylvia That lived in the other, Colonel So and So lived there, and Orson Welles was here.

And so we'll ride and ride and get back to the hotel, and go to our room and lie on our separate beds and read separate books, and he'll look at his watch after a while, then turn around and say in that coarse, thin voice of his, "Well, you about ready to eat?" And I'll say, "I don't know, George. I'm not very hungry."

18

The ferries were like tides, they went back and forth, back and forth. But they were not as variable as tides, for they held stark precision; you could have set watches by them. If a difference showed, the ferries would have been right and the tides wrong. Coins were paid, twenty-five Hong Kong cents was paid, a hand came out of a coop to accept money or return change. If you patronized this upper deck you could smoke, provided you were at the smoking end of the deck; if you goofed and were at the nonsmoking end of the deck a midget official appeared, as if somebody had rubbed a lamp to fetch him. He would point to the nonsmoking sign, and then you would become a nonsmoker for the rest of the seven-minute trip.

Ferries carried their names forward on their hulls. This fleet glimmered as a galaxy, one being called the *Midnight Star*, and there twinkled the *Evening Star* and *Morning Star*, and *Silver Star* and *Golden Star* for all July knew.

What am I on?

Her imagination told her.

A ferryboat named the *Belle Starr*.

Gad, not that!

True. Belle Starr.

But Belle was an outlaw. A murderess! Burton Rascoe wrote a biographical book about her long ago, and we had it from the college library when we were merely kids-living-in-a-trailer.

And she had a lover. Named—

Jim—

Jim what?

Belle Starr had a lover—or husband—named Jim *July*.

He was insanely jealous of her. And—

Well. Howdy, coz! Happy greetings from this July.

> *Speed, bonnie boat, like a bird on the wing,*
> *"Onward" the sailors cry;*
> *Carry the lad that's born to be king,*
> *Over the sea to Skye.*

Carry the woman who's born to be—

Off to the Hotel Skye.

Woman who's born to be—

Woman who's—

Whatever are you doing on this ferry, my dear?

Salisbury Road and Chatham Road beyond. She walked with purpose, conscious of her fairness, her finery, traveling with the pride and confidence and assured dignity of a woman sought, a woman admired and desired.

She drifted in high assertion of self and sex and still did not know what she would do when she got there.

Memory of the Singapore kiss was sportive, and in brief reverie she felt Cliff's mouth moist upon hers.

She turned her lips in at the thought and pressed them hard together.

Rebuff.

Let me continue as immaculate.

She dodged and drifted with recognizing that in this moment she was going to meet a man who was not her husband . . . going to meet him in a hotel room. She had never done that before and would have deponed that she never would.

But the very act now instigated gave her the notion of identity with sisters of her species previously unowned. She felt a brighter, brisker claim upon this moment and strangely on her future.

She was eager to rally Cliff, to sweetly upbraid him.

To taunt and worry—employ all arts.

She felt brilliant in skills she had never flaunted earlier, or at least had refused to admit that she held.

She progressed as more perceiving, more knowledgeable. She wanted to be excessively girlish and desired to hum a tune. She was aware of affectionate pity for all beings who were not herself.

She had a weird notion that she was graduated or emancipated from circumspect existence, that already she was a product —in inclination if not in actual performance—of gleaming and desirable vice.

A driveway or courtyard or roundabout was carved out of building space directly in front of the Hotel Skye, and here, as

July danced in her turning, a bus had pulled up and passengers were being discharged.

Directly in front of her stood a woman wearing an orchid. Evidently these people were newly arrived—probably they had come by air—and this was their port of reservation. The woman was fat, old, stuffed, sagging; apparently she had Let Herself Go in the change of life, as so many of them did. Yet someone had been glad to adorn her with a badge of admiration, to send her beflowered on this portion of her tour.

The Orchid Bazaar. Room 462.

May you amble contentedly with that drooping bloom upon your stuffed bosom.

Your face is a cream puff, swollen as a pie. But someone wished you well and wanted you to go gaily.

We meet for the moment, are gone in that moment, cleaved, will never meet again, will never pass and come nigh to touching elbows. I shall never circle past you in the future. Yet there bloomed a kinship in this incident.

Because I imagined it so.

Little Sisters of the Flowers.

July had become wholly a woman when she was only eleven-and-a-half, and she entered high school at the age of thirteen. Screamingly, in the fashion of the young, she was sought and courted. The boys brayed coarsely, friends giggled about it; the less attractive girls (many) often came courting her in jealousy and in hopes that they might gain approval by association with her. Then they censured her when associating with others of their ilk.

Mainly July stood serene and well-loved. She was not yet permitted to go out on dates, but cut her own rich swath at school parties. Raptly she worshipped courtesans they read about, whose status as courtesans was at least hinted in the European histories to which students were exposed. In searching for an accurate quotation she discovered a two-volume edition of Samuel Pepys' diary in their little library, and as donated books these were unexpurgated. July stumbled across some references to Pepys' loves and admirations; she was permitted to draw the volumes out on her card, only because the woman librarian had no accurate notion of what they actually contained.

Promptly July fell to imagining herself as a seventeenth-century charmer who exuded those benefits that the diarist found in her. When he professed delight at viewing petticoats of the king's mistress, which had been displayed when airing, July's own excitement at the prospect made her breath come short and hot. She was more than willing to imagine herself occupying the position of that enchantress.

Forever she was proud to be female, proud to be herself. Her splintery dark eyes glinted with admiration of her own status, and her hair seemed to boast a new metallic glistening when she brushed it with passion next to fury. In later times she dared not speculate as to what would have happened to her if Don Lundin had not come along when he did.

In accord with the preaching of family elders, wicked women should have looked bitter and exhausted, humped beneath the scorn that a rigid society awarded them; yet strangely this seemed not to be fact or truth. People did not say, "There goes Mrs. Passy" as they would have said, "There goes Mrs. Smith or Mrs. Jones." They said instead, "There goes *that* Mrs. Passy," and the use of the pronoun had an implication beyond common power of scorn.

One would have considered to observe Mrs. Passy as cringing or kicked or despoiled, the despondent victim of popular opinion, tawdry in admitted wickedness. But Mrs. Passy walked with lounging grace, as if more than satisfied with herself, and her voice was low and rich. She wore her clothes prettily and displayed convincing grace in voice and manner.

July's father had a box at a branch post office of the town where they were living when July was in her earliest teens. Mornings, before he went to his office, Mr. Banfield stopped at the post office to get his mail. His box was number 118, and one morning he received a surprise and momentary endowment. Withdrawn to a correspondence desk to examine mail that might be deemed urgent, he tore open a fat envelope and found a fold of United States currency in the amount of fifty dollars. Also there was a letter to accompany this bequest.

My Dear Little Girl,

It is so long since I have seen you and I am nearly beside myself with anticipation. I will be in the Capitol City on Monday the twenty-ninth, and expect to remain there at least two days. I have made a reservation for us two at the Hotel Kirkwood. Mr. and Mrs., under my own name.

Don't say that you won't meet me there on Monday or I would explode. Just get on the parlor car of the noon train and ride down in bliss, and I will probably get there about the same time you do. It will be wonderful to be together again after all this gap in our mutual scenery. In high hopes and excitement.

Yours ever,

Buster

July's father mooned over the letter for a time and relished the notion of receiving an extra fifty dollars as a gift from evil gods. He needed an extra fifty dollars sorely, as always. However he was not quite cut from that bolt of goods and finally took the letter to the window and said to the clerk casually, "Sorry I opened this. I see now that it was addressed merely Box 119, and that's right next to mine."

"Well, by golly!" said the clerk. "I wasn't on distribution this morning, so it ain't my fault. Here, I'll seal it up." He did so, and found a stamp "Opened Through Error" and applied that to the front and rear of the sealed envelope.

Mr. Banfield wasn't about to ask to whom Box 119 belonged because he had a pretty good notion that he knew to whom it belonged. He had encountered the woman sometimes when they were both gathering mail simultaneously. He stuck around the lobby awhile, opening other letters and dawdling until, sure enough, Mrs. Passy came in, elegantly and calmly, her dark blue eyes tender, as if examining a pleasant landscape far beyond this humdrum street.

She opened Box 119 and got the newly sealed letter, along with her other mail, whatever that might be. July's father told his wife about it when he got home in the late afternoon, and his wife told Grandma, and the girls heard her telling and were eager to tell their own acquaintances. Soon it was all over town. Mrs. Passy had received five hundred dollars in cash and was going to Washington, Chicago, New Orleans, Hollywood, to meet the millionaire who endowed her. July did notice one peculiar thing. She had never been aware that her father spoke to Mrs. Passy when encountering her on the street. She had walked with him often, and had seen the woman, and thought that her father ignored Mrs. Passy. Now he always addressed her, made a manner in smiling, and the woman smiled in reply —most readily.

This seemed very odd to the young girl. She wanted to ask somebody about it, to have the matter explained properly, and yet there was no one whom she might ask. She kept it as a small and secret puzzle.

In that moment, entering the ornate Hotel Skye, she felt an immense and rewarding kinship with all the Mrs. Passys of existence, and the ornate wenches who'd preceded them, and all the actresses who lived openly with their producers, or agents, or with other actors, and even had children without being married to their partners. She felt tenderness for young girls who Made Mistakes, and wished that she might do something to enrich them in their bodies and their souls.

This was utterly surprising. She was ready to giggle about it and found difficulty in restraining humor, because who would expect to see a middle-aged woman walking through a lobby giggling to herself? It would almost be a case for the police.

It was inordinate to suffer this affinity because July Lundin was circumspect in manner and appearance, and pure in practice, and all she was doing was going upstairs to meet her old friend.

And— And—

She hadn't Done A Thing.

She didn't intend to Do A Thing.

No one should dare hint that she might.

Cliff opened the door of Room 462 in response to her ring. She bobbed and beamed in fancied Oriental daintiness and addressed him as Madam Wow.

He said, no, that was all wrong, he was Golden Boy.

"Why, you are gold! Gold slacks, and kind of gold moccasins, and a kind of gold sports shirt of a different shade."

He embraced her after the door was closed, and she had feared and dreamed and hazarded that he would kiss her in exactly the same fashion he did in Singapore, and she was undecided as to whether she should resist and turn her face away; but all he did this time was to put his arms around her and hold her motionless and tightly so that her face was united with his wide hard chest.

He released her.

She said, "I think I may have got some lipstick on your golden shirt. Yes, I did. Just a little bit. See?" and she showed him.

Cliff said, "I shall not sponge it off. I'll wear it as a badge of honor."

"Not—" Her voice wavering a bit. "Not dishonor?"

"You know. Like ribbons or miniatures."

She said, "I didn't think I'd come."

"I knew you'd come."

"Don't be overconfident. I can always turn around and go home."

"You won't go home."

"Order me to go home."

He said in childish glee, "Go home! Go home! That's an order."

She said, "If it's an order, I'll have to have my orders cut. Isn't that what you say? And you haven't got any lieutenant to cut them for you. Or I guess I mean any sergeant to cut them for the lieutenant."

He was in such a different mood, he was not as he'd been in Singapore—tense and compelling in approach. Today he kept smiling, but not rigidly. He said something about, I was certain that you'd come, and she said feebly that she was not at all certain that she'd come, and he merely chuckled and put his arms around her again, but gently, gently, and this time he didn't even press her against his body. He just looked down mutely, and she'd never realized that he might appear so boyish and almost pathetic in welcoming.

He asked, "How did you get loose?"

"There was no problem whatsoever about that. If a day of leisure in Hong Kong and Kowloon means a day of shopping, there are others who can shop, too. When I said to Don that I was going to Kowloon at the invitation of a modiste named Madam Wow, he merely said, 'Well, I guess that gives me the opportunity to buy some clothes. Everybody's been needling me about it. The men are all getting silk suits, and I don't own any silk suits, and Mitz says that it's high time I had some. So Mitz and I are going shopping.' You see, Mitz is Dr. Mitzheimer, and we've become very close friends with the Mitzheimers on this trip. I think they've gone to Connaught Road to some tailor's. And also they were talking about some peculiar place called Fenwick of Hong Kong, Limited."

Her glance flashed beyond to where wide windows of the balcony were drawn back. "Why, it's a party!"

"Of course it's a party. You're thirty-five minutes late."

"Did you wish me to appear overpunctual? It's just a per-functory lateness."

A table was arranged with a champagne bucket next to it, and July ran to see what was offered.

"Shrimp salad—"

"Got two salads," he said. "Shrimp and chicken. And a very English chef downstairs makes— Look, here they are. Little bits of sandwiches like you get in Claridge's or somewhere when you're in London: little wee tiny thin things with watercress in 'em. And some of them have hard-boiled egg yolk and some have— I think it's minced-up chicken and bacon. I must confess I'm getting hungry because I didn't have much breakfast. I was up fairly late last night. Slept fairly late this morning, and tomorrow I've got to be gone."

"Why, it's a party!"

"Golden Boy Special."

"You're not Golden Boy, you're Madam Wow."

"Madam Wow has something to show you. Madam Wow show madam special designed orchid garment."

"Cliff, you're worthless and extravagant. That absurd invitation of yours. I nearly fainted. You had it engraved—an engraved letterhead. Is that the way you spend Meg's money? I'm glad I'm not related to you, I couldn't afford to be."

"Rice grains," he said. "Just a few. You go to Little Engraver, and he does it all in a day. All you pay him is little-bowl-of-rice."

"You're appalling."

"No, I mean that. Little yellow man—not yellow boy, because he's old—little yellow man who works cheerfully and willingly doing engraving for people like Madam Wow, and all he wants is rice."

"Cliff, you're a menace. Full of extravagant pretense."

"I," he said, "am deeply dedicated to international relationships. That's part of my business. Suppose I were offered an opportunity—or dreamed up an opportunity—to employ Little Local Engraver to do little local job, and didn't do it. How would I stand internationally? My dagger would be all wound up in my cloak."

"'The Orchid Bazaar.'" She quoted from the letterhead. "Really I should make a pun on that and call it 'the orchid bizarre.'"

"Merican lady make puns and make Golden Boy and Madam Wow feel bad. Also both feel thirsty. Want champagne."

They were operating their lives half a world apart. There could be no protraction of any relationship established this day.

Until Singapore they had not seen each other for many years, and violent odds stood against their seeing each other again.

But miniature awareness kept asserting itself to July. In secret rose a constant affirmation.

I didn't know he could be so gentle.

I didn't know he could be so tender.
For all his warring and his scars he is boyish.
It was impossible to realize he might be so boyish.

She could continue in innocence, and there could exist that same innocence between them, so long as they maintained it.

Or she could be the complete woman in this moment of his life, as he desired that she should be.

They owned mild mischief, the boy-and-girl sharing of jest, a lightness rising like sparkles in busy wine.

Middle-age? Ha. What was middle-age? Thirty-five? That was youth untried. They felt as young as kittens.

She said that she didn't know champagne could become too cold.

"Oh, yes. It can."

He was from one of the eldest Air families in the business. His father had served in the Army Air Service before the infant Air Force or even the Air Corps was born. One time his father had gone down, in a primitive aircraft, somewhere in the Rockies. The pilot died but Sergeant Cliffert walked away. He kept walking, broken but not pulverized, until he stumbled upon a lonely cabin. There he was made welcome by two trapper-miners, and was nursed until they were able to march him out through the snow. These men had whisky, and the weather grew so cold, according to the father, that the whisky froze.

"Had icicles in it. Turned to ice."

"So you believe champagne could freeze?"

"Of course it could."

Theirs was unfrozen. It nettled them, and they looked at their glasses intently, touched the glasses, uttered infant toasts in various languages, were merry, drank again, and ate sandwiches.

"And these salads are so very *good*."

"You haven't eaten much."

"Yes I have. But I wasn't as hungry as you, because I had a good-sized breakfast."

"What did you have for breakfast?"

"I'd never had it before. They called it oatmeal, Oriental style."

"With an egg in it?"

"A coddled egg, and bits of roast pork all through the oatmeal. It was wonderful."

"That's good with cream."

"Oh, I didn't dare take cream. I asked for skim milk but I don't think I got any. I think I got the regular milk."

"Now you'll grow fat and sassy."

"I'm always sassy but I shall *not* grow fat."

They continued sporting. They sparred at being lovers when they were not truly lovers.

Oh, of course *he* was willing, in certainty he was. He'd instigated the whole thing, and planned and probably preened himself in the planning, and knowing that she should pretend to chastity until they were actually caught up in the toils of his contrivance.

So he told her about whisky and splinters of ice and how those wild gentlemen taught his father how to eat the splinters and not drink them. She said: "You're kidding me. You're teasing. You're taking advantage of a paddlefoot. I don't believe a word of it."

"More champagne?"

"Certainly not!"

He refilled her glass.

His gift was a negligee of orchid tints—the best, he swore, that Madam Wow might design, and he insisted that she try it on then and there.

"But I love the dress you're wearing. It's so rich and brown. Brown silk."

"No, it's not silk. It's some phony kind of stuff—dacron or pylon or tryon or heaven-knows-what. I guess it's probably made out of dust. Coal dust."

"But it feels like silk."

She whispered, "You mustn't stroke it with me in it."

He'd just smile and take his hand away.

Finally she went into the bathroom and removed her dress in order to put herself into the dainty wrapper. Then she came out seriously, posing for him, retying the sash as she posed.

"You look lovely in that. I knew you would."

"Cliff, I can't forgive such extravagance. You've got to let me pay for it."

"Then it wouldn't be a gift."

"Yes it would."

"You came to see Madam Wow as you might visit any other designer."

"But—but—but—"

"No—no—no!"

Their challenge and their mimicry.

He'd even prepared a box for her to carry away the negligee, and it had that same tinted card from Madam Wow pasted carefully on the top of the box. She said she'd need a receipt when she showed the negligee to Customs, and he had not thought to prepare any receipt but said now he would make one on a spare sheet of Madam Wow's stationery, and so he did, checking it out carefully for an extravagant sum.

"Think of all the duty I'll have to pay!"

"We dare not insult the integrity of Customs officials when you clear in Hawaii."

"Will I have to clear in Hawaii? I thought—San Francisco—"

"You forget that you're entering the United States when you land in Honolulu."

"Why, so we are. They'll make us go through Customs then?"

"Sure. But baby, these are Hong Kong dollars."

She was big-eyed.

"You see, you paid twenty-five cents to come over on the ferry."

"Ohhh."

"But that was twenty-five cents in Hong Kong money. Five cents in our currency."

"Ohhh."

"Can't you say anything but ohhh?"

"Ohhh!"

His arms around her, he lifted her off the floor, put her down again.

There must be a choice, and she must define it.

She touched one of his scrolled old wounds and exclaimed, and she was becoming maternal. So in turn he was the youngster a-telling and confessing and nigh to bragging quietly. Not only was he willing to speak about the scars and how they came to be, but he resounded with the powerful strident past through which he had lived and which was his echoing present (as all violent pasts declared their hold upon an individual amid his every waking moment).

He went back two generations, told about his father helping to refuel the *Question Mark*. "That was a great feat in anybody's language."

"I can't remember. It was before my time."

"Definitely they remained in flight for something like 150 hours. It was an old— Well, not old then, I suppose it was more or less brand new. But it was a three-engine high-wing monoplane, a Fokker."

"And it did the refueling?"

"Negative. It carried those individuals to their record. General Spaatz, then a major, was in command. Then there were Pete Quesada and Ira Eaker, a guy named Halverson, and Sergeant Hooe."

"And your father was with them?"

"He helped to refuel the biplane that carried the gas. You know, putting the fuel into it on the ground. I've even got an old snapshot that Dad saved after they'd made one futile trip. It was painted on the fuselage. 'Moon had trouble with hose. He has gas this trip.' Oh, there were a lot of funny things happening in the old days; I grew up hearing Dad tell about them. He said that when word finally reached Mrs. Spaatz, there in California, that the flight with her husband in command had exceeded the world's record for hours aloft, she dashed out into the yard with the news. Her daughters were playing in a sand pile, and Ruth Spaatz rushed up and exclaimed, 'Your Daddy has just passed the world record for sustained flight. They've been aloft longer than any aircraft ever before!' And one child kept pouring out her sand in the sand pile somewhat critically. Mrs. Spaatz said, 'Oh, isn't it wonderful?' And the little daughter shrugged and said, 'Sounds kind of dumb to me.' See? That's typical. That's the way the world greets great accomplishments."

They were entwined when he told her this.

Preference and decision were to be hers.

Should the episode conclude amid tender reminiscence, in affirmation of love and duty shared somehow through the years?

Or finish with tempest?

July could be her own private Mrs. Passy in heart and recollection.

Or never.

Whatever happened, she wanted only to be kind to him.

Kind, like a lady shepherd of antiquity, wearing a smock amid lambs.

But sometimes the sole solicitude you might invoke within yourself would be a yielding to frenzy, and there were those who called all sexual frenzy Wickedness, and thus were stultified, and never really knew the act because they were unable to practice it appropriately.

Their Riot might mean crying Darling, Darling, Darling, with choked breath and whispering it over and over, and it might mean his hands going over her and over her (*Oh God*) to denude her, or it might mean her denuding herself, or might mean her saying, No, Please, I want To Keep My Slip On, Just My Slip, and might mean his hands sliding the straps down from her shoulders, or maybe putting the lacy top of the slip below her breasts, and his mouth and tongue busy at her breasts until the little points stood out as firm and aching-aching as pebbles (Do pebbles ache-ache in sport like this?), and it might mean her hands exploring the blemishes of his mottled body but tenderly, oh tenderly. And then the hardness of first penetration for which she would have sold her soul, and had sold her soul, and would have sold a vast aggregation of other souls. First heady hardness adorned with its natural mucilage, and all the flouncing and gyration that went with it, and cooing of simple expressions that lovers have always used and will forever employ, the nondescript gasping of "Oh, my darling" and "Oh, my sweet" and "That's right, that's right, that's right, do it that way, oh yes, that way, *that* way." And final suffusing in glee as urgent as the activity of our constellation itself, or maybe even contigent constellations whistling beyond.

Two hours later; two days later; two weeks, two months, two years, two centuries afterward; she walked aboard a ferry and saw Hong Kong signaling across those 420 seconds of water. Signaling "here I lie" (What? *Lie?*) but never counseling and chiding. Never saying, "You were an idiot to do what you did." Never saying, "You were an idiot not to do what you did not do."

Small woman, poised and docile, with the orchid-colored box containing an orchid-colored negligee held as trophy beneath her slender arm.

She thought of the Hotel Skye and then of the Isle of Skye. With Don she had driven nearby one rainy day; they held reservations in distant Oban and did not cross to the island.

She found herself wishing now that they had visited Skye. Sometimes they must do so.

19

Sometimes Rab thought his party was composed of baboons, sometimes starvelings. Often they were fugitives from a fight that he could not designate (but why had these refugees been visited directly upon him?). Sometimes they were blossoms. Rarely there had been tigers, but yes, he had suffered tigers as ominous as any little meter-length clouded tiger of his native Formosa (or not truly his native Formosa, but his wife's; and surely it was his own two children's native Formosa, but today designated as Taiwan in graphic modern term). He owned so few solitary moments that when they came he was at a loss as to how to spend them. He carried books along but there was a certain detachment required for dedicated reading, and Rab had not yet mastered that art.

He said, "I cannot get myself loose from my gang."

Constantly he yielded to devilish prompting and went out to poke his way along corridors. Often he met convivialists and was invited to have a drink, to have many drinks, but he dared not yield to the many drinks because he would then be unfit to accept horrendous demands dumped upon him the next day.

This night, have discharged every reigning obligation, he brooded in love for the companionship of his beautiful wife. Ah, if she were there with him! But yell Rebuff! Such fancy recurred often, and he needed to discipline it away.

A friend in the hotel's management had sent him a fine basket of fruit that stood upon the bureau of his neat, tight room, and there beneath shielding fabric he found a very small pineapple but still neat and ripened, and the top had been cut off, and the rich sweet pulp carved loose and rearranged in jackstraw bits, and then the top replaced like a lid to discourage air and insects. It was fun to nibble at carvings of pineapple which you lifted out with bamboo slivers, but you could not eat pineapple all night.

He drifted to the thin balcony where there was barely room to stand between doorway and high railing, and he listened to sounds of four million people (but more Chinese defected yesterday) and sounds that came up from water squeezed among and between them, and witnessed lights of late boats moving.

Then rose rabbit misery from the room next to his, where balcony doors were pushed open as well. Who could be keeping rabbits for pets in this hotel? Perhaps not rabbit conversation, perhaps a rat squealing, but that was unpleasant to contemplate. He liked neither rats nor mice and was a little afraid of both, congenitally; whereas his collection of cobras gave him no real terror and might not, even had they been true cobras instead of fancied ones. Nevertheless, this was some nature of animal, indolent and pathetic, and Rab wondered if it were one out of his own traveling collection, and if so should he march at once to learn what was wrong.

He could not lug the plan of billeting in his head—they all mulled together—so he went to look at his card of assignments. He found that Miss Sarah Buckles was next to him. Was she ill? He'd best go to see. He was wearing his dressing gown of light gray-and-rose silk—his wife had made it for him, and she was proud, and so was he—and he glanced at himself in the mirror, tightened the belt of the gown, took his key and went into the corridor. Room 305 was next door, his own room was 303. He went to 305 and tapped lightly and kept his voice low as he spoke.

He said again and again, softly but still with power to reach through the paneling, "Miss Buckles. Oh, Miss Buckles. It is I, Rab. May I see you, please? Is anything wrong? Are you ill, Miss Buckles?"

But it seemed a long while, reassuringly as he might address her and address also the late silence surrounding them in room and corridor.

It seemed a *very* long while.

There occurred some kind of flurry inside. He heard her cry tremulously, "Yes? Yes? Who's there?" as if she did not know already. So he recited his name again, feelingly and warmly. As if saying, "Please open the door, you have nothing to fear from me." But of course she would have known that all along, so finally the door did open up.

Her dressing gown was saffron agony, wrecked lace with limp bows and frizzles, and she wore a kind of nightcap, and her miniature lined face peeped up, as if desiring some brand of vindication. Don't beat me, you beat me last time we met, I ache in every portion of my shrunken self because of it, please don't beat me again. And that was stuff and nonsense because he had not beaten anybody in nearly three years, and then it was a hulking panhandler in Bangkok who endangered two women in the party, and had to be disciplined by hasty, rigorous means.

Then Rab was in the room with her and she was such a wisp that it was no wonder he'd thought of mice.

Saying now, "Miss Buckles, please tell me. What is the matter?"

"I didn't mean to—"

"Dear Miss Buckles. What did you not mean to do?"

"I didn't know I woke you up. Didn't know that I was waking anybody up."

"But you were crying."

"I guess mmmaybe."

"Are you ill? Please tell me what is the matter. What can I do to help you?"

"I guess—I guess— I—don't need any—help."

"But there's something wrong."

"I'm sorry."

"Please tell me."

"Oh, I am so sorry."

Then she began blubbering afresh, except her blubber was not the sort of weeping where the word is often employed, but it was a cringing, whining squeal, worse than any child's. She bent her face down against her hands—poor scrawny little old hands—and there wasn't much light in the room, but enough came in from outside, and the light had been left on in the bathroom and the door was partly open, and so she was crying in that reflected bathroom light, and hiding her face, and stuttering and stammering somehow through her nose, as if such feat could be managed, and this was a dreadful thing to hear.

He thought he said, "Oh my dear, my dear little woman, please allow me to help you." Maybe that was not what he said, but it was what he intended to say, and surely the sounds he uttered were tender and sympathetic, he wanted them to be so, and she was such a wizened pile of rags that it was no effort for him to draw her over to the bed, and back her against the bed until the edge of the bed came against the backs of her legs; and he pushed and disciplined her until she was in a sitting position.

Then he got down and sat beside her, and put his arm around her, and she was tense like a little steel spring but still a rather weak one, an unbelievably weak metal spring, and he wanted her to throw herself against him so she could sob and sob, and possibly he might comfort her. That took several minutes; then in utter collapse she lay back on the bed, and he was very near to lying beside her as he tried to stroke her hands, and strengthen her frail shoulders by exerting strength against them. Foolishly he still kept asking her if she were ill, and she couldn't answer, uttering only that muted crooning.

After a long while she had quieted into gulping and sniveling, and then she spoke to him comprehensively.

She said, and he was amazed to hear her say it, "I haven't got anything. Anything."

"You haven't—?"

"I haven't got anything. I mean I haven't got anybody."

"Anybody?"

"It's just that I'm so—so alone. I'm all alone."

She wailed, and burst out spitefully. "I can't just keep sending postal cards to the doorman of the building, and to the maid, and the two men in the bank! And the—the lawyer, my nephew's attorney. Just can't keep sending them postal cards! They'd think I was crazy. Oh," she chattered, "maybe I am crazy. Mr. Wong, Mr. Wong, do people feel like this when they're going crazy?"

"Well, now," he said.

Later, with continued soothing. "Well, now."

"I hate this trip," said Sarah Buckles. "I'm so scared. Those big airplanes and— and everything. It just seems to me that I don't have anything, and I was so scared when we landed here in Hong Kong, I mean over there in whatever they call it—that place across the water—and I saw all those big buildings coming up at us and I got so scared cause I thought we were going to hit some of those big buildings. I would have screamed but I couldn't even scream."

She said, "You're young. You're so much younger than I am. I don't know why I'm telling you this, but I don't feel old right now. I mean I'm an old lady but I don't feel old. I just feel like I was a little girl—like I'd been a scared little girl all my life. Oh, I wish I could tell you what I mean. I mean, I wish I could tell somebody, but there isn't anybody to tell because I haven't got anybody. Don't you see what I mean?"

Consistently she shivered, and one claw of her came against his hand, and seemed trying to tear the fingers off his hand, and the other claw was barbed against his chest farther down.

"Oh, I'm so lonely! Or is it lonesome? I mean, what is it when you feel that everybody else in the world has got something—I mean somebody to love—or to tie to. And all the friends I once had— I used to think I had a lot of them but I guess I didn't have very many, but they're either dead or gone away somewhere and I'm so—I don't know what to call it. There was a word we used to use when we were joking. Anchoress, we'd say. Or anchorite or something like that. Dora said it, my friend Dora, but she's been dead for years. She got emphysema, and she had to take oxygen and it was awful.

"I mean she had to use that oxygen all the time in order to stay alive, because she got to smoking too many cigarettes. But she had always smoked, I mean ever since I knew her, and then Dora died, and Miss Klabbe died before her, and only one of the girls from the library is still alive. She's out with her husband and children and grandchildren, out in Clovis, New Mexico, so I never get to see her. I did go there once. She invited me to come, but I had the feeling that I was kind of in the way. I can't make you understand what I mean about being so lonely. I've got some money—"

He thought that he was a mother or a grandmother talking to this elf, trying to counsel her, if indeed elves had mothers or grandmothers. But yet he didn't know what to say.

He had helped and encouraged other frail people along the line, many times. He didn't know how to cope with this one.

He considered the adjurations of Buddha, and yet they did not seem to suffice.

If suddenly he did not shudder in his body, he quivered in his spirit at recognizing the fundamental terror inherent in all humanity.

They were not only afraid of other people, they were afraid of themselves.

In knowing that very space itself held a threat when you were loose in it, just as surrounding walls threatened you when you were jailed by them—

In having here demonstrated again before him the persistent complaint which ensued when one was lonely past endurance.

He saw in an encompassing flash the entire race projected in their cringing and realized that only the stupid walked unafraid and only the insensitive were adequately armed.

He wished to cry, Why do people march in pageants? And fly flags or kites? Or haul dragons?

Their vast spasm was merely an attempted reassurance. All people sought and needed a strength outside themselves, and so they bowed to the sun, or saluted the moon in some degree of fright, or merely looked at stars, and were still scuttling in surrender.

"Now, my dear," he managed to say again.

She gave a frail utterance that he might have expected.

Why did he call her Dear?

She wasn't anybody's Dear.

She had no one.

No one.

"Miss Buckles—"

"Yyyes?"

"What is your religion?"

"We were Episcopalians."

"Why do you say 'were' instead of believing that now you are still an Episcopalian?"

"I'm just not anything. I'm alone."

"Didn't you ever find a comfort in your religion?"

"It frightened me," she said.

He considered, and then asked if there had always been pain.

"Yes, that's it. I was taken to Sunday school and left there when I was little, and a bigger girl was mean to me, and I cried. The Sunday school teacher wasn't in the room when it happened."

What had the child done to her?

"She scratched me with her fingernail."

Dumbly he recognized that Miss Buckles was always being hurt, all her life long. Finally he mustered sufficient courage to ask if this were true.

"Yes," she said. "After the third time at Sunday school I said that I didn't want to go anymore, and my father wanted to know why. I was afraid to tell him the real reason. I just said that it took too long. He didn't think that I should criticize the idea of Sunday school, and made me go up to my room and think about it. Then I felt so lonely up there in my room—just all lonesome— That's the way I feel now, but it's a lot worse. I guess the longer people live the worse it gets. I know when my mother was killed—she was run over by a truck from Fanwood— I mean she was hit by the truck after she stepped off the curb, and it knocked her a great distance, and she was dead in the street, and I saw all the lights, and the police came with a siren and things, and I wondered why all that crowd was around, and I went downstairs, and ran over there, and there was my wonderful mother."

He wished to know if her mother was truly so wonderful.

She was long in giving him the answer.

It was a bare whisper. He had almost to lie against her face to hear it.

"No. She was mean and selfish. She wanted everything her own way, always. She didn't care what happened to me. And then, when they had the funeral service—"

Miss Buckles struggled away from his clutch and tried to sit up, but she fell back against the bed again.

"When they had the funeral, I was sitting there kind of blank. It was just like I was in a stupor or something, and I didn't hear them coming down the aisle and pushing that—that coffin—under the purple cloth they had over it. And all of a sudden, just like it came out of nowhere, I heard the rector saying, 'I am the resurrection and the life,' but he said it in a kind of hollow voice, and it didn't sound like he was the resurrection and the life. It sounded like he was the resurrection and the death, and how could there be any resurrection if there was only death? And his voice so hollow and kind of booming like he was in a barrel. It hurt me. It went right through me like—"

She said at first "like a sword" and then she thought wearily awhile and said, "No, not like a sword."

But it went right through her.

"I—don't—know—why I'm saying these things. I never said them to anyone else. But I just haven't got anyone else. I'm just as lonesome as can be." And again she mourned about it. "I'm just afraid of everything," she said.

A great truth had come to him, and now Rab himself was shocked at voicing it.

"I know what the trouble is. I know what's wrong fundamentally."

"Oh, what?" she asked. "What?"

"You're selfish."

"Oh, no." She wept. "Don't say that. Don't upbraid me. Please don't say such things. I can't face it. I'm so weak. And you—and so many other people—you're all so strong. I'm all alone."

Fairly he was prying the truth from her.

"That's the trouble. You keep saying '*I, I, I. I'm* so lonely *I* don't want to do this, *I'm* afraid of that.'"

"Oh, I *am* afraid!"

"Don't you think everyone else is afraid? Why do people turn to all these gods, why do they welcome leaders and exhorters, why did your people try to depend on Christ, and my people on the teachings and guidance of Buddha? And before the Buddha they depended on spirits and suns and moons, just the way your people did. I remember one of my people, I mean one of my passengers, on a trip from the United States. He was an Indian. I do not mean East Indian or West Indian, not from any Indies, I mean he was an American Indian. He was what you call a Sioux, but he came from the state of Dakota.

"I think now that he called himself a Dakota, too. But he had not earned any money. He said that no other Indians of his tribe or region ever made any money, but he had married a girl from another Indian nation. She came from the state of Oklahoma, and her people had grown rich from oil in their lands. But what I remember most of all about him—he said to call him Jim, so we called him Jim. He said that when he was small his grandmother had taught him or tried to teach him that the mice ate the moon every month. The moon grew full and large and yellow, and then the mice began to chew. They kept on chewing and chewing, night after night, and that was the reason the moon went from large to small. Because the mice were eating it. And I remember Jim said he was frightened by this story. Just as you were frightened when you heard that hollow cleric saying that it was the resurrection and the life, and you knew fundamentally that it wasn't the resurrection and the life."

After a time her flimsy voice spoke his nickname. "Rab."

"Yes, Miss Buckles."

"Rab, somehow you—you comfort me."

She wept again, and then said, "No one else ever did before. Not in this way."

Then she was quiet for so long, quiet both in speech and in body that he thought she had gone to sleep, and maybe she did sleep for a time, but when she awoke he was still lying there with her. And she sighed and whispered, "I'm glad you didn't go away. Please tell me more. Tell me again that I am selfish."

He told her, and she trembled with a new sobbing which was half laughter.

---

1 4 3

20

This wanderer's name was Martin Luther O'Gleen. He had joined Alcoholics Anonymous several times, but it didn't do any good, and he couldn't stand all that prayer stuff. He thought maybe it was like a prayer meeting in church, but of course he had never been to a prayer meeting in church, and two of the bunches that he got with in AA went in very heavily for prayer but the other ones didn't. But anyway, if they had, Marty didn't think that he could have survived and clung to AA for very long. Some friend cut out a cartoon from an old magazine and sent it without identification through the mail. He guessed it was a friend who sent it, because how would anyone else know his home address? The cartoon showed a drunk—you know, the way they show drunks in cartoons always, with just little crosses for eyes—and this drunk was walking along in a railroad station or an airport station or somewhere, and Marty guessed that the drunk was supposed to be just arriving in New York; he was escorted by two policemen. They had him held up on both sides and were leading him on, and the drunk was saying, "Hey, give me the address of the nearest Alcoholics Anonymous." And the cops were saying, "What's the matter, Buddy, you want to join?" And the guy was answering the cops and saying, "No. I want to resign." But it couldn't have been a very good friend who sent him a cartoon like that, and Marty was really quite hurt by it and thought, "Who the hell would do a thing like that to me?"

Carstairs
Blended
Whiskey
3.99

They were quite informal in those AA deals. Excessively informal if you want to call it that, because everybody addressed everybody else by their first names. Lots of them didn't seem to have any last names, and they said, "Good morning, Marty. Gee, it's great to see you again. How you doing, Marty?" And then they'd say, "Oh, Marty, you haven't met Ted. Hey Ted, this is Marty. He's a new member." And Ted would say, "Well, hello Marty. Welcome, welcome, welcome." And then Ted might add, "Oh say, I don't think you've met Agnes. Agnes, this is Marty." And Agnes would say, "Hi there, Marty. How's about a cup of coffee?" and pretty soon they would all be sitting around drinking coffee together and talking avidly.

Windsor
Supreme Canadian
4.99   Full Quart

And then Jerry and Amy would join the group and sit down and have coffee, too, and they'd say "Hi Marty" because they'd met him before, and he was supposed to remember who was Jerry and who was Amy and who was Grace and who was Eloise and all that kind of crap. And the way they drank coffee and coffee and more coffee, and had those big urns going out in the back room all the time. And then there was Tony, and he wanted espresso all the time, and he finally brought along his own espresso set so they could make espresso. Tony said that he had it straight from a coffee importer who knew his business about coffee, and he said that espresso wasn't actually as strong as the other coffee—it didn't have nearly as much caffein in it as the other milder-tasting coffees. Because in espresso the coffee had literally been baked to death; all the caffein or most of it had been baked out of that dark stuff they used for espresso, so you weren't getting as much caffein, even though it did taste black. Thus Tony insisted that it was a lot better for you to drink espresso, but none of the others went in for it. They had a lot of little cans of condensed milk kept in a cupboard, and they'd get those out for the people who wanted cream in their coffee, because it was hard to keep cream without an ice box or an electric refrigerator or something. Because they didn't have anything like that in the AA where this particular bunch was always meeting.

Calvert
Extra
86 Proof
Blended
4.99

And then a guy named Prescott—that actually was his first name, really Prescott, and Marty tried calling him "Pres," but Prescott didn't like that too well. He'd just say, "Call me Prescott and be done with it." And then everybody would laugh, and Prescott would say, "All right, you guys and dolls. I want to say something. You know, I woke up about six o'clock this morning—you know how it is—and finally I went out and fixed myself some coffee, and I was looking at the calendar. It was hanging right up above the stove while I was making the coffee, and it said today was the twenty-seventh. And I started figuring out the day and month and everything, and believe it or not, it was six years ago this very morning that I got picked up for the last time. I was in the gutter. Literally in the gutter. It was down on Fourteenth Street, somewhere over east of Union Square. So it wasn't very far for them to take me to Bellevue. Yes sir, literally in the gutter six years ago. And you know what? I just signed a new contract last week, and they're giving me the whole territory, and if I do all right the next few months, there's a very broad hint that they might give me the Caribbean area, and then I'd get to travel a lot, which I'd really love to do. Quite a change in six years, eh, guys and dolls?"

———————

1 4 6

Then everybody would cheer and laugh, and there prevailed the general idea that they knew how it was; except with some it might be nine years or seven years. But in cases where it had only been five months or five weeks or something like that—those people would remain silent, because no one was very much interested in what they had to say about it, because they hadn't been Off long enough to make any difference. And anyway, most of them were wise enough and experienced enough to recognize the true philosophy, which was that there was no such thing as a Former Alcoholic or a Reformed Alcoholic. The best you could call him or her was to say that he or she was an Arrested Alcoholic, and they weren't meaning to make any crack about the Arrest. As in the case of those two cops escorting the drunk who wanted to inquire about Alcoholics Anonymous.

Mattingly & Moore
Straight Bourbon
4.19

Mattingly & Moore was almost as cheap as Carstairs but what the hell made the difference?

They drank enough coffee—absorbed enough caffein to sink a battleship. But probably battleships never carry caffein anyway.

Sometimes they had get-acquainted sessions in the meetings; in fact, they usually had them for newcomers, and you were supposed to stand up and tell something about yourself and say how glad you were to be there, but some of the folks were too shy. They'd just get up and say, "Call me Tim," or, "My name's Babs," and then sit down again; and of course some of them were so scared that they wouldn't stand up at all when they were asked. They'd just feebly wave their hands, or make a sidelong gesture, or shake their heads or something.

Old Crow
Kentucky Straight Bourbon
4.79   Full Quart

"Where we going this morning, Siggy?"

Marty's wife, Sigrid, read from the tour guide. " 'Kowloon and New Territories toured by motor coach. This with English-speaking guide. All wishing to take the tour report to Mr. Wong in hotel lobby at 0845 hrs. The following are points of view: Crossing the Victoria Harbor by vehicular ferry. Then visit the Refugees Resettlement Area.' "

"What the hell good does that do for us to visit the Refugees Resettlement Area?"

"Marty, you've been drinking already. Where did you get it?"

"Now, just where could I get it? I'm all cut off at the bar. You know I'm cut off at all the bars in this hotel. You talked to the management and made them cut me off. And for all I know, Rab talked to the management, and he made them cut me off."

Philadelphia
White Label
3.99

"Well, you got it somewhere. I can tell! Ooohhh—"

"Siggy, lovey, honeybunch, don't go to bellowing."

"Ooohhh—"

"Now, it won't do any good. I just had a little nip or two, just to keep me in shape. What do you want me to do? Go around to Refugees Resettlement Areas when I'm not in the pink of condition? Why, honeybunch, you want me to be in the pink of condition, don't you?"

"—And I took all your money and hid it, and the Traveler's Checks are in my name, and you can't write one, and you haven't got any money, and I don't know where you got the stuff—"

He'd fetched several $100 bills from home and had them hidden beneath a shoe lining where even yet, even after all these years, she'd never think to look. Then, when she was away from him, he had a way of removing the shoe lining and taking out a

148

$100 bill. And then of course they had separate passports; and when she wasn't around, he'd just take his passport and a $100 bill and go to one of the cashiers, and break his $100 bill and get some smaller change, and thus far he'd needed to break only two $100 bills, and he had more left, so he wasn't worried about anything. And he hid his bottles in the very best places, but, my God, it was lousy whisky sometimes; it had queer names, not like the good names from home.

J. W. Dant
100 Proof
4.99 Each

Sigrid dried her eyes for the moment, trembled slightly, and began again to recite the points of interest on the trip to come. " 'Tsun Wan. An industrialized district.' "

"You read in a very Tsun Wan voice," said Marty. "Hey, that's a good joke. Isn't it?" He laughed uproariously, then went on to speak in comment, because he was still able to comment sensibly. "Industrial district. I'll bet they haven't got a one of our signs, and God knows we've done quite an export business, but I bet we don't see any of ours. Faulkner Plastics Incorporated might have sold them some— I don't think they've got the facilities for reproducing over here, especially the Plexiglas stuff. Plexiglas is the best material for plastic signs, and everybody knows that, and the Faulkners even use it in their ads. Even yet in phone books. They had an awful lot of neon in Singapore. I guess they've got quite a lot here, at least from what I've seen."

Siggy said wearily, "Nighttimes you've been too plastered to see any signs."

He kept chuckling. "You made a good joke out of that one. You realize it?"

"No, I don't."

"Too plastered to see plastered signs. I mean—plastic signs.

See? It gets to be quite a joke. Plastered. Plastic. Plexiglas signs. See?"

"Marty, have you got something hidden on you right now? You promised you wouldn't."

"Sure I promised you. You can go over me like a cop. Go ahead—go over me. I've got my jacket on now and everything. Say, we'd better get down to the lobby."

Siggy tried to go over him like a cop.

"See?"

"Well, you haven't got a pocket flask, at least."

"Why, doll baby, you think I'd try to kid you?"

She spoke again in worn-out, fruitless, rewardless vexation and ignominy. "Oh, shut up."

Guckenheimer
3.99 Quart

Early that morning, momentarily clear of head, Mr. Martin Luther O'Gleen had found which bus they would be taking on the trip, and had searched out the driver and bribed the driver to hide a bottle under his seat in a bag along with the driver's ration of lunch; and it would be available to Marty O'Gleen when he left the bus behind the others or came back earlier than the rest.

Quart
Paul Jones
3.99

Siggy tried to read dutifully, as they moved toward the door. " 'Un Long, a farming village. Lok Ma Chau, for a glimpse of the People's Republic of China.' "

Outside the door Sigrid left off reading to start fumbling for the room key.

"I picked it up," said Marty.

"You weren't supposed to take charge of the keys! You promised me! You promised me you'd let me take charge of the keys and everything!"

"Oh here's your damn key."

She locked the door.

He said meditatively, "You know, when my brother Terry was still alive, he used to be keen all the time about our devoting more effort to export. He wanted to export just the way a lot of the bigger companies do, but I'll bet he wouldn't have stood a chance with that People's Republic of China."

Sigrid locked the door firmly and put the key deep in her purse. Marty looked at the door and smiled with a natural quaintness. What he called his room bottle for the day was hidden beneath Siggy's long skirts and evening slacks in Siggy's biggest bag, and she wouldn't be fumbling around down in there. It was rather a flat bottle anyway, of some unknown make by some unknown distiller. Because he'd heard her talking with some other women, and none of them was going to dress up that night, because the party was going on a sunset cruise in a Chinese junk and eat dinner at a floating restaurant, which was really another great big junk, down near Aberdeen. So she wouldn't be dressing up in that special evening stuff, and there would be the bottle safe underneath. After she went into her exhausted sleep, he could quietly take as much as he needed to go to sleep himself—just two or three long, slow, sweet ones out on the terrace or in the bathroom, and of course he could still lock the bathroom door when he chose, pretending that maids or room boys might come in.

"Then," she said on their way to the elevator, "we're going to Tai Po, a fishing village, and then Shatin, with its famous Amah Rock. And there's some kind of ancient walled town, and a university to be seen en route."

"And not a God damn one of our signs," said Marty. He was still able to joke, and suggested that they make a bet. "Bet you ten bucks."

"All right," she said, "but if you win the bet I won't give it to you until we're home. You're not supposed to have any money."

"I know that, honeybunch," he said most humbly.

Ten Years Old
86 Proof
Old Hickory Straight Bourbon
Quart 4.99

His father and mother had been embattled Irish Protestants, and probably that was why they named him Martin Luther O'Gleen. He supposed that if they were young and alive today they would have been functioning fiercely as embattled Irish Protestants up in the north of Ireland, that is, if they hadn't ever emigrated to the United States; and he couldn't imagine them leaving plastic bombs in grocery stores or anything like that. Though they were both fiercely combative by nature—and his father had been quite a heavy drinker, too. But it was sporadic with him. Just big occasions, like when the Orangemen had a parade. Then he'd go out with some cronies and have to be helped into the house when he came home, and the father and mother would row and yell at each other about his drinking, and then the mother would get to drinking, too.

It was funny, but so many of the people in AA came from homes where they swore there wasn't any liquor flowing. But liquor had certainly been flowing at the elder O'Gleens! Marty's brother, whom he'd mentioned as dying earlier, had really died of acute alcoholism, but Marty thought he himself was made of sterner stuff. Most of all, what he couldn't stand in one of those praying AA groups were the kind of prayers uttered by a big heavy Scandinavian-type named Krnjagel or something like that. Krnjagel would speak with quite an accent and always tell about how they were a bunch of brothers and sisters who shared a common cause and had made common errors, and they were asking the Lord's blessing that they might not make any more common errors.

Once Marty attended such a meeting when he was a little bit

in the wind; he had sneaked some drinks ahead of time, and then taken some kind of antiseptic dental fluid and rinsed his mouth frequently, hoping to kill the odor. But when he smelled of dental fluid that was just as bad as liquor. The rest thought the sweet, antiseptic smell was liquor, because he saw them shaking their heads; and the kind of leader in the group whose name was Rennie came up to Marty, and said, "Come on now, chum. Speak up. You had a couple of quick ones, didn't you? You know you're not supposed to come to a meeting after you've had a couple of quick ones."

All Marty could do was try to look pious and sinned against and say that he hadn't had anything.

Trouble was with the sign business: it just went ahead full tilt because they had some good men running things—people who knew the trade and the stock and the entire demand of the sign business. Whatever else those boozing O'Gleens were, they were good judges of men. Good judges of employees. Especially when they were sober, and of course they had been sober more often when they were younger.

So the Norwegian would lead in prayer and speak with his accent and say, "Father, we pray to Thee not only out of necessity, but out of love for Thy spirit as well. We need Thy help, but everybody needs Thy help. We are as little children, and we need to be led. We need to be punished when we are bad. And surely Thou hast punished us or let us punish ourselves."

He was always talking about wrath. He was always saying, "The fierce wrath of the Lord is upon us," and "Great is our trespass," and "Our trespass is great, and there is fierce wrath against us."

The others weren't too keen on what he had to say. Often they shuffled nervously, but on the whole they sat back and were patient. More patient than Marty would have been. Marty didn't know much about the Bible, but he heard a couple of other guys talking about the Scandihoovian later, and laughing, and saying that he had been exposed to too much Old Testament. He was always saying that the brothers and sisters should sanctify themselves, and cleanse the House of the Lord, and bring out all the uncleanness that they found in the Temple of the Lord.

One of the men said, "What the hell. I didn't come to AA to listen to Chronicles, and I wish Mr. Krnjagel would just plain shut up and not give us all these Chronicles."

So it seemed that the big old guy was quoting from Chronicles, and Marty decided that he wouldn't read any Chronicles himself if he lived to be a hundred. He stopped in a bar on the way home and had a couple of quick ones—or maybe it was three—and he never went back to that particular AA unit again. He didn't resign or anything. He just didn't go back.

Ancient Age
Quart
4·99

They had so many signs in Kowloon that he got dizzy looking at them. It wasn't just because the O'Gleens had been in the sign business all their lives, and it didn't have anything to do with his drinking. It was just that there were too many signs. It seemed as if those Chinese—and they formed 98 percent of the population—weren't happy unless they put up signs. They put them up everywhere, and on top of each other and in between each other. Masses, masses: a landscape and cityscape oozing and dripping with signs. Sometimes there were signs in English, too, but mostly it was Chinese script. And lights everywhere you looked, day or night. They were dazzling. Every color of the rainbow but with a predominance of glaring blacks and reds and yellows. They had signs starting at the ground and going all the way up to the roofs and across the streets and down the other side and back up again.

Whenever people in a building were having a birthday or a wedding or some other kind of festivity, they would put up new signs and decorations, until the whole neighborhood was

1 5 4

just a mass of decorations. It seemed to Marty that if his company could have sold just one-tenth of the amount of signs spread around Kowloon, he would have been a millionaire several times over, and so would everyone else in the Chinese sign business.

He grew so dizzy—made dizzy by all those signs, and the rabble of people scrambling or walking or staring or trotting among them—that he would have appreciated a little drink to quiet his nerves. He thought, "By God, I've got sign nerves," and wanted to tell others about his sign nerves, but disciplined himself into silence.

After a while they reached the Resettlement Areas, and comparatively there were very few signs. The Graduate Tours Incorporated sightseers strolled around, and Marty found a narrow court where he could stand amid waste and take a leak. Big buildings towered all over the hillsides, and people on the top floors would throw their garbage out, and it would land on canopies extending out from apartments of the floor below, and then it would drip off and fall down onto the next floor, and so on. It was funny to see. Those were pretty new, those buildings, and it seemed like they could have had some other method of handling their waste, but maybe they just didn't care.

One of the tourists cried out about rats. He saw some big ones hastening away, and asked aloud, "What do these people do about rats, anyway?" And somebody else yelled, "Eat them."

There was a lot of laughter about that, as they reboarded the bus. Marty tried to join in the laughter but his head was hurting now, the way it did sometimes, and he thought, "Boy-oh-boy, if I could have just a little drop out of that bag under the driver's seat."

He could see it if he bent down and looked up the aisle toward the front—a little cloth bag, kind of denim or something—and the driver's lunch was in there, and Marty's own bottle he'd stashed away. But a lot of good it did him up there under the seat.

So they went on past a crowded spasm of warehouses and

factories, and he didn't know what it was they made in those factories. The local tour guide was explaining about them, but the guide didn't know how to use the microphone very well, and he sort of quacked when he employed it, and it was tough to try to listen, especially if your head hurt.

Then the highway climbed some hills and went down the other side of the hills, and up two more hills, and down, and there were some estates hanging high above the seashore where very rich Chinese lived, and maybe some of those rich Chinese were in the Chinese sign business, and Marty O'Gleen tried to beguile himself with the idea.

He played around with it in his mind, and sponsored a vision of a whole host of Chinese—thousands and thousands and thousands of them—all sitting down at presses and lathes or kneeling in front of tiny easels, and all of them making signs. And then more thousands of Chinese trot-trot-trotting, bearing those signs to customers; then more thousands of Chinese putting up the signs; and those were signs nobody could read except the Chinese themselves, but they kept on making more of them.

Marty bent forward again, and Sigrid wanted to know what he was looking for. So that frightened him, and he sat up straighter.

He didn't try to peek at the little blue bag any longer.

He just said, "I saw something kind of blurring in the aisle, and I was afraid one of the girls had lost a pin or a ring or something, but I guess it's just silver paper or cellophane."

That seemed to satisfy Siggy for the moment, but he realized he'd better be more careful and not bend down to contemplate that blue bag when, after all, he wouldn't have a chance to get the bottle out for a while.

As a matter of fact, he started thinking about brandy for the first time in ages. Usually he thought in terms of rye or bourbon, but now he endured a vision of a big snifter glass with his hands around it, and there would be brandy in the glass, and his hands would warm the glass until the smell of the brandy came up all around him, and he drank it in slowly, slowly.

V.S.O.P.
Imp. France Phillipe
3.99 Fifth
47.75 Case

Despite hills and curves, and more hills and curves, and for a while just curves, and then for a while just hills, the highway was sticking pretty close to the shoreline, and there was oppressive traffic. Apparently enormous hordes of Chinese were having a holiday, but maybe some of them were going to work or had just come from work. And there were a lot of public beaches in this area, and so many of the people in their little flashy cars or little beat-up cars, but mostly flashy ones, were going to the beaches.

Lots of boys and girls in bathing trunks and bikinis—you could see them gathering as if for picnics—and probably they were going to have picnics on the beaches, and Martin Luther O'Gleen wondered whether they had anything to drink, along with all those baskets of fish or rice or chop suey or whatever they took on their picnics.

In New York City there thrived a fine little chop suey place only a block and a quarter—just a few hundred feet, really—from the side door of the O'Gleens' apartment building. Sigrid liked to order *"moo goo gai pan,"* but Marty didn't like *"moo goo gai pan"* too well. He liked "sweet and pungent pork" and he got that often; or another kind of pork that was cut up into smaller pieces; and then sometimes he liked "pork snowtop," too. He usually had beer along with that. So maybe that was what all these Chinese kids were taking on their picnics to the beach: "Sweet and pungent pork" maybe, and probably they had beer.

He supposed that they had a lot of beer, and suddenly he could see a great big stein of beer, all nice and chilled, except he really didn't care whether it was chilled or not, just so it was beer. But beer was hogwash, really. There wasn't much power to it, except when they went to Luchow's down by Union Square, but they hadn't been to Luchow's in a long time. It was funny: Luchow's sounded like a Chinese place but it wasn't, it was old-fashioned German. They had imported German beer, whole barrels of it—not just in bottles but it came in barrels— and when they brought out the steins they were all frosty and nice, except it didn't really matter whether they were frosty or not, because beer was beer.

Once the bus was halted by a stagnant wedge of vehicles for a long time; the driver pulled off on the edge, next to a grove, and several men got out and went amid the shrubbery to take a leak, and Marty accompanied them, walking tranced and aching.

Tucked away around curves and pinnacles existed more extravagantly built private dwellings, and some that seemed to be motels or clubs. Evidently the private dwellings had been built by people in the sign business, and they had manufactured all those signs that choked the area of Kowloon; and at one place you could see a lot of people sitting out on a kind of balcony or verandah, and it appeared that they had some bottles on the table. They were drinking and kind of congratulating each other on how well the sign business was going.

Suddenly Marty was swept by the scalding feeling that the Chinese, having completely filled the Kowloon and Hong Kong areas with their signs, were now thinking of exporting signs to the United States. Maybe they would put the American sign companies out of business by sending in those cute products which they paid about two cents an hour for, to hired help, here in the Orient.

Suppose they did that, and undersold all American competition, and then the O'Gleens would go bankrupt, and what would happen to the company?

Suppose that he and Siggy would have to go to work at something else in order to survive?

Because, if they went bankrupt, all their holdings would be

taken from them, and their furniture and everything, and they wouldn't have a cent, and he wouldn't even have any $100 bills left under the sole of his sandal or moccasin or whatever you call it—

These little easygoing shoes.

And so they'd have to go to work at something else.

Maybe he and Siggy would have to get jobs in a Chinese restaurant.

Maybe he could get a job as bartender in a Chinese restaurant. So that wouldn't be too bad.

He spoke the thought and said, "That wouldn't be too bad."

Sigrid looked at him suspiciously and wanted to know what he was talking about.

"Just thinking about all these Chinese going into the sign business."

"What? Honestly?"

"Well," he said, "you saw all those signs back in Kowloon."

"But what's that got to do with it?"

"Oh, never mind," he said. "Never mind." Then he added weakly, "It was just a business thought. We'll talk about it later."

The last word kept echoing in his brain.

Later. Later. Later. Later.

Southern Comfort
100 Proof Liqueur
59.75 a Case

But that would be a case of fifths, not quarts.

He heard Sigrid's voice. Wearily she spoke, but there was a patience in her manner, too, a sort of weak and pitying patience. "You're going to sleep sitting up, Marty. Lean your head back against the cushion."

So he did lean his head back against the cushion, and there was peace for a time.

A lot of signs swam briefly before his eyes. He saw them,

the wild Oriental characters glaring and dancing, and momentarily he held the notion, "Why, I can read them. I can read
Chinese, so that means I can talk Chinese, too."

He opened his mouth, or thought he did, to say a few words
of Chinese, and then it was easier to remain in the semidarkness
given him by closing his eyes and putting his head back against
the cushion as she had instructed him, as she had told him he
must do, as she had told him he must do, as she had hold him he
must do.

Later he jerked back into comparative consciousness and
looked out and saw that the sky was clouded over. It had been
fair when they started on this trip, but in elapsed hours the
clouds had blundered up and filled and festered, and also it was
darker in the southwest, very dark down close to the watery
horizon.

Their coach guide was telling them that they were soon going
to stop for a brief rest.

"It is a ship," the guide said, "a little ship. It is moored
against the shore, and there is a dock where we can walk out.
There are both ladies' and men's rooms for your convenience,
and also there is a bar for the convenience of the boat," he
added, making a jest, and the load of people chuckled along
with him.

The bus stopped, and there were several other buses parked
there also, alongside a rickety wharf. There was a rickety kind
of gallery or gangplank going out to where the ship was moored,
and it too was a rickety ship. Beyond it, the rickety sky was
turning rapidly from blue to black, although it hadn't been a
real blue before but a dark blue that hurt and hit and bit you
when you looked at it. That dark blue or purple was an oppressive mass of solid clouds, and there was going to be some kind
of culminating storm.

Women were squealing to each other, "My, look at that sky,"
and they seemed to be talking to each other in rickety voices,
and so did the men, and they were talking about whether they
should take their rickety raincoats and umbrellas, and Marty

He thought briefly of Mr. Krnjagel and Chronicles and things—

The AA's.

I don't think you've met Agnes.

He held the bottle in one hand, then used his other hand to twist off the top and he bent forward and put his lips around the top of the bottle firmly. He tilted his head back and, boy-oh-boy-oh-boy, he took one swallow of the straight stuff and coughed a little, hanging onto the bottle, and then he kept swallowing three or four more times, big gulps.

A warmth of reassurance went through him.

The driver said, "Good, huh?"

"Yes," he said remotely, and heard his own voice coming back to him and repeating itself in a jabber, saying "yes, yes, yes" very rapidly. He stood there and belched, and the driver grinned to see him and hear him do this and ducked his head.

"My name Lee," he said. "You remember?"

"Sure. Lee." His own vision was clearing, and he looked out at the sky critically, and said, "Going to rain real hard."

Lee said, "Ess. Rain come. Rain."

"Yes," said Marty, and swallowed again. "This is great," he said, "Great."

"Gate," said Lee. "O.K., O.K., O.K."

Marty thought it was silly and dreadful for people to cut him off at the bars. This tasted awfully good. This felt perfectly wonderful. This was helping him. His vision was becoming keener. He saw Sigrid appear at the distant door of the surfside vessel and look out, but hell, with all those people around she couldn't see him through the window.

A renewing whirl of storm drenched close.

"Gate?" asked Lee.

"Yes. Very great." He took another couple of swallows and belched again. Lee giggled, and said, "Gate. Gate."

Marty had worried about getting the shakes before, but now he wasn't at all worried about getting the shakes. He felt so much better, and Siggy had gone back inside the boat or ship or restaurant or whatever they called the place. My, it was a filthy hole, and look at all that garbage! Enough to make anyone sick to his stomach. Water and wind stung the windows again. O'Gleen took one more swallow, then held the bottle up critically to the light to see how much was left. There was plenty left, they'd be stopping somewhere else, so he'd better save the rest for when he might need it later, although cheerfully he could have drunk the whole bottle down.

"Well," he said, "I guess that's about it."

"O.K.," said Lee.

"Just one for the road," said Marty.

He took one for the road, and then a sort of half a one, which would be good for half a road. That was a fine joke, and he smiled, appreciating it, and then reluctantly he gave the bottle back to Lee, and Lee put it away.

Kahlua
Mexican Coffee Liqueur
9.25 Value
6.99 Per Fifth

Nothing could be sweeter and heavier than Kahlua, and if he hadn't had those several short ones just now, he would probably have exploded at the mere thought of it. It was in Mexico City or Cuernavaca and those other places down there that Sigrid first began cutting Marty off on liquor when they were traveling. All he'd managed to put away secretly was a couple of bottles of Kahlua, so he drank Kahlua until he was dizzy.

On their wedding trip earlier they journeyed abroad, and it was a lot different back in those days. Sigrid's maiden name was Sigrid Tolstrup. She had been a cashier in the office of their company. Marty O'Gleen had been engaged to a couple of other girls before the Sigrid days, but they both broke up with him because of his drinking, and since he didn't know Sigrid socially to begin with, she wasn't as aware of his heavy drinking as she might have been.

Usually when he saw her at the office he was functioning pretty well. When he felt sick or overcome, he'd just stay home in his apartment and sort of live it off, so actually she didn't know what she was in for. After his second bust-up with a gal he was engaged to, he didn't want to get entangled anymore, and he played it all at a distance. He even picked up a few women in bars from time to time, and took them home, or in some cases went to their apartments.

Once it was a house with servants and everything, and the woman was a widow and very rich, and she lived all alone, and she too was a drunk, but she was a mean drunk, real spiteful and cross when she got to a certain point. She did a lot of queer things. Once, wearing her long sable coat, she went out with him, and it turned out that she didn't have anything on underneath it. Marty was in mortal terror that they'd get picked up by the police and there'd be a big stink in the papers, but they managed to escape that. Still, he didn't want to go out with that babe any more, although she called him up a few times.

Siggy was a good, solid, substantial soul, and quite pretty in a pale-blonde fashion. One day he kept looking her over in the office and thinking, "Well, why don't I try a chunk of that?" But when he thought of a chunk, he just thought of a chunk, and wasn't thinking of matrimony at all.

One night he felt morbid and lonely when he was taking her out to dinner, and he asked her to marry him. That's all there was to it. They got married a couple of weeks later and went to Europe on their honeymoon. Had a lot of fun, too. She evinced a desire for their being photographed in front of churches, because this was their wedding trip, and so they stood in front of St. Paul's and St. Peter's and St. Mark's and Notre Dame and all those big old churches, and each time they'd have somebody photograph them, and they'd be standing solemnly there, holding hands. Sigrid put it all in a little book, but he hadn't seen her looking at that book for a long time. He didn't even know whether she had kept it. Maybe she'd thrown it out or burned it when she was mad at him.

She was mad at him a lot of times.

Now she wasn't mad at him at all, and that was a great relief. Because she just said, "Well, did you have a good rest here in the bus? I'll bet you slept while we were in there."

And he said yes, that he did sleep awhile, and he just smiled at her, and felt exalted and vibrant. He looked out at the storm because it was really storming now. He thought, "I'm big and powerful, and I could brush away this storm with one hand," and he made a motion as if to do so and then checked himself.

"No," he said aloud. "It's better to have it storming."

"But this is really a terrible rain. I don't know when I've seen it rain like this."

"I heard a couple of people talking about typhoons. Maybe this is a typhoon."

"It's certainly coming down in sheets."

They drove past a lot of little villages and clusters of tiny houses strung along the highway. Back beyond the houses you could observe the wide fields. The guide said it was mainly rice they were seeing, and people working with the rice doggedly. Men and women, both, bent over under those big straw coolie hats, and some of the men were trying to plow or grub or do something to the crops with the aid of some great big hump-backed animals. Siggy wanted to know what the animals were, and Marty told her that he thought they were buffalo.

"Buffalo? Have they tamed them to work on the farms?"

"Looks like."

First the ditches were full of water, then pretty soon it was all over the fields. The people who tried to work there, rain or no rain, were practically swimming, as they knelt and bent. Then pretty soon the bus came to a village where water was all across the road and the bus sloshed through it at a crawl.

By this time most of the inhabitants had taken refuge within doors or were standing under projecting roofs of small buildings. They looked out with dejected patience and blankness at the bus and its cargo of visitors. Even when the bus stopped now, it was raining so hard that no children came to beg or offer

God knows what for sale and say, "Dollar, dollar." Marty still felt lofty and eminent but he thought it might be better if he dozed briefly, and so he did doze. When he woke up, passengers were standing in the halted bus and peering out through momentarily lessening rain, and talking about the People's Republic of China.

Where was it?

"We've come as far as they'll allow us to go. The border is right up there ahead."

"Ahead? Where?"

"Now look past those children. See? There's a long white gate across the road. That marks the border."

People said that they didn't see any guards or things and they had believed that the Chinese border would be guarded heavily, but their guide told them that the guards were just around a corner up ahead. You dared not go past that white gate because the guards would then come out of their sentry house and arrest you.

"But folks are walking there. There go two or three more. Right around past that white gate across the road."

The guide explained that those were farmers who lived in the area. The guards knew them and let them go back and forth freely. But any strangers would be halted.

"Well," folks were saying, "so that's the People's Republic of China, beginning right up there."

And others said that they didn't want to go to the People's Republic of China and were glad that the bus wasn't splashing any further.

A gang of children had broken loose from their homes and were gathered in the road. A few were cringing and uncoated, but most of them wore little capes and caps or hoods of plastic in rainbow hues. They were pretty in their dancing colors. Really, they weren't begging, but it wouldn't have done them any good to beg or offer things for sale anyway, because the people were all stowed tightly in the bus and no one had any desire to venture outside with all that rain still pounding. It was coming down so solidly that you could only see the white gate of Red China and the few people walking through, and then beyond that there was just rain.

The kids were playing on a hillside. There was another road that went up a hill—maybe it was to the north. Anyhow, it was on the right-hand side of the bus as they sat there, and kids had made a cart out of two wheels that didn't match, and they were coasting downhill on that cart amid laughter. Just a couple of old boards put together and tied somehow between the wheels; one of the wheels was little and one was big, so that made the cart lopsided, and three or four of those children in their shimmering pink and red and green and white and golden little raincoats would pile on that thing, and try to ride, and they'd fall off, and the cart would get upset but nobody cried.

They were just raving about it, and then some of the bigger boys would run and haul the cart up the hill again, while whole gangs of children would go tagging after, and more of them waited down below, circling and cheering and clapping their hands. Then the cart would come lurching and upsetting and waggling and upsetting and twisting and upsetting again.

The lake across the road became a deep brown ocean, and owned frequent geysers to wrench and drench the children as they capered.

Geysers?

Splash.

Dash.

The bus was turning back, inching into a narrow space to wheel and assault another road that poured its river down an adjacent hillside. The guide was quacking about it over the microphone.

Children danced to safety in their plastic garb.

Plastic garb?

Plastic signs.

Marty O'Gleen felt a fierce surge of confidence. It was great, feeling confident like that. He didn't know when he had felt so confident. If he felt that confident when he got back to New York he would be known as a—

They might call him a confidence man!

He chuckled at the idea and remembered vaguely that Sigrid had asked him what he was laughing about, and he hadn't been able to tell her.

His brain was fevered and alight with its panorama of plastic children in pink, and plastic children in hazel colors and grass-green and pea-green, and bright as stars and older than time and younger than new-fledged foetuses, or however doctors and scientists talked about the beginnings of human life. They were also aqua-colored and varying shades of carmine and rose. He could think of a lot of colors because he was in the sign business; and now he would be in the sign business in a big way, bigger than ever before, but he mustn't let the Chinese get in first.

Because how many Chinese restaurants were there in New York City? Hundreds and hundreds and more hundreds, and new ones seeming to open every minute. There was North Chinese food and South Chinese food and some kind of queer new Chinese food. He couldn't think of the name now but there was a name for it. And there was Mandarin cooking, and he played with an echo of that name for a time, and then came up with the word "Sandarin," and liked the sound of it.

Plastic Chinese children, in color, on every Chinese sign.

There would be some way, or should be some way, to copyright or patent the idea, and he'd take over and do just that.

The O'Gleen Company would originate and grab all the business and not give the Chinese a chance.

Color of tea and color of straw and color of cherries and sky and clouds and the rich fierce grass all around, except it would be plastic glass instead of plastic grass, and how those children would wink and dance and beckon. Not just funny Chinese characters looking like a misshapen alphabet that an idiot had constructed, not looking like broken dried trees or half-baked dragons. No, these would all be children in their little olive and sunny plastic coats, and whenever you saw one of those squinting, wavering children—he meant, whenever you saw a whole mess of them together—that would be the Chinese sign, and you wouldn't have to say "chop suey" or "Queen of Asia" or anything like that. You wouldn't have to say "On Leong" or "Hip Sing" or any name of any Chinese lodge or group or fraternal order, because the children would be enough, and some of them might be silver as well and some tinted like strawberries and some like oranges in bags in a market.

Siggy was saying, "Marty, please. Marty, please."

"What my doing? Whass matter?"

"You're making such queer noises, you're kind of humming and grunting."

"Juss got wonderful idea."

"What is it?"

"Juss wait-an-see," he said aloud to her, and secretly to himself.

He began to prepare a plan.

After a time he told his wife bravely, "Iss got children in it. Juss got that idea right on edge of Peeps Republic of China." But by this time she was indignant and hurt and bruised, the way she was always being, and she turned her face away, and he saw her mopping at her eyes, so he didn't want her to mop his eyes too, and he closed them and pretended to be asleep.

He was asleep and leaning leaning leaning leaning against her.

When he awakened the bus had stopped in East River Hudson River because cars were broken down and stalled and two cars appeared to have gone off the road ahead. Passengers were talking about it and grouping up front to look out through Niagara and see Maid-of-the-Mist stranded cars. The driver managed to work their own vehicle ahead and to one side, until he was next to a kind of platform built for a professional bus stop, a regular ordinary-duty bus which traveled that way and brought Chinese people to villages and took Chinese people away from villages again.

Along that platform people could walk to a restaurant beyond, and many of them were going there now to use the facilities and facilities and a number of men men men were saying that they wanted a drink and would get at least some beer

inside or maybe some of that Chinese whiskey. They said it
wasn't half bad, and Marty nodded sagely sagely to hear them
say so.

The space next to him was empty.

Siggy had gone too.

He saw Lee grinning at him. Lee, small, beaming, but
shriveled star in the firmament beyond. Why did they say
firmament? Did they mean firm as mint less say firm as mint?

Marty held his head low and slightly behind his hand, and
he kept signaling to Lee. He would signal by bending his finger
and then moving it back and forth, as if he were pulling a
thread with his bent finger. Finally, Lee left his seat at the front
of the bus and edged and staggered and galloped and flew
toward Marty O'Gleen.

"You bring bottle," said Marty. "Heap big bottle."

He kept saying things like that—"bottle" and "heap big," and
trying kind of to talk Indian talk to Lee because Lee was a
foreigner.

Then Lee got the idea and said, "O.K. O.K. O.K." again in
his rapid fashion, and he went and got the bottle and brought
it to Marty O'Gleen, and Marty O'Gleen drank everything that
was left in the bottle. He drank all the rest, big swallows, and
it made him feel so much better.

He sat bent, bottle cemented in his hand.

Bottle cemented.

Cemented.

Until he heard a kind of squeal, and he looked and some
women were dissolving and forming in the aisle, but they had
halted halted because Siggy was ahead of them and she was
frozen frozen there, kind of stiff, and then she groped up with
one hand and put it over her eyes.

Lee and the guide and two of the passengers got him off the
bus at the hotel entrance, where Rab was pacing in concern.
Because the bus was nearly three hours late in arriving back
at the hotel. There were rumors about a huge mud slide up

on the mountain they'd come past, somewhere near the Amah Rock, where some woman had been solidified long ago and was still standing, made entirely of stone. There had been an enormous landslide of mud, and some tourists near the university had been swept away, and were said to be buried deep, and Rab was praying that none of his own party was under that mud as well.

So they got Marty off the bus, and then the big doorman took charge and called two of his more capable bellboys, and their arms went around Marty, and they held onto his sides and walked him at a slow pace to the elevator, and took him up to the O'Gleens' room and put him on the bed.

Dr. Kayce turned and wiped his needle. "Now comes the big question. Where do I get this sterilized, in case I have to use it again?"

Mitzheimer asked, "What did you give him, Doctor?"

Kayce smiled and said, "A hundred milligrams of Sparine. I thought that might help for the moment, Doctor."

And Mitz smiled and bowed, and said, "Sounds good, Doctor."

And then they sighed and kind of smiled, and went out together. Mitz was asking Kayce how he happened to have that Sparine with him, and Kayce said wearily, "Oh God, these things are apt to happen. A couple of trips ago when Mona and I were in the Mediterranean we had an alcoholic woman aboard—I mean, along with the party. So I thought it might be a good idea to come prepared."

Outside there were women, and one of them was Mrs. Mitzheimer, and she said that she and Mrs. Lundin would take charge of Mrs. O'Gleen and get some food into her, because they all needed food badly, and she, poor dear, needed magic and no mistake.

Don Lundin said bitterly, "Better give O'Gleen a shot of embalming fluid while you're about it."

"Oh," said Kayce, "the undertaker'll be doing that before long."

Back in the room and on the bed, Marty stirred slightly and kind of gargled, and before he went into apathy he thought of the colors of all those Chinese signs to mark the restaurants in New York City. Colors of tulips, colors of cocktail crackers, and nut-colored colors too—not just plain brown or yellowish nuts —but gorgeous dyed nuts and candy-tinted too. What a bewildering variety of colors, like on a fancy old-fashioned birthday cake.

Little dots.

Some had anise flavor in them.

Anise.

Anise.

21

At the International Airport in Taiwan excitement ran among those travelers who loved Rab in varying degrees or who assayed him merely as bizarre and unique, according to their previous experience. Taiwan was Rab's home, and when he was asked if his wife and children would be there to see him at the airport, he could only say, "I hope so," and his dark eyes would be a-gleam.

"But don't we stay any length of time in Taiwan?"

"I am sorry to say that we do not."

"Well, I should think you would be sorry."

"Yes, I am sorry."

"But why couldn't we stop, at least overnight?"

"This I dare not do. I would not be permitted to do so. I would not do so myself, were I permitted. You people are my obligation."

"I think that's a damn shame," said July, and other women seconded her roundly.

Rab explained, "Truly it is not as bad as might appear on the surface. Once I have put you aboard your airplane, departing Japan for Hawaii and the other United States, I shall then fly from the same airport back here to Taiwan and be with my family for a brief vacation."

Passengers who were merely en route and not stopping were barred from the rest of Taiwan with precision. Those who were most interested approached the barrier along with Rab and watched him confer with officials.

An understanding arranged previously was made apparent. A slender girl—she seemed so young to be the mother of that pair—was escorted through the wicket, along with her sons. A police officer collected three passes offered by the woman. She was dainty to the point of perfection; she wore Western dress, benefiting it by appearing in it; her eyes were slanted and sparkling. Her mouth—

"I keep thinking," said Erna, in a voice controlled to un-accustomed softness, "of something written by James M. Cain."

Don Lundin asked, "James M. Cain? The novelist? I guess he's been dead quite a while, hasn't he? What on earth makes you think of him? Didn't he write *The Postman Always Rings Twice*?"

"There was someting about a girl," she said. "Maybe it was in some other book he wrote. There was one called *Mildred Pierce*. Anyhow, he said about this girl, to wit: 'Her lips stuck out in a way that made me want to push them in for her.' A purely masculine reaction and rather brutal too, but—"

You could observe both pride and longing in Rab, because his wife was a work of beauty and his sons attentive and attractive and disciplined. Sun and Moon were their nicknames. Sun was ten, Moon was eight. Moon was having his teeth straightened and presented a blaze of metal whenever he smiled, which was persistently.

They stood side by side in the navy blazers they wore to school. They spoke winningly the few words of English, the politenesses in which they had been instructed. They said, "Yes," "please," and, "Thank you," and "How do you do, sir" (or "ma'am"), and things like that. People wanted to buy them Cokes and ice cream. They looked earnestly at their mother, and she shook her head firmly. No, this was between meals. But women clustered and cried, "Oh, this once, Mrs. Wong! They don't come often to the airport, do they?" and it seemed that they did not come too frequently.

Finally, Susan Wong relented and let them be treated, and travelers honored the boys in their treating. The nervous but affectionate lawyer, Semple, hastened to the gift counter and purchased twin revolvers in holsters and armed the boys with those. The parents looked at each other hopelessly and gestured, as if to say, "Well, what can you do about this? Nothing." Soon the refueling and aircraft inspection was completed, of which they were informed firmly by mechanical means, and Rab was crying.

It grieved the rest to see him cry, and he made a great show of polishing his glasses and putting them on and taking them off, and wiping his eyes in the process, and then, as an honest lover, he embraced his wife. If you were standing near you could see his hands tighten convulsively across her lovely shoulders. He pressed her against himself and whispered something—probably saying that they would be together in just three weeks and have a glorious vacation.

Then he was all business, marching his little ones and the wife of the eleven years they had spent together (but it didn't seem that it could be possible)—taking them back to the gate, where folds of paper were duly inspected and some remark was made about the weapons with which the boys were endowed

---

and adorned. One official questioned another—rather angrily, it seemed—and the senior official smiled and made gestures of reprobation and passed the Wong family, guns and all, while the stern little official stamped away in disappointment; the strictness of his approach had been ignored and apologized for.

The Wongs were gone, devoured by oncoming processions of passengers for other flights and maybe a few for their own. Rab was checking to see that all his people held their boarding passes prominently displayed and that those who carried newly bought liquor in hand containers had had their liquor duly stamped and passed. Then one by one and two by two and in groups the Graduates were marshaled to their bus and stowed aboard.

Now they would leave this one-time Formosa, and wouldn't even have seen the Incarnate Buddha named Chih Hong, and how the bolder of them had wished to see him, and how the women said Ugh at the idea. He had died in 1954, contemplating, and that was a perfect way for a monk to die.

"Do not bury me when I die," he said. "Do not bury me after I'm gone. Merely seal me up in a receptacle," he told the nuns. Then promptly he was transformed, even while sitting in his attitude of contemplation, and the nuns followed his instructions to the letter. They found a jar big enough to put him in, and there he was kept for the five years specified.

Promptly on a traditionally rainy May day in 1959 they opened the jar, and the body of Chih Hong was perfectly preserved; at least that is what they swore. They swathed him in silk and put what they described as a permanent coating of gold leaf on him, and there he is sitting even now, and no wonder the women in the party said Ugh, and no wonder impish men wished that they might have visited him.

22

The eminent deeds of Wye Rabarti Wong included a brief interview with the Mitzheimers in a Tokyo hotel.

"Please to forgive me. But I could not help overhearing when you spoke about your boat. You do have a yacht?"

A chuckling Mitz accused Rab of flattery. "We're not exactly in the yacht bracket, but we do own a little cruiser. It'll sleep four. We keep it way over on the east shore of the Chesapeake. Too much local traffic near our home."

"I was thinking about Miss Buckles."

Erna cried, "Up the Divine Sarah! Does she crave yachts?"

"Permit me to explain. If you could be so considerate as to invite her aboard, once you are reestablished at your home. She is so very lonely, although it is actually her own fault. But she fears and hates our constant flying. Forever she is going back in memory to the one cruise she took when she was younger and visited ports in the Caribbean Sea."

The Mitzheimers decided on Smith Island and Tangier Island. "You'll love every minute of it, Miss Buckles," Erna proclaimed. "The original English settlers' descendants are still there, smack in the middle of the Chesapeake. Especially that's true of Tangier."

"But I thought," said the wee voice, "that Tangier was a place in North Africa. With mosques and—caliphs—and—international banking."

"Not *our* Tangier. The people still speak with South Country accent and mannerisms. Devonshire, unless I miss my guess, and I very seldom miss my guesses. And their front yards are gaudily filled with gravestones. Their ancestors are all buried there, right in each family's front lawn. And they boast the most overpowering masses of blue and purple hydrangeas to be seen anywhere, any time."

Sarah Buckles wept in a glee of sacred contemplation. Boldly she tried not to cry, but her shoulders quivered, and moisture spilled from her eyes. "I never was invited on such a trip before," she managed to gasp. "I mean—a trip like this. I promise not to be seasick. I don't want to cause anyone any trouble."

"But you'd like to go, my dear? We'll have a ball!"

"I never wanted to go so much in all my life," the little voice was wailing. "Not even to Vassar. When I was a girl."

"We've been planning to ask you for weeks," lied the valiant Erna.

In the middle of that night David Mitzheimer thought that he was sitting in a place, and he didn't know who he was sitting with. The presence was impressive. Maybe it was God he was sitting with. Some sort of priest or president or commander.

His main question was, "Why was I selected?"

"Of course you were not selected."

"Then how did it happen?"

"That is a mystery which you'll have to prove."

"You don't prove a mystery, you solve it."

"But you'll have to prove that the mystery exists."

"Oh, I see."

There were two windows or wide sets of windows in this den or office or Post of Command. Through one of them you could see the colors of dawn coming up and offering both promise and derision to creatures who witnessed it, and through the other row of windows the colors of sunset could be seen.

Mitz asked, "How many days and how many nights?"

"Well, statistically you can figure it out."

Mitzheimer figured and figured. "Somewhere around twenty-eight thousand. Apiece."

"That's a lot of days and nights. Enough to make a pattern of conduct?"

Mitz replied testily, "I don't like that. It sounds as if it came out of IBM, some kind of computer. Little businesses oozing up and down with talkative regularity."

"You know, don't you, that the majority of the people with whom you have been intimately associated are now dead?"

"Yes, of course. One has to admit that."

"But you don't like it?"

"No, I don't."

"What would you do, then, if you had your way? Would you retain life? Keep these people going on and on forever?"

"A lot of them—I guess the vast majority of them—didn't wish to die when they did die."

The proctor or prompter was close to sneering. "You know, you're getting nowhere fast. You're not even thinking straight."

"No, I'm not. Let me tell you, sir, that a long life is extremely confusing."

"Ha-ha-ha! A lot of short lives are, too. But what would you have done now, in the middle of the night, the long lonely darkness, and still the comfort of night? Suppose you'd come back from the bathroom and slid into bed beside Erna and found that she was gone? I mean that she had died while you were in the bathroom, or possibly before you went, and you hadn't known it. And there she was, all cold. What would you have done?"

"Guess I would have screamed, and turned on the light."

"Would you have screamed deliberately?"

"The cry would have been torn out of me."

"Are you sure? Maybe you wouldn't have said anything."

"No, I guess you're right. Maybe I wouldn't have screamed. But certainly I would have turned on the light."

"And then you'd know that you were alone as you were alone after Cleo died, and you hadn't wished or expected to be alone again, although certainly you had considered the possibility on many occasions. That's one thing which life is all about. Isn't it?"

"Boss, you mean—?"

"I mean that a lot of life is considering the possibility of death."

"By golly, you're right. It's the first thing that confuses children. I remember an anecdote concerning Walt Whitman. Ever hear it?"

"I'm not too sure, sonny boy. Go ahead and tell me, if it will please you in any way."

"Well, I can't remember just where I read it, or when, but it was long ago, and Whitman was living there in Camden, or wherever it was he lived after he became decrepit— Yes, Camden, New Jersey. I think it was his brother who died. Anyway, the body was laid out in an old-fashioned coffin, probably up on chairs, the way they used to do. And Walt was sitting there beside it in his wheelchair, and a little child came into the room. The child stood solemn-faced, staring at the dead body in the coffin. Then Walt was heard to say, as if speaking directly to the child, 'You don't know what it is, my dear, do you?' And then he was silent for a moment, and then he added, 'Neither do we.' "

"Hell's bells. I was in the room when that happened."

"Oh, I suppose you were. You've been everywhere, no doubt."

"Are you making fun of me?"

"Certainly not. I'm just a little resentful."

"Mitz, you've been a lot of places, yourself."

"Yes I have."

And then he thought about the places where he'd been, and the people he had known along the way, and the process removed him from the clinic, confessional booth, conference chamber, and from its Worthy Patron. At home in their country place they had a pet cat, and for a time Mitzheimer fancied that Melissa was there in this Orient in bed with them. He felt the small warm weight of the cat, down somewhere between his feet and Erna's, and he moved his feet around the cat's heftiness. Of course Melissa was up on top of the covers, but he could wriggle his feet slyly past. Then his feet encountered Erna's leg and ankle and foot. He stretched them down, his foot pressed against hers. There ensued her slight waking, a responding demonstration of warmth, softness, affection. She sighed, and resumed breathing regularly in sleep.

The big question still remained in his heart and in his fancy. Why had he been chosen? It seemed in some way that he had been selected rigidly.

His next thought was, "I didn't deserve to live this long. And yet I've done so. And what a joy it all is."

Even taking into consideration the pain, the terrors, the uncertainties, the dun seasons and ambuscades, the reiterated awareness that this was a constant protracted "examination day," with no way out.

"Forget it," he counseled himself, and smiled calmly up into the gloom.

23

July said, "That charming information girl in the lobby."

"Glad to hear she's charming."

"Haven't you talked with her?"

"I've never even seen her."

"Well, Erna and I decided that it would be delightful if we went to the Sambo In. It used to be a summer palace."

"Sounds like a place where they might serve good pork chops. But look, pet, I'm not going to any more palaces. Or shrines. Or pagodas. Or temples, wats, ghats, or such."

"You won't have to go to this one and neither will Mitz. Erna and I are going alone."

July explained that the Sambo In was a retreat for the royal family long ago. "It's on a beautiful hillside, and they have all sorts of miniature tea houses and ceremonial places scattered over the slopes and in the groves and along ponds and streams. I suppose the sacred family used to go and have lunch or tea or whatever they wanted to have in a different one every day. Anyway, it's not commonly open to the public. You have to go with a group, and there's something about your having to be invited."

Don thought it sounded rather complicated. "If all you get to see are a flock of tea houses."

"They used to let you go into the residence. But some tourist stole something that was uncommonly holy in the family annals, so they won't permit sightseeing parties to go into the main building anymore. I guess you can peek through windows but that's all. But it sounded unique, and Erna and I decided that we should go. Thereupon ensued all sorts of technical complications, but that lovely girl in the lobby has overcome them all. Erna and I are going this afternoon by taxi."

She said later, while she was deciding what to wear and then dressing after her shower, "You should feel an especial soft spot in your heart for that little information girl downstairs. The one who is facilitating our trip. She's your slick little Japanese sister. Because her name in Donna."

"Maybe she's a kissing cousin."

"Well, don't you dare try to kiss her next time you're in the lobby. She's very popular with these hordes of tourists; there are always people standing in line by her desk, and she's such a pretty thing. Has the most lovely mouth."

"I'm compelled to admit that a lot of them have."

Mitz wanted to go to the zoo. He said that he had picked it out by use of a map and a tourist street plan, and a study of

Mrs.—" She had a little trouble with the name Mitzheimer. "But it is you with whom I wish to speak."

"Well. Sure."

The next question was surprising. "May I please come to your room? It would be difficult to talk here in the lobby."

"Why—why—certainly. Come ahead. You know it's mixed up. You have to take two sets of elevators."

She laughed. "I know. I am well acquainted with the manner."

Don chuckled. "I'm stupid. I was just sort of dozing. Come right along."

He didn't know what on earth she could wish to speak to him about. This was odd.

Suddenly it struck him. Since July and Erna had gone on a side trip by special arrangement, and were paying a special fee, she probably had something else—some other proposition, some other strange place to go—in which she thought they might be interested. That could be it. It might be a more expensive deal, and that was probably the reason she wished to talk to the husbands first.

Don laughed to himself. "Quite a saleslady. Maybe that's the best way to work it—go up to the customers' rooms and—"

Amid these musings the doorbell rang its song.

Yes. The young lady was pretty and trim, except she looked a little actressy or night-clubby. Because she had those great dark spectacles masking the upper part of her face.

Why on earth do these gals insist on wearing dark glasses? It's tiresome. I wish they wouldn't do it. Oh, I suppose the big lobby is too bright with sunlight and—

"How do you do—ah, Mrs.—"

She gave her name again. "Takami."

"Won't you please sit down?"

"Thank you." She seated herself on the edge of one of the stiffer chairs. She wore a cherry-colored uniform with a very short skirt, and had lovely legs, and wore slippers of a color to match the uniform. A dish.

He asked, "Now, please. What can I do for you?"

the landscape from his own high windows with binoculars. '
a nice stroll, maybe a mile or something like that. We can
back if we feel too lazy to walk. Maybe we'll see a gaur."

He and Don admired especially the bears, and felt sorry
raccoons imported all the way from America, and felt sorry
vultures and condors on general principles.

Back at the hotel once more they drank a couple of cockt
and had a leisurely lunch on the lobby balcony.

"Nap in order for me," said the doctor. "You take th
habitually too, don't you, Don? I saw you dozing again on t
bus yesterday."

"I take naps whenever I can manage, which isn't often on
trip like this. Let's go up and stretch out."

They went through a tiresome routine of elevators and cori
dors. A huge addition to the hotel had been built on the hillsic
above, and thus the transportation system occupied differer
levels. You had to go up in one elevator to certain floors, wal
through inclined corridors, and take one of another series o
elevators in the wings, and then walk some more.

The men waved in farewell when they parted at a corridoi
juncture. Don Lundin went to his room and stretched out in a
chair near the window—a chair which had soon come to be a
favorite. He shoved a soft stool beneath his feet.

He dozed contentedly, magazine fallen from his hand, when
the telephone gave its musical tinkle.

It was the voice of a stranger, a woman. "Mr. Lundin?"

"Speaking."

"Mr. Lundin, excuse me, please. I am Mrs. Takami, the information clerk in the lobby."

"Oh, yes, Mrs. Takami."

"I wonder if it would be possible for you to speak with me
for a few minutes? I should like to talk to you."

Don couldn't understand this. He stood sleepily, blinking.
"Are you sure I'm the one you want? Don't you wish to talk to
Mrs. Lundin? But she's gone off on that trip."

"I know, sir. She came to me for arrangements. She and

Her hands were mangling straps of her bag. Slim, dainty hands, twisting in and out, out and in.

"The name was of great interest to me. Lundin." She pronounced it with care. "One does not often encounter that name. I have never known of a hotel guest before with that name."

"Probably not. It's an old Scottish name. Sort of obscure. Not important Scottish, you know. Like Bonnie Prince Charlie Stewart or anything like that."

Donna Takami said, "I have here a letter," and she drew it from her bag and gave it to him, and he took it in his hands and looked at it with curiosity.

He saw the well-worn envelope, the address, saw a small attached snapshot.

Saw the handwriting on the envelope.

He looked at the snapshot again. Two white-hot boxer's gloves struck him simultaneously in both eyes. The double blow split through head and brain. Through past and present and the yowling future.

For a moment he couldn't see the room or the woman.

"Letter—" he croaked. "Letter."

Dear Suguran-san,

I shall write to you, as you requested a brief note, and send you the little picture I promised to send. How is your English? Doing any better? I cherish the picture you gave to me and please thank Mamma-san again for letting me have it. I had thought to come back to you but now that is not possible. We are deployed to the United States and must clear the base by next Wednesday according to latest reports.

If and when I return to Japan I shall come to you again. The memory of you will be forever fragrant in my mind and in my heart. I hope that somehow, somewhere, you will find great happiness. You are a lovely girl and I am proud to have known you, and pleased as well.

With great fondness,
Don

She said, "This was of my mother."

I—I—

Where in hell did you get this letter?
And this picture?
I'd forgotten—
Who gave them to you?
Where in hell did you get them?
What is this, anyway?
A frame-up?
What—
What are you coming to me for?
I mean—
Where did you get this stuff?
I—
I don't understand—

Slowly she removed her dark glasses, and she stood up and looked down at him, then he looked down at her as finally he managed to rise.

She said softly and slowly, "Mr. Lundin, I am your daughter," and the inherited, challenging, round gray eyes of her looked up into his.

24

Don.
> In *tanka* manner
> I would tell you, new daughter,
> Of birds in a coop
> Given me in far Siam
> (But you would call it Thailand).
> *

Jest so lewd I cried,
So casual in laughter,
Inconsiderate,
Wounded by homely poultry
More pitiful than plovers,
*

Chattering brown wrens,
Doves that wail in deep mourning,
Doves that coolly cry,
Or breed within the morning,
Or trot the furze of pheasants.
*

Donna.
Tokyo lost her:
Kyoto was not destroyed.
Her parents had moved—
And Mamma-san was their friend.
She was pregnant. She went home.
*

Blossoms flowered fair,
And I remember many.
Daintily I walked
Carrying chrysanthemums,
The year my mother wilted.
*

So many tender
Perfumes to be remembered;
They have colored deep
The loneliness which wrapped me.
But my pale eyes shone always.
*

Do not turn away
And weep, my Yankee father.
There is more to tell
And I will sing it coyly.
An instrument I cherish,
*

Pluck, and then caress
The cautious string so bland.
Filled with happiness,
I tell you now of children:
First a girl and then a boy.
*

Choice fruit in jelly:
Mikiko, your granddaughter:
We call her Miki.
Eel so busy in the sea:
Kenkichi is your grandson.

*

So very tiny—
But you shall see them running—
Shadows on the grass—
The dancing figures fleeing:
Only three years old, and two.

*

My husband Tatsu
Studies anthropology,
Teaches in a school. . . .
Father, do not turn away.
You should be lilting also.

*

I am your daughter,
And I wear your blessed eyes.
Embrace me, parent,
And we shall not own sadness.
We shall pick petunias.

*

In this Kyoto
We need feel a benefit.
You will come to own
The Ken and Miki fortune.
We have a lawn with greenness.

*

25

"Mitz, how do I tell July?"

"I don't know quite how you tell her, but you've got to tell her."

"How do I tell her?"

"You couldn't live with her and not do so. You know that."

"Doesn't seem real. Seems like a dream. Can't believe it."

"You do believe it. You saw the girl's eyes."

"Yes. And the letter and snapshot. It's all real. But I actually couldn't believe it until she took off those dark glasses."

"Erna was raving about her, Don. I mean raving. You know how Erna carries on when she gets started. Announced that she was such a darling little thing. When they talked with her— I don't know: several times."

"My God. How do I tell *my wife?*"

"July's made of good stuff."

"But Mitz, we haven't been like other couples. I haven't been like—a lot of married men. Most married men. I haven't played around."

"And you don't believe that July has played around."

"No. She hasn't."

Mitz strolled to the window and halted in contemplation. (As if counting high-rises and discovering disgraceful new ones.)

He swung quickly and spoke with roughness. "Come on! You're no child. This is something you have to face up to."

"But I feel like a child. Feel like a baby. A great big bawling baby—"

"There's no way in which you can revert to infancy. You can't escape this. The knowledge will be with you all the time. July would notice something complicated in your relationship. Immediately."

He pondered, then added, "Maybe that's one way of doing it. Wait until she questions you, asks you what's wrong. No, that wouldn't be good either. It would be—what's the word? Cumbersome?"

"No. Cowardly."

"Maybe both?"

"Cumbersome *and* cowardly."

"Don, I'm telling you again. July can take it. Get your spirits up. Don't just linger here sniveling."

"God damn it, if I'm bothering you, I'll get out!"

"At least you're showing a little spirit. No, don't get out. That, too, would be cumbersome and cowardly."

He came over and patted Lundin's shoulder. "Maybe I'm selfish. I've never had this to contend with. I've had a lot of other things. How do you think it feels to have to say to a patient—a sweet, trusting patient who has every reason for wishing to live on and on, every inducement in circumstance— And yet there are times when you can't keep the secret. Times when the patient has to know. I've had to tell them."

Lundin took out his pipe, filled and lighted it. The doctor was glad to see him do this.

Don looked up, trying to smile. "Guess I'm just a born sniveler."

"No, you're not. When you were up there in the air over Japan at the age of seventeen along with those B-29's—and again, a few years later, when you were flying over to bomb Korea. Boring through those typhoons, and getting all black and blue from it? You said one guy had a broken arm, and another a broken shoulder in one typhoon. And where was that target where the flak was bad?"

"Pyongyang."

"And the time you got all that ice and were going down? Over that water? The bay?"

Don said, "Wonsan."

"Well, you weren't a sniveler then. Or were you? I think not. They would have kicked you out of the crew."

Don's pipe had gone out, and he stood up again and relighted it. "But if July and I had been like most folks— But we weren't. Not like any others we knew. Maybe it's because we started out so very young—just a couple of kids, in our teens. Of course I've seen it happen the other way a lot of times, too. Kids starting out, thinking they were madly in love because they held a violent physical attraction for one another. And then, with the cares of the world around them, they all became different.

"But it didn't happen to us. We were together right from the start. Oh, there was the usual woman across the street who made passes, and another two or three who let it be known, as you might say, how they felt. I know that there were guys after July, too. I saw it happen. I mean I saw them try. You know. Kids going to a party at school, a little party in somebody else's trailer. Everybody working hard and then trying to have a big time with a couple of bottles of booze, and midnight suppers that seemed luxurious.

"Somebody says, 'Well, we'll go over and get those records. Come on, Priscilla, come with me. We'll go over to our place and get that—you know—maybe a Bing Crosby album or something.' And then they'd be a long time in coming back, and everybody would smile wisely and say, 'Well, where have you two *been*?' Sometimes there might be a row about it later.

"We had those things happen—saw them happen. But we were together. Unified. There was so much pressure from the outside. Illness. And certain reassortments you have to make. And poverty was always there, sniffing outside or just around the corner—the wolf, coming in and trying to get in bed with us. But I never stepped all the way over the line. And by God, I'm certain July never did either. And now—this. I had no notion that it ever existed. I couldn't have believed it. Until she put that letter and the snapshot in my hand."

Mitz said, "Overseas. It was different business."

"Yes. It was different in a way. It didn't start out to be that way. I mean I had no intention, at the time. I thought we were just going to be entertained. Hear some nice peculiar music, and smell the flowers, and drink *sake*—"

The doctor interrupted again, abruptly. "As I said, overseas was a different business. I was first untrue to my first wife, Cleo, while I was overseas. There was a nurse, a British woman. We got acquainted while we were working in a dressing station together. We liked each other very much. She was married, too, but her husband was elsewhere on the Front. Anyway, we had a love affair, and it's all so long ago I'd almost forgotten. She was four years older than I, too. God. She'd be eighty now, if still alive."

Soon he said gently, "Go ahead. Tell me about it. If it'll help."

Don hadn't known how matters worked at a geisha house. There were a lot of rumors; and there seemed to be a lot of different attitudes reflected in geisha houses as well. Suddenly and unexpectedly his crew got a forty-eight hour pass because the bombardment schedule was slowed down for the moment, and they owned the highest aggregate of missions of any crew in the squadron. So they were tapped for it. One of the officers had a brother-in-law who had been on active duty in Tokyo for several years. Arrangements were made.

The place was beautiful. Really entrancing. A fairyland of gardens and flowers and pools and everything. The works. Suguran's father was a business executive on a Tokyo newspaper, but he was crippled and couldn't take part in the war. The night of the fire-bombing of Tokyo the family home was burned, and Suguran's two younger brothers were killed. The body of one was never found.

"It seems too strange to be believed. There we were, talking together and on the verge of intimacy—which we didn't know or realize yet—and I'd been up there in one of those 29's that same night and morning. And her brothers died in the attack. But we talked about it."

The father had studied business administration at UCLA and thus he was conversant in English, and had insisted on teaching English to his children. He prophesied that English would be the business and professional language of the future Orient.

The family's livelihood, as well as their sons and their home, was destroyed. The survivors decided to go to Kyoto, where the mother had relatives. But they were in utter destitution.

Mamma-san entered the picture. She was an old friend of the family, and a connection through a series of marriages. She insisted that she would take good care of Suguran-san. There was no disgrace contained or implied in the proposal. The true complexities of the geisha world could not be commonly understood by people who were not of Japan.

Suguran returned to Tokyo, and this was considered an upward step by friends and neighbors. Eventually she might become possessed by a kindly and generous patron. Starvation prowled in many directions. The races of birds and rats and cats and dogs were disappearing momentarily from Japanese life.

"Mitz, you must understand that it was good for her to be well fed and taken care of."

"Anyone should understand that."

"There was a pride about it. And she was just beginning in the business. If you call it a business. It's hard to explain."

"Don't try."

"See, it wasn't a whorehouse. Some of our guys thought so, before they went, but others said no."

"Don't apologize for it. There was a war going on."

"Yes. But this geisha situation is difficult to explain."

"God damn it!" said Mitzheimer testily. "Quit trying to explain!"

The other officers exhibited their natural liveliness, propounded the obvious in jokes. Take it easy or you might have to get married. It would be a shotgun wedding instead of a *shogun* wedding. They savored flowers, *sake*, and music, and the bathing. But Lundin and the girl wished to leave the others, and did. Soon they huddled alone in a little *shoji* room, and their talk went on and on. Each found in the other a dignity, a doughty humanity, a wonder.

"We'd been together only those few hours. And, before we were intimate, she actually said to me, 'Don, I love you.' "

"And you said—?"

"I told her that I loved her too."

And I did love her.

So quickly.

She was a wonderful girl. Just as I wrote in the letter.

Divine.

I—

I guess our daughter is like that.

That's how it all happened.

In the early morning we made love, and it was a rare thing.

As if some god had—Ennobled us.

And so—

Her pregnancy was an act of deliberation.

I understand that now.

She did it a-purpose.

Didn't take any precaution.

My God, Mitz!

I never thought I'd be telling anybody about this.

Anybody in the world.

The telephone bell gave utterance—truly a mild and poetic melody. But it sounded like gongs and war bells rung by priests invoking slaughter.

The voice of Erna echoed with inflective drama. Where, indeed, was her husband, where was July's husband? Two lonely and exhausted women demanded surcease and companionship.

"We have just emerged from the ladies' room, which, I regret to inform you, is drenched with the odor of previous urinations. The Eastern world is reluctant to part with its bodily perfumes. Is Don with you? Good. July tried calling him in their quarters. We crave attention and companionship. We are in the fifth booth at the rear of the balcony, and a discerning young waiter has kindly plugged in a portable telephone. Immediately we have cast him as Guildenstern because he 'here gives up himself in the full bent, to lay his service freely at our feet, to be commanded.' What shall we order for you?"

Mitzheimer cut off the telephone with his plump but still-a-musician's hand, and said, "The babes. What will you have to drink?"

Lundin closed his eyes tightly and shook his head as in spasm. "Jesus Christ on the rocks. I mean vodka."

"Don'll have vodka," said the doctor when he had uncovered the transmitter. "On the rocks. For me a Margarita, straight up." He looked at his friend again, and added, "Make them both doubles. Very well, mad Ophelia, we're already on the way."

He hung up and smiled at Don, and made an effort to be casual and reassuring. "Come along, Don, and get scrubbed. As Erna might say, 'God be at your table!' "

26

"Don, are you ill?"
He's acting so funny.
"I really don't know."

Mitz was correct, she would detect something amiss. I wonder when she first became aware of it. It doesn't matter, she has sensed it and that's all that matters.

"Well, you didn't eat anything. You ordered only chef's salad and only nibbled at that."

Maybe he's drinking too much. But he's always a mild, steady drinker when we're away on a trip and having fun, and ordinarily it doesn't really seem to bother him.

"Maybe I should have ordered only a head of lettuce. Like in that old story about the guy who sold himself so ardently to the gal, and bragged about his sexual prowess, and could only perform with a fraction of the power that he'd boasted about, and then when he was ordering breakfast next morning over the telephone in their hotel room, Little Hon-Bun called to him, 'Don't forget that head of lettuce,' and he turned to her in surprise and asked, 'Why should I order a head of lettuce?' and she replied, 'Because I wanted to see whether you *ate* like a rabbit, too.'"

Stupid. I would go blabbing a sex story.

"I'd forgotten that one."

I haven't forgotten it at all, but suddenly he goes running off at the mouth again, as he did at dinner. Maybe I'd better call Erna and see whether she's got some kind of oral or verbal Kaopectate to relieve his condition, whatever his condition may be.

"July."

Imagine that I was pulling back the charging lever on quite another sort of gun.

"Yes?"

He's going to tell me something, tell me something.

"There's something I've got to tell you."

Mitz was pretending that I was a surgeon and telling me to get scrubbed. Scrubbed in surgery means getting ready for an operation. Not like scrubbed in combat, when suddenly you're wiped off the board and don't have to fly the mission.

"Darling. Tell me."

Please tell fast, tell rapidly, this isn't any fun hanging

suspended. Is he going to tell me that he's had a heart attack which nobody knows about—?

"Don't you want to lie down? I mean, sit down?"

I mean Don't Just Stand There Looking At Me, Don't Just Stand There Looking, Don't Just Stand There, Don't Just—

"Don! Tell me!"

I mean Please Have Some Regard For My Heart and Feelings. How can anyone wait like this? I mean for Pity's Sake Have Some Regard—

"You know that lovely girl in the lobby, the one you and Erna were raving about—"

This weapon is fused improperly but I don't know how to fuse it correctly because I never fused a bomb before; some other people always did that, it was their job. By 1950 half our bomb fuses were strictly for the birds or the beetles or somebody; half of them weren't worth a poop in an old privy or out of it, the Delayed Actions exploded on immediate contact, a Three-Second-Delayed-Action was best to use on bridges, and we hit that long bridge up by Seoul I don't know how many times, but if we hit the super-structure Whop went the bomb right then and there, instead of permitting the bomb to descend down into the mud underneath, the way a Three-Second-Delayed-Action fuse was supposed to do, and Lordy Lordy, when we used to VT's, the Variable Type fuses, the fucking things might detonate yay seconds after they were loose from the cocking shackles, and we'd have them explode directly beneath our aircraft, and plenty of times we got fragged by our own bombs, and that's what I mean when I say fused improperly—

"Don! Have you heard bad news about her? Why didn't you tell me before? Has she been in an accident?"

I teased him about her and said, She's your slick little Japanese sister because her name is Donna, and he said, Maybe she's a kissing cousin, and I said—

"July. She's my daughter."

In the Buddha book compiled by Bukkyo Dendo Kyokai it says,

These feelings of dislike do not often end in acts of violence, yet they poison life with feelings of hatred and anger that become so deeply carved into the mind that people carry the marks to the hour of death.

A muted voice remarked presently, "I think I will lie down on the bed after all," and she sat on the edge of the wide bed, which so luckily they had been awarded for their long stay in Kyoto, though it wasn't really a double bed, it was two beds drawn tightly together and then arranged separately as to sheets and pillows, but if you were close close when you lay there, and if you wanted to join each other more intimately it was a simple thing to do, because already you were near and affectionately neighborly, and maybe you had been holding hands as you lay asleep or nigh to sleeping, and July pulled off her slippers first in dainty gesture, and you could hear the tiny falling of her slippers to the carpet, just a light, mothy sound, and then there came the pretty curve of her lower body, as she settled it inside the pale rose-colored skirt, and that skirt itself was a savory thing to see, with that mere fraction of lace on her slip or petticoat exposed, and she said she said soberly, wisely—

She said, "Her mother was the Japanese girl you knew. In the geisha house."

*

Recognized at once,
The power of your knowledge!
Casual you speak,
But tender words are demons.
I need to weep like rainfall.

*

It did not sprinkle
As tiny fingers spraying;
Delicate it sprang,
Memory annointing us.
Flowered years are twenty-two.

*

Sweet Suguran-san,
Endow me with your courage.

1 9 8

Ah, let me capture
Our daughter and her children,
That we may hold them tightly!
                    *

You remain aloof,
Oblivious to battle.
Not in contending,
But wiser than human strife,
Remote among the lilies.
                    *

"You say you've known all the time. I still can't understand it. But when you tell me to believe it, then I've got to believe it."

"Not quite all the time. But from the next year."

"Who told you—? How did—? What—?"

"Inez."

"Who?"

"Don't you remember Inez Cliffert?"

"Cliff's wife? That screwball Latin type with the vicious temper."

"Cliff was with you. When you all went. To the geisha place."

"God sakes!"

"Cliff and Inez got into a fight."

"But they were always having fights."

"Yes, they were. I recognized that, as soon as I came out to Spokane, at your behest, to greet you. Then— It was a while afterward. Just about the time we were going through all that negotiation about adopting Charley and Lottie. And Inez wrote to me. She told me then."

"You mean to say you've known it ever since that time? Jesus Christ, my head is spinning. But how did Inez *know*?"

"They were having one of their many terrible times, and in a rage Cliff told her. He said he had been with a Japanese girl, and told her about the place you all went to, and everything. He must have been more or less out of his mind with resentment of some kind or he wouldn't have told her. She said he bragged about it, but I don't know whether he really did. I guess he might have when he really lost his temper. Maybe Inez thought I'd descend on you with all four feet. But I didn't."

Long silence.

Don went to the window and back to the bed and stood looking down at July, and walked back to the window and stood looking out for a time. July uttered a smothered sound that was half a sob, or so Lundin thought, and he came back again and stood looking at her once more, and then he dropped down on the bed and flung his arms around her, and he thought her face would be wet with tears by this time. But it wasn't wet with tears, it was a dry face, but warm, maybe too warm for the moment, but he wondered about her dry warm face only vaguely.

He said, "My daughter's got two children."

"I know. She told us about them. Erna and myself. The day we were first talking to her. She's such a darling."

"That means I've got two grandchildren."

July said, quietly and nearly with complacency, "How wonderful for you."

Later.

"How wonderful for us both."

"You still feel that way?"

"Sure do. If they're yours, they're mine."

Don spoke in continued explosion. "July. You're angelic. You're supreme. What's the word I want? Iridescent? Yes, you're iridescent. I told Mitzheimer about it. Late afternoon. He said I had to tell you. I knew I had to tell you, and now I've told you, and God God God you've made me feel— I could walk on top of the world. I guess I will walk on top of the world—"

July drew loose from his restraint, and sat up quickly.

"Oh, I want to see them. The children— I mean, our *grandchildren.*"

"One thing. What did you say to Inez when you replied to her letter?"

"Never replied. Not one line. Not one word."

"Boy! I bet she was mad."

"Don, I want to see our *grandchildren*. And Donna. And her husband. Right away. Can't you arrange it *right away?*"

He chuckled. Well, let common sense prevail. They couldn't see anybody that night; they didn't even know where Donna lived. It would have to be arranged.

"Oh, of course. I'm just suddenly silly."

Don mumbled that it was all so strange. "I was untrue to you that once, that one time. And instead of misery, it'll yield us an enormous happiness. And you— In all these years you've never been untrue to me. Not once."

She laughed lightly. "My dear, if I was, you'll never know."

He began gabbling. "You mean—? You actually—? Why, Christ, I thought that you— And I was telling Mitz, and bragging—"

She laughed lightly. "You'll never know!"

"But, look here! Come on! Give, baby, give—"

" 'Arise, arise,' as Erna might say. I'm going to furbish myself a little, and you shall take me up to that high-and-mighty corridor where we can look out and see myriads and myriads of lights. I don't know what you want, I want a champagne cocktail."

Don Lundin tried to blunder after her as she retreated to dressing table and bathroom. "But I've told you everything! Gave you the works. It isn't fair for you to—"

The door closed.

She laughed lightly.

27

Don Lundin wrote a note to the tour conductor and put it under his door.

Dear Rab,

I have tried to get in touch with you, but was unsuccessful because as usual you are away looking after people, and being fatherly and motherly and generally noble. I want to make a fool's confession. You are aware naturally of my deep-seated aversion to Orientals, or call it deep-rooted to be more correct. I don't quite know how this thing got going within me, but there it was. We only came on the trip because July was dying to come, and of course I am lost without her so here I came tagging along.

You witnessed that fucked-up mess with which I offended the party in Bali, and offended myself even more in the perpetration thereof. There was no excuse for such an antic, so I won't try to offer any. Suffice to say that it all stemmed from abhorrent prejudice; and if such prejudice is to rule our world then may all the gods and Buddhas and Jesuses and dragons and celestial images show mercy.

Rab, I have just discovered something which leaves me quivering and nakedly humble. I am the father of a beautiful woman, here in Kyoto, and I didn't know that she even existed. Her mother, long since dead, was a geisha girl with whom I spent one night in Tokyo during the Korean War. More than that: my daughter is the mother of two tiny children; we haven't seen them yet but will go shortly.

Here stand I, craving the mercy and benevolence of entire races whom I have scorned, and some of whom I helped to slay, and all survivors of whom we must embrace earnestly; or we shall perish, and become mere fragments of history instead of a wise and prevailing force.

You are already acquainted with my daughter I am sure, and I rest entirely on your discretion in not approaching her *until I tell her that I have told you.* She is Mrs. Donna Takami, the information girl in the lobby. Bless her, bless her busy scrambling nation, bless all Japanese and Chinese and Wyes and Rabartis and Wongs who will ever become Wight. See you later.

Don

28

They drove down the familiar course of Sanjo Street and turned right on Higashi-Oji. Lundin sat blindly and could not have told whether his eyes were open or closed. There was some prank about imagining that he was in Tokyo rather than in Kyoto. Suguran-san had been a portion of the Tokyo area during that single night when Don was an active portion of her life, and she of his. He knew nothing of Kyoto in those days, except that the city marked a region through which they flew when journeying on multitudinous hours of missions, beginning often initially off islands that draped the south coast of Korea. Kyoto was a thing on charts, a point on the pilot's flimsies, on everybody's little directive flimsies—pale, tough, wrinkled paper printed with the jargon of instructions. The airmen made a minor happiness of Kyoto, as staunchly they tried to discover fun in bombardment and its death-dealing termination of human and structural life. They were old pros, and no old pro dared find fault with the grimness of his embraced chore. Should he do so, he had no rank or status as an old pro, and who the hell would want him around anyway? So Kyoto was funny; call it "coyote" in three syllables, and make like you're howling like one. Except that none of them, except Magnussen in Central Fire Control, had heard coyotes howling commonly, and Magnussen came from Wyoming but he was no good at imitating the critters. He'd just say "You guys don't do it right."

Lundin was seeing Kyoto signs and advertisements and designations, at least when he did have his eyes open, but the few he noted started a riot from Tokyo remembrance and kept it fulminating. Toyota. Tatsumara. Interior Fabrics. Asakusa Station. Columbus Ltd. Mazda. Toppan. Tohan. Honda. Stork. And the word "telephone" spelled out, always; and they had characters for words and characters for letters and sometimes characters for numbers, but he was confident that they had no characters for the word "telephone" because they spelled it out eternally until eternally became painfully. Sometimes—oh, maybe once in a while—they said just Tel, but that was rare. Telephone (941) 7030. Telephone 624-5756. Telephone (216) 2926. Tel 553-1931. Telephone (813) 7561. Plus. Lipton. Sanyo. Mukai-Kum. Yutaka.

Amazing thought exploded within his brain—it had never been there before, never puffed, never detonated. *Why not ask your daughter about the telephones?*

Leica. Dunlop. Konica. Suntory. Telephone 843 1831. Tel 941 2140. Telephone (943) 5521. Bireley's. Ito. Ichida. Y.K.K. *Ask Donna about the telephones.*

July said, "Darling."

He found her damp, clenched, clawlike tiny hand and took it in his dry larger one. "Whassa matter?"

"You were breathing hard, and kind of snorting."

Drink Fanta. Snack. Chinzan-so. Hitachi. "It was something about telephones. Something sort of funny. Tell you later."

When the taxi turned at the Imadegawa Street intersection, July cried aloud with delight of recognition. "Don't you recognize this, Don? We came this way before, I'm certain. Yes, I'm more than certain, the bus took us right over that way to the Ginkakuji temple, and you said no more temples for you, the way you're always saying it, and then finally when we parked and you said we weren't too far out of the pattern of modern existence, and Mr. Semple said, 'What the hell, Lundin, you crab, you seldom have anything good to say about modern existence anyway—' "

"He didn't say that."

"Yes, he did. We all heard him."

"Well, he didn't."

"Did."

"Didn't. Well, if he did, he didn't mean it in a mean way."

"Of course not. He's crusty and sort of always tearing around with an intense look on his face, but at heart he's a dear. You can tell that by looking at Amy."

Don said sourly, "And he lugs one or another of those bloody damn cameras of his, wherever he goes. Click click click, every waking moment."

"But you walked back. You said it was only a mile or so, and you didn't want to see any more nasty old temples, and you said you'd be waiting at that last main intersection, on the left-hand side of the road where you belonged, and we could pick you up when we had to stop. You were waiting there, waiting and grinning, and you said you'd had a pleasant stroll among modern Japanese backyards—"

He said sharply, "We just turned again."

"Yes, I saw."

"July—"

"What?"

"I walked this way. I was down this street a little farther. There are little fences, and grass and flowers."

"Don—"

"Yes?"

"How does the driver know where to go?"

"She sent me a card in an envelope, with the address written out in Japanese."

Her damp, clenched, clawlike tiny hand was a lizard within the clutch of his dry larger hand, and it squirmed around and tried to get loose, but you shouldn't let it loose because somebody might step on it, as in the case of a miniature chameleon at home in Florida. And you wouldn't want to have it squashed because if it were pulverized damply in instant ugliness it would become immediately a thing of horror, and you didn't wish it to become a thing of horror because then never could it wear another fresh, new, fitful, colorful coat as it crept along the trunk of the palm.

"Don—"

"Yes."

"The taxi's stopping. We've got to get out. I'm scairt."

"So'm I."

*

> In this Kyoto
> We need feel a benefit.
> You will come to own
> The Ken and Miki fortune.
> We have a lawn with greenness.

*

Donna stood at the head of the outside stairway before they reached the foot of it. She was wearing a lavender-flowered dress, Western style, as the majority of young Japanese wives were garbed these days, and her small figure shone milkily moistly as Lundin turned his hard gaze up and upon her. He felt July's captive fingers jerk within his clutch. No, no, don't let the incredible beauty of this specimen get away, never let it run free and run dangerously at large, remember that it might be damaged. He wrenched his stare away from his daughter and tried to turn it upon his wife, but found only that she too was concentrated in the same attention; and by the time he looked at Donna again she was a bird (Ho, not a dove of *tanka* verses!) in full downward flight.

The family's apartment occupied the upper story of this

bright line of white stuccoed buildings. The yard, the lawn, the neat-clipped grass were properly fenced and sidewalked for all tenants, but the only toys in sight belonged in truth to Donna's children. The short stairway broke at a platform halfway down, and it seemed that the slim, trim, patterned figure halted her descent there for seconds; then took fresh courage, fresh intention, yielded to renewed assurance, and then came on whisking. On the balcony above her other figures large and small seemed materializing from inside. Lundin could not identify or count them—they were a muddle.

He heard the marvel of his wife's low utterance. Her captured fingers drew from the caging he'd put upon them and flew to freedom. Lundin could not have sworn to the identity of her utterance, but in considering it afterward, so many times afterward, building the entire experience into a permanent renewal, it seemed that she must have said, "Oh, my dear," and that was all. Beside and around him, while he halted at the core of this pageant, the two women came together. Donna's cry was muted and was wordless. They clung instantly, fiercely, and being women, both were crying.

Don Lundin could not remember climbing the stair (might there not exist an escalator unsurmised?) but then they all were there unchecked. This seemed so singular but still exalted, and his foolish and triumphant knowledge shot like an arrow within him—Japanese arrow fired from horseback as the draped wild bowman came at lope or canter—

Why, here they are, we are, here we are.

A family.

I had not thought to own a family.

"Father."

And slowly slowly I go down upon my knees.

The small folks staring. They are shy but—

Eel so busy in the sea:
Kenkichi is your grandson.

"This is Ken. And this is Miki."

Choice fruit in jelly:
Mikiko, your granddaughter—

I have become a toad. No, not a toad (in frightful faking
Bali episode that I contrived). A frog. For I can only croak. The
eyes, the eyes—

"Yes, they both have my eyes. Your eyes. It is in-her-it-ed."
And now light laughter as July is all among them. She is a
monster with four arms, six arms to wrap around them. Still
they are shy, but laughing lightly, as they squirm and try to
draw away, and looking up at their own proven elders for
guidance, and their great-grandmother admonishes them in
their own language, hoping to give guidance, as still they writhe
as if they chose to retreat into native babyhood again.

Then July is on her feet, with moisture on her cheeks all
marring makeup, and reminding, saying, "Manners, manners,"
as if I had not even one lone "manner" to offer, even after I'd
been briefed.

My son-in-law, Tatsu Takama, Takama Tatsu, is taller than
remembered Orientals of another epoch. So tall the Japanese
are growing, very thin so many of the young, but taller by the
minute. He is bespectacled, severe of countenance with face re-
posed, but when he loosens up with smiles and joy, I think he
looks just like an oversized Boy Scout informed upon the
moment that he has won a contest.

"My grandmother, Takako Miyoshi, Miyoshi Takako."

I bow. July has briefed me how to bow.

Bow low, bow low, we are all bowing.

Bow low again. All bow so very low again. Then we are
shaking hands in modern style.

And she was mother of the dead and lovely, oh so lovely but
long-vanished Suguran. She wears her best kimono, tan and
purple intermingled, her wispy hair is knobbed in ancient style,
her squinting eyes are starred with crinkles underneath the

glassy wafers that hold them trapped. She ripples run-together words, the brown Jap words, I don't know what she says.

I helped to burn her house.

So what's her age? So Suguran was seventeen, I think that she was seventeen, I can't remember, cannot think, my mind is puddled. All kindliness and clear affection in her face and corded hands, the busy very busy hands, so much they have to do, the chores, the household tasks, the waiting on these babies, *my grandchildren!* Striving for them busily, so Donna goes to work, so Tatsu teaches in his classes, studies in his other classes, the yen do not come pouring into coffers, we must be neat, her face says that, she'll want to serve us tea now we are come—

I helped to kill her sons.

The answer? Answer?

Try to find an answer.

Seek once more in Buddha.

The Spirit of Buddha is the great compassion and love to save all people by any and all means. It is the nourishing and protective spirit of a mother for her child; it is the spirit that prompts it to be ill with the sickness of people, to suffer with their suffering.

I'll find it in the Bible, find it in Isaiah.

Behold, I will send a blast upon him, and he shall hear a rumor, and return to his own land. . . .

Whom has thou reproached and blasphemed? and against whom hast thou exalted thy voice, and lifted up thine eyes on high?

Donna saying primly, "Now we shall drink tea."

Tatsu escorted Lundin to the balcony to indicate the wealth of universities at hand. "We are so close. Kyoto University stands near. You cannot see it, but it is behind that wall. And

2 0 9

over there, a short distance to the west, beyond the Kamogawa River, can be found the Ritsumei. It also is a university. Then also near the Old Imperial Palace, some small distance north and west, there is the Doshisha. Then one more, due to the north some longer distance, and also beyond one other river, the Takano-gawa, one more university, the Kyoto Kogeiseni. As boys at Harvard would say, we are up to the ass in universities."

"Tatsu, you went to Harvard?"

"One year only. I was on a fellowship."

"And now—?"

"Three days each week I study, three days each week I teach in children's school. One day each week I have for home and family, but sometimes it is very difficult to have the same free day which Donna has. For also it is very difficult for her to know which day is free for Donna, for often there are conventions, and sometimes two girls are necessary, and another information service must be—must be—in-aug-ur-ated. Yes. Sometimes two whole desks."

But sometimes both he and his wife owned their leisure together, cramped little hours of leisure precious and so dearly bought, and then they took the tiny ones to see the great works of the past, the shrines and palaces. But little people tire easily of shrines and palaces— "Big people, too," said Don, and both found merriment in that. And to the zoo— "They like the bears," said Tatsu. "And the go-rill-a with face so black. The lion, too. And those American raccoons, sometimes American raccoons will wash their food, not always, but the children love to see them washing food—"

Don interrupted roughly. "We have them in the yard."

"Not children?" Tatsu was exclaiming. "What children in your yard? Do you have other children? Grandchildren?"

"No, I mean raccoons. Old Florida coons, the wild ones. But these are very tame; they'll eat out of your hand. You'll see them when you come to us."

Tatsu smiled, and bowed, and shook his head. "I am afraid that will be a very long time."

"God damn it, no. What do you want to study? You want anthropology? You want to study for a doctorate? You'll need a doctorate, that's right. Look here, God damn it all to hell anyway! You want to return to Harvard?"

Tatsu said, as if telling secrets, "I have a dream sometime of going to Stanford or to the U of C at Ber-kel-ey. Those are best for my now purpose."

A teabell made its remote jeweled sound.

"They call us to drink tea."

You haven't quite got the idea. Look, I don't mean to rush in where angels fear to tread, I don't want to appear foolish in your eyes or Donna's. But you've got to get this straight: I'm Donna's father, you're her husband, we're one family, those are my grandchildren in there, July's and my grandchildren. What's good for one is good for the rest. I mean what's good for us is good for you. Oh, Christ, I don't know how to say this correctly. So as not to offend you. You're a man, you've got your life, your work, your ambitions, but you've got to give us the opportunity to do what we can to help you realize your ambitions, both of you, all of you. If Grandma-san wants to stay here at peace in Kyoto that's O.K., she can do whatever will make her happiest, or if she wants to go to Tokyo, why that's O.K., she's wonderful, or she can come to the United States along with the rest of you, if she wants to come and you want her to come, or she can do anything in God's green world that she pleases, it's all O.K. with us. But I want you to go to Stanford or the University of California or Harvard or Oshkosh or where the hell ever you decide to go and get that doctorate, so you can have a good life doing what you want to do, because you're wonderful for Donna, and wonderful to her. Anyone can tell that by the way she looks at you. And I want to see the kids and have them close to us and in our life, because God sent me here, I tell you that He did, or Buddha led me by the hand—

July emerged to act the role of Buddha and take her husband by the hand, and lead him in.

Tatsu Takami was late in coming.

July asked of Donna, "What are the children wearing? Those aren't kimonos."

"We call them happi-coats," and she was chuckling at the idea of happi-coats. "My grandmother fitted them, and cut them out. She also did some sewing, but not all. I sewed as well. You might not believe it, but sometimes I have some hours when I am not too busy at my little booth, and I can sew."

Miki's happi-coat was of flowered blue, the small Kenkichi wore a robe of mainly scarlet. They stood solemnly, side by side, and turned inquiring glances on their mother and on the older woman who was rearing them.

"They now will sing for you."

So miniature, and they can sing?

"They know a song or two."

"It is—it is three songs they know," said Tatsu. "But some-times—they grow fright-ened."

July told them all, "I bet I couldn't sing when I was two or three. I bet most people can't."

Their father whispered, "They sing—well."

"We'll have them sing the Sakura song." Donna explained that it was about cherry blossoms.

Miki put up her arms, as if she wished to whisper, and her mother bent down to hear what she had to say.

"It is another song they wish to sing."

Side by side they clasped their hands, fairylike the words came forth. Ken might barely manage them because he was so young, but still he sang.

Uchi-e kaero—

Donna said tenderly in translation, " 'Let's go home—' "

Tiny people, tiny words, the breathing as if in terror, no, not in terror but in intensity of purpose.

" 'Since it's close to the sunset—' "

Otete tsunaide.

" 'Hand in hand.' " Donna's gray plaque eyes challenged the room but never with offense. "It is a song known to children of Japan. 'Let's go home, since it's close to the sunset. Hand in hand.' I sang it when very small. My mother sang it."

Tatsu. "I also. Sang it." His utterance was shivered into brittle fragmentary syllables since he had stood upon that balcony with Don.

The great-grandmother spoke lengthily in her clear but tone-less voice, and the younger relatives smiled at hearing her. "My grandmother declares that she too sang it long ago."

July. "Then we all must adopt it. I can learn it, it's so short." And to her husband, "Could you learn it, Don?"

Lundin. "Affirmative. Will do."

He thought, And I had seen them clearly on that other day as idly I went strolling, the infant-portioned tricycle, the infant-portioned wagon, blue and white they were as I looked over flower hedges, I saw them in the yard so clipped and clean, abandoned for the moment, I must be the first, the first stark staring grandfather of all recorded time and that greater portion of experience which goes as unrecorded, the first to ever see their toys and not know that they were their toys, the pint-sized wagon glinting bashful in the sun, the quart-sized tricycle a-challenging and bold, Ah come with me and take a ride, we're waiting for the Little Folks to climb on us and go a-journeying, they know not where they go, we know not where we go, but we can guess, they pedal and are hauled amid their perfect world, go round and round as children playing games go always round and round, and little do they recognize the circle which they represent, the bulbous aspect of their universe and ours, the planets and the sun and stars forever stormed in their vast course.